SEEING MISS
Heartstone

A REGENCY ROMANCE

NICHOLE VAN

Fiorenza Publishing

Published by Fiorenza Publishing
Print Edition v1.0

ISBN: 978-1-949863-01-7

To my Woodland Hills friends—
Even though we're half a world apart,
I love that words bridge the gap.
I miss you all.

To Dave—
Thank you for being
my touchstone of sanity
in this crazy life.

PART I

APRIL, 1816

PROPOSALS

. . . My lord, news of your current financial pressures has reached many ears. I know of an interested party who would be honored to discuss a proposed joint venture. They have asked to meet you along the Long Water in Hyde Park tomorrow morning, where they shall endeavor to lay out the particulars of their proposal . . .

—excerpt from an unsigned letter posted to Lord Blake

In retrospect, Miss Arabella Heartstone had three regrets about 'The Incident.'

She should not have worn her green, wool cloak with the fox fur collar, as Hyde Park was warmer than expected that morning.

She should not have instructed her chaperone, Miss Anne Rutger, to remain politely out of earshot.

And she probably should *not* have proposed marriage to the Marquess of Blake.

"P-pardon?" Lord Blake lifted a quizzical eyebrow, standing straight and tall, rimmed in the morning sunlight bouncing off the Long Water behind him. A gentle breeze wound through the surrounding trees, rustling newly-grown, green leaves. "Would . . . would you mind repeating that last phrase? I fear I did not hear you correctly."

Belle straightened her shoulders, clasped her trembling hands together, and sternly ordered her thumping heart to *Cease this racket.*

Swallowing, she restated her request. "After much consideration, my lord, I feel a marriage between you and myself would be prudent."

Lord Blake stared at her, blinking over and over. Belle was unsure if his reaction denoted surprise or was simply the result of the dazzling sunlight off the water behind her.

Silence.

Birds twittered. Branches creaked. Leaves rustled.

Eternities passed. Millennia ended and were reborn.

Belle gritted her teeth, desperate to bolster her flagging confidence. *You are strong and courageous. You can do this.*

In the past, her passivity over the Marriage Matter had nearly ended in disaster. So, Belle had set her sights on a more forthright course— propose marriage herself. Yes, she struggled to talk with people and preferred anonymity to attention, but her current situation was critical.

She needed a husband. Decidedly. Desperately. Immediately. As in . . . yesterday would not have been soon enough.

At the moment, however, her mental encouragement barely managed to convince the swarming butterflies in her stomach to not free her breakfast along with themselves. Casting up her accounts all over his lordship's dusty Hessian boots would hardly nurture his romantic interest.

At last, Lord Blake stirred, pulling a folded letter from his overcoat. He stared at it, eyebrows drawing down, a sharp "V" appearing above his nose.

"You sent me this message, asking to meet me here?" He flapped the letter in her direction.

"Yes." Belle bit down on her lip and darted a glance behind at her companion. Miss Rutger stood a solid thirty yards off, studiously facing the Long Water. "Well . . . uhm . . . in all truthfulness, Miss Rutger wrote the letter."

Lord Blake raised his eyebrows, clearly uncaring of the minutiae involved. "So you are *not* a gentleman interested in my business venture in the East Indies?" He unfolded the letter, reading from it. "'*I know of an interested party who would be honored to discuss a proposed joint venture. They have asked to meet you along the Long Water,*' et cetera. This 'interested party' is yourself?" He returned the letter to his pocket.

"Yes, my lord." Belle commanded her feet to hold still and not bounce up and down—the bouncing being yet another effect of those dratted nervous butterflies.

Lord Blake's brows rose further. "And you are offering . . . marriage?"

"Yes, my lord," Belle repeated, but she had to clarify the point. Apparently, she had no issue with being thought forward and brazen, but heaven forbid Lord Blake imagine her a liar, too. "Though . . . I *am* proposing a joint endeavor."

"Indeed," he paused. "Marriage usually implies as much."

Lord Blake shuffled a Hessian-booted foot and clasped his hands behind his back. A corner of his mouth twitched.

Was the man . . . amused? If so, was that good? Or bad?

And at this point, did it matter?

Belle soldiered on. "There would be significant advantages to both of us with such a match."

More silence. An errant draft of wind tugged at his coat.

"You have me at a disadvantage, Miss . . ." His voice trailed off.

"Heartstone. Miss Arabella Heartstone."

"I see." He removed his hat and slapped it against his thigh. "And why have we not met in more . . . uh . . . typical circumstances? A ball, perhaps? A dinner party where we could be properly introduced and engage in conversation about the weather and the latest bonnet fashions before leaping straight to marriage?"

"Oh." It was Belle's turn to blink, absorbing his words. *Oh dear.* "We *have* met, my lord. We were introduced at Lord Pemberley's musicale last month. We did discuss the weather, but not bonnets or . . . uhm . . . marriage."

She hadn't expected him to recall everything, but to not even *recognize* her? To not remember their brief conversation—

"How do you do, Miss Heartstone? It's a pleasure to make your acquaintance." *Lord Blake bowed.*

"The pleasure is all mine, my lord." *Belle curtsied.* *"Lovely weather we're having."*

"Indeed, we are."

It did not bode well.

The butterflies rushed upward, eager for escape.

"Right." Blake let out a gusting breath and shook his head, sending his hair tumbling across his forehead. The morning sun turned it into molten shades of deep amber, curling softly over his ears.

Lean and several inches taller than her own average height, Lord Blake was not classically handsome, she supposed. His straight nose, square jaw, and high forehead were all too exaggerated for classical handsomeness.

And yet, something about him tugged at her. Perhaps it was the breadth of his shoulders filling out his coat. Or maybe it was the ease of his stance, as if he would face the jaws of Hell itself with a sardonic smile and casual *sang-froid*. Or maybe it was the way he ran a gloved hand through his hair, taking it from fashionably tousled to deliciously rumpled.

Mmmmm.

Belle was going to side with the hair. Though sardonic smiles were a close second.

Regardless, her decision to offer marriage to him had not been based on his physical appearance. She was many things, but *flighty* and *shallow* were two words that had never been attached to her.

Replacing his hat, Lord Blake studied her, blue eyes twinkling.

Yes. Definitely amused.

That was . . . encouraging? Having never proposed marriage to a man before, Belle was unsure.

"Enlighten me, if you would be so kind, as to the particular reasons why you think this . . . joint endeavor . . . would be profitable." He gestured toward her.

Oh! Excellent.

That she had come prepared to do.

With a curt nod, she pulled a paper from her reticule.

"A list?" His lips twitched again.

"I am nothing if not thorough in my planning, my lord." She opened the paper with shaking fingers, her hands clammy inside her gloves.

"Of course. I should have expected as much. You arranged this meeting, after all." He tapped the letter in his pocket.

Belle chose to ignore the wry humor in his tone and merely nodded her head in agreement. "Allow me to proceed with my list. Though please forgive me if my reasons appear forward."

"You have just proposed marriage to a peer of the realm, madam. I cannot imagine anything you say from this point onward will trump that."

"True."

A beat.

Lord Blake pinned her with his gaze—calm and guileless. The forthright look of a man who knew himself and would never be less-than-true to his own values.

His gaze upset her breathing, causing something to catch in her throat.

Belle broke eye-contact, swallowing too loudly.

"Allow me to begin." She snapped the paper in her hand. The words swam in her vision, but she knew them by heart. The paper was more for show than anything else. She had done her calculations most carefully.

Taking a fortifying breath, Belle began, "Firstly, you have newly inherited the Marquisate of Blake from a cousin. Your cousin was somewhat imprudent in his spending habits—"

"I would declare the man to be an utter scapegrace and wastrel, but continue."

"Regardless of the cause, your lands and estates are in dire need of resuscitation." Belle glanced at him over the top of her paper. "You are basically without funds, my lord."

"As my solicitor repeatedly reminds me." He shot her an arch look.

"It is why I am trying to fund a business venture in connection with the East India Company, as you are also undoubtedly aware."

"Yes, my lord. That is why I am proposing an enterprise of a slightly different sort. Allow me to continue." Belle cleared her throat, looking down to her paper. "My own family is genteel with connections to the upper aristocracy—my great-great grandfather was the Earl of Stratton—though we have no proper title of our own, leaving my father to make his own way in the world. I, as you might already know, am a considerable heiress. My father was a prominent banker and left the entirety of his estate to me upon his death three years past."

Belle clenched her jaw against the familiar sting in her throat.

Blink, blink, blink.

Now was *not* the time to dwell upon her father.

"Are you indeed?" he asked. "Though I do not wish to sound crass, I feel we left polite discussion in the dust several minutes ago, so I must enquire: How much of an heiress are you, precisely?"

Did she hear keen interest in his tone? Or was Lord Blake simply exceedingly polite?

"I believe the current amount stands somewhere in the region of eighty thousand pounds, my lord," she replied.

Lord Blake froze at that staggering number, just as Belle had predicted he would.

"Eighty thousand pounds, you say? That is a dowry of marquess-saving proportions."

"My thoughts precisely, my lord."

Her father had originally left her a healthy sixty thousand pounds, but she was nothing if not her father's daughter. Numbers and statistics flowed through her brain, a constant rushing river. She had used these skills to grow her fortune.

It was what her father would have wanted. Refusing to see her gender as a barrier, her father had taught his only child everything he knew—financial systems, probabilities, market shares—even soliciting her opinions during that last year before his death.

By the age of sixteen, Belle understood more about supply-and-demand and the mathematics of economics than most noblemen.

Knowing this, the conditions in her father's will allowed her to continue to oversee her own interests with the help of his solicitor, Mr. Sloan. At only nineteen years of age, she currently managed a thriving financial empire.

She could hear her father's gruff voice, his hand gently lifting her chin. *I would give you choices, my Little Heart Full. A lady should always have options. I would see you happy.*

Belle swallowed back the painful tightness in her throat.

Now, if she could only land a husband and free herself from the guardianship of her uncle and mother.

Family, it turned out, were not quite as simple to manage as corn shares.

Her mother, hungry for a title for her daughter, was becoming increasingly bold in her attempts to get Belle married. She had all but forced Belle to betroth herself to a cold, aloof viscount the previous Season. Fortunately, the viscount—Lord Linwood—had asked to be released from their betrothal.

But the entire situation had left Belle feeling helpless.

She *detested* feeling helpless, she realized. And so she used that unwelcome sensation to suppress her inherent shyness and overcome her retiring personality.

Belle would solve the husband problem herself. She simply needed to reduce the entire situation to a statistical probability and face it as she would any other business transaction.

"Eighty-thousand pounds," Lord Blake repeated. "Are husbands—particularly the marquess variety—generally so costly?" He clasped his hands behind his back, studying her. "I had not thought to price them before this."

"I cannot say. This is my first venture into, uhmm . . ."

"Purchasing a husband?" he supplied, eyes wide.

Heavens. Was that a hint of displeasure creeping into his voice?

"I am not entirely sure I agree with the word *purchase*, my lord—"

"True. It does smack of trade and all polite society knows we cannot have *that*."

A pause.

"Shall we use the word *negotiate* instead?" she asked.

He cocked his head, considering. "I daresay that would be better. So I receive a sultan's ransom and your lovely self, and you receive . . ." His words drifted off.

"A husband. And in the process, I become Lady Blake, a peeress of the realm."

"Are you truly so hungry to be a marchioness? Surely eighty thousand pounds could purchase—forgive me, *negotiate*—the title of duchess." His words so very, very dry.

"I am sure my mother would agree with you, my lord, but I am more interested in finding a balance between title and the proper gentleman." She cleared her throat. "You come highly recommended."

"Do I?" Again, his tone darkly sardonic.

Oh, dear.

But as she was already in for more than a penny, why not aim for the whole pound?

"I did not arrive at the decision to propose marriage lightly. I had my solicitor hire a Runner to investigate you. I have armed myself with information, my lord."

Belle wisely did not add that, after crunching all the statistical probabilities, Lord Blake had been by far and away her preferred candidate. She was quite sure that, like most people, he would not appreciate being reduced to a number.

"Information? About me?" he asked.

"Yes. For example, I know you recently cashed out of the army, selling the officer's commission you inherited from your father. All those who served with you report you to be an honest and worthy commander—"

"As well they should."

"Additionally, you are a kind son to your mother. You send her and your stepfather funds when you are able. You visit regularly. Your four older sisters dote upon you, and you are godfather to at least one of each of their children. You are a tremendous favorite with all of your nieces and nephews. All of this speaks highly to the kind of husband and father you would be."

After her disastrous betrothal to Lord Linwood last year, Belle was determined to not make the same error twice. She learned from her mistakes. Her mother and uncle would not browbeat her into accepting one of their suitors again.

If nothing else, eighty thousand pounds should purchase—*negotiate*—her a *kindhearted* husband of her own choice.

Lord Blake shuffled his feet. "I-I really am at a loss for words, Miss Heartstone. I am trying to decide if I should be flattered or utterly appalled."

Belle sucked in a deep breath, her mouth as dry as the Sahara.

Stay strong. Argue your case.

She pasted a strained smile on her face. "Might I suggest siding with flattery, my lord?"

. . . you cannot imagine the goings on, Cecily. I am feted and sought after at every turn. Just two months ago, I was a humble captain in His Majesty's Army and could not garner an invitation to dance at Almack's for any price. And now, Lady Jersey herself sent a personal note requesting my presence there Wednesday next. I cannot fathom how other men actually seek and desire this sort of notoriety. I should be glad to leave it all behind . . .

—*excerpt of a letter from Lord Blake*
to his older sister, Cecily Radcliffe Phalean

Colin Radcliffe, Lord Blake, stared at the girl—er, woman?—before him.

Valiantly, he tried to remember being introduced to Miss Heartstone. For better or worse, his newly-acquired title of Marquess of Blake placed him firmly near the top of polite society, above an earl and just barely below a duke. This meant he had been introduced to hundreds of individuals over the past few weeks. Add in the fact that his memory for names and faces was somewhat poor, and Colin wasn't quite sure he would recognize the Prince Regent himself, much less a mere miss.

Though in his defense, Miss Heartstone was utterly nondescript. Forgettable. Brown hair, brown eyes, neither short nor tall, figure neither plump nor thin. Her round face was not unattractive, but neither was it conventionally pretty. More baby-soft than striking.

The only thing exceptional about her was the expensive cut of her pelisse and the height of her audacity. He still struggled to decide if he should laugh at the absurdity of this situation, salute the woman for her daring, or give her a blistering set-down.

But as with most things in his life, Colin chose to laugh. Life was difficult enough without taking himself too seriously.

Marriage, eh? He was twenty-three with barely two farthings to his name—marriage was his last concern.

Yes, the marquisate was paupered, mortgaged to the hilt. Yes, an advantageous marriage would set his finances to right almost instantly, but at what personal cost? Tied for life to a woman he barely knew?

No. That was not a life he wished to live.

He was accustomed to being let in the pockets. He had no desire to dig himself further into debt in order to attend the opera and balls every evening, socializing with people he hardly knew.

Colin desired more from life than that. He wanted freedom and adventure and purpose. His current course offered all three—a chance to voyage to far-off India and recoup his finances.

The multiple country houses he now owned were let with responsible tenants who oversaw the land. He made no money from them, as all available income went to debts, but neither did they require money *of* him. Once he secured funding for his venture, Colin intended to hire a man-of-affairs to oversee his lands while away in India. As for family, his mother and sisters were wed and cared for.

In short, there was little to tether him to England currently. He most certainly didn't need or want a wife. No matter how much money she brought to the match.

Which brought him back to the young woman standing before him, all but wringing her hands in nervousness. To be honest, it was that very nervousness which endeared her to him. She was clearly facing her fears in confronting him. The least he could was hear her out and respond politely.

"Miss Heartstone, I do believe it is the time-honored tradition to express gratitude when receiving an offer of marriage, no matter how . . . irregular." Colin fought to keep dry humor out of his tone. "I am not insensible to the honor you do me."

"That sounds like the beginning of a rejection, my lord." Miss Heartstone folded her hands primly and lifted her chin. "I would beg you to reconsider."

She was courageous. He chose *that* word over its less flattering cousin—*brazen*.

He couldn't help but appreciate her straightforward manner. She was honest and refreshingly direct. After weeks of fawning flattery from the *ton*—aristocrats who had only considered his acquaintance valuable once he inherited the marquisate—Miss Heartstone was a breath of fresh air. Her genuine sincerity and obvious trepidation were the only reasons he hadn't sent her packing already.

Any woman who would seize the reins of her own destiny like this was to be admired. Just the machinations that had gone into arranging their current meeting spoke volumes about her capabilities. With those two characteristics and a fortune to boot, why did she need him?

His father had been a commissioned officer in His Majesty's Army and, therefore, constantly overseas fighting in one war or another, leaving his family safe at home. Colin had been raised by his mother and older sisters. He knew, better than any man of his acquaintance, the capabilities of women.

That didn't mean he was going to accept a marriage of convenience.

"Yes, Miss Heartstone," he said, "I fear I must refuse your kind offer."

She opened her mouth to speak. He held up a staying hand. *Allow me to explain myself.*

"Why do you feel the need to purchase a title?" he asked. She wasn't the only one who could be refreshingly direct.

She winced, the motion barely visible but still obvious. Clearly, that was not the question she had anticipated.

Her spine straightened even further, if possible.

"A lord may marry for money or physical beauty. How is my proposal any different?" she scrambled to say.

She was a nimble thinker. He'd give her that.

"Forgive me. I phrased that poorly." He clasped his hands behind his back, contemplating the Long Water for a moment. "Why do you respect yourself so little that you would eagerly enter into a loveless marriage with a man who—no matter how well researched—you do not know?"

She inhaled a sharp breath. "Pardon, my lord?"

"You are a young woman in possession of a tremendous fortune. It is also obvious you are courageous and intelligent." He waved a hand toward her. "Why do you wish for a husband?"

"My mother wishes to choose my husband for me. I find her judgment somewhat lacking and prefer to find a husband for myself."

"Yes, but your mother's wishes aside, why must you have a husband? Why marry at all?"

Miss Heartstone opened her mouth. Shut it. And then frowned. Clearly struggling to answer his question.

Such foolishness. How could she embark on this path without knowing her own motivation?

Honesty was paramount for him, in all its forms—in his interactions with peers, with his family, and most importantly . . . within himself.

The unexamined life is not worth living—the famous phrase Socrates uttered when he chose death instead of renouncing rigorous mental debate.

Colin wanted to have the quote engraven on a plaque where he could see it daily. He refused to allow himself to be anything other than painfully truthful with himself. That meant carefully examining his reasons for actions. And to the occasional dismay of friends, his tendency to favor frankness over affectation or polite inanities resulted in awkward silences.

There was no other acceptable way to live.

"Women must marry, my lord," she finally replied. As an answer, it was a poor one.

"Why?" he countered.

Miss Heartstone's eyes flared. "Society expects a young woman to marry—"

"You appear comfortable flouting the expectations of society. Your proposal this morning proves that. You needn't live any part of your life according to a strict rule book, Miss Heartstone. Marriage doesn't *have* to occur before a certain age . . . or even at all, for that matter."

She blinked. But Colin was just getting started. He had listened to his mother and sisters too many times over the years. He started pacing, hands still clasped behind his back, trampling the fresh green grass under his boots.

"You, as a person, are worth far more than a marriage of convenience." He shook his head, gesturing toward her. "*I* am worth more. Marriage is a lifelong contract. It should not be entered into lightly. I do not want a *convenient* wife who will feather my nest with her money. When I do finally marry, money will have no place in the decision. I value myself more than that. I cannot imagine entering into such a binding agreement for anything less than the deepest love and respect. Why would you settle for less?"

"As I said, my mother insists that I must marry; she is most persistent—"

"Does your mother control your fortune?" he continued, pacing. "Is she forcing you into this somehow?"

"Aside from her constant henpecking?" A wry smile tugged at her lips before melting away. Miss Heartstone shook her head. "My father was wise enough to ensure my mother had no control over my inheritance. My late father's solicitor and I make all decisions for my estate. But until I reach my legal majority, obviously my mother and uncle must give approval for my marriage."

"At what age do you take sole possession of your fortune?" Colin knew that legal majority and assuming possession of her fortune were not one and the same thing—the former was set by law, the latter by her late father's will.

"If I am still unmarried at the age of twenty-one, the entirety of my father's estate comes under my care."

"At the legal age of majority then?"

"Yes."

Colin wanted to shake some sense into her. Heaven save him from young women! She did not remotely understand the power she held.

"Though your mother deserves your regard, it does not follow that she be allowed to control your future, telling you whom to marry and when," he said. "No one can force you to marry unwillingly, even before you reach your legal majority. Our English laws forbid forcible marriage at any age, under any circumstance. So if and when you *do* marry, it will be of your own choice."

Despite her nervous demeanor, she was definitely pretty enough to capture a husband, even without her enormous fortune. But could a marriage that started out so loveless bring true contentment ten or twenty years from now?

"Miss Heartstone, allow me to paint a clear picture for you. If and when you do choose to marry, your fortune will pass to your husband's purview. You will cease to be a person in the eyes of the law." He stopped pacing and studied her. "If you continue in your current course of action, you will marry a man you do not know and, perhaps, gain entrance into the highest levels of the peerage. For the dubious honor of taking another man's name, you will turn over your fortune and freedom. Under English law, your husband will control not only your money but your every move.

"I know that many women have no choice but to marry or face lives of penury. However, an unmarried woman of fortune has the world at her feet. Without a husband, you remain a person under English law. You can hold property, make decisions, and retain control of your estate. You simply must take courage and decide to marry when you wish to, not when Society or your mother dictate."

Miss Heartstone's eyes had grown three times in size as he spoke.

"But such a thing would be highly irregular, my lord. I cannot establish my own household as a single woman. 'Twould not be proper."

Colin shot a glance at the older companion behind Miss Heartstone. The tall woman might have been a ways off, but she kept a hawk's eye on them both.

He raised his eyebrows. "You most certainly *can* establish your own household, madam. If you are properly chaperoned, no one will think ill of you."

Her forehead creased.

He held out a staying hand. He was not quite done. "Marriage is an admirable state, Miss Heartstone, but given its lifelong permanence, it is not something to be undertaken lightly. If you fall in love with a man who respects you—a man who sees you as his equal—then by all means marry. If you reach a point where you want a permanent companion or children, then seek out a man to share your life. But only marry because it is your heart's desire, not out of some societal notion that marriage is required of you."

"You are a revolutionary, my lord." She shifted on her feet.

"Perhaps. Though you must be something of one yourself, given your behavior this morning."

"I concede your point."

"I ask you, Miss Heartstone, to be honest with yourself. When you imagine your future in ten or twenty years, what do you see? Is it truly marriage with a stranger? Have you taken time to listen to your heart?"

That stopped her. She froze, eyes darting out to look over the large lake beside them.

Her pause was telling.

"You need to think beyond your narrow sphere." He pressed his advantage. "My mother and sisters are tremendous followers of the writings of Mary Wollstonecraft. I have never been able to view women as mere subordinates of men. My mother would box my ears. She has always insisted that women have tremendous intellect and fortitude. You are capable of amazing things, Miss Heartstone. You merely need to believe in yourself."

The young lady blinked at him. A cool breeze floated off the Long Water, ruffling the feathers in her fashionable bonnet.

She clearly did not know how to respond to his words. Granted, few people did, which is why he rarely voiced them. He knew his ideas were . . . *revolutionary*, to use her term.

"For myself, I am more than merely a title and handful of estates," he continued. "You researched my life and fortunes and, from that, have extrapolated a series of behaviors and attitudes. But, at the end of the day, I believe myself to be greater than the mere summation of numbers and a handful of desirable qualities. You do not *see* me, Miss Heartstone—the man I truly am. So, though I am sorry to disappoint your expectations this morning, I am also quite sure you will one day thank me for my reticence in accepting your suit."

She raised her chin a notch, shoulders straight. She was so *young*. So untried in the ways of the world.

"My lord, I would ask you reconsider—"

He cut her off. "God has granted you wings, Miss Heartstone. 'Twould be a shame if you never learned how to fly."

He did not wait for her response. Instead, he tipped his hat in her direction and, clicking his heels together, gave her a short bow.

"I bid you good morning, Miss Heartstone."

... I value your opinion, daughter mine, and desire to know your insight into the matter. You say that the muslin fabric designs from last year were drab and uninspired. Do you truly feel that a more lively pattern would boost sales by 73 pct? Have your calculations led you to that conclusion, or your unerring sense of intuition as a woman? Please tell me your thoughts. You possess a brilliant mind. I feel you are destined for great things, my Little Heart-Full ...

—excerpt of a letter from John Heartstone to his daughter, Belle, age 16, on the purchase of a cotton mill outside Harrogate.

Belle walked briskly to her London townhouse, needing to return home well before her mother awoke. Not that Mrs. Heartstone ever rose before noon, but Belle refused to take any chances. The mere thought of the raptures—and Machiavellian machinations—her mother would resort to if she knew Belle had stolen out to meet with a marquess.

Ugh. Just the *thought* underscored why Belle had taken the drastic risk of seeking a husband herself.

Miss Rutger was quiet and gave a comforting pat of her hand, clearly understanding that Belle's conversation with Lord Blake had not gone as Belle had hoped.

Belle swallowed back the disappointment burning in her throat, thankful for her friend's silence.

What to do now?

Lord Blake had been by far her best choice for a husband. She had prepared an extensive list of potential grooms—cross-referenced with their financial need and statistical probability of being a caring spouse—but no other man met all her criteria quite so readily. Did she want to move on to the next candidate? She chewed on the inside of her cheek.

Lord Blake's words hummed through her head, a buzzing hive.

You are courageous and intelligent.

I ask you, Miss Heartstone, to be honest with yourself. When you imagine your future in ten or twenty years, what do you see? Have you taken time to listen to your heart?

She could see him yet, rimmed in morning light, the wind tugging at his greatcoat, chestnut hair curling from under his top hat, eyes alternating between humor and firm belief in his opinions.

A crusading angel, fighting for *her*. A woman he did not know.

God has granted you wings, Miss Heartstone. 'Twould be a shame if you never learned how to fly.

Her heart gave a painful thump.

What had he truly meant by that? What would it mean to fly?

Blink, blink, blink.

And why did his words bring her to *tears*, of all things?

She handed her bonnet, cloak, and pelisse to her butler, still fighting the tightness in her throat.

"I believe I shall lay down for a moment," she murmured to Miss Rutger. "I fear a headache is coming on."

"Of course, dear." Miss Rutger's tone was soft. Belle didn't miss the concerned, knowing look in her companion's eyes.

Belle all but fled to her bedchamber. She intended to rest and sort through her next course of action.

Instead, she paced the floor.

Lord Blake's words would not be silenced.

You are worth far more than a marriage of convenience.

When was the last time Belle had said such a thing to herself?

And why did it take a complete stranger stating something before one actually believed it?

Lord Blake's words had taken the neat box of her life and upended its contents upon the floor, leaving all the uncomfortable bits and pieces of her bare to the glaring light of truth.

She paused, staring sightlessly into the back garden below her window.

She *was* worth more than a marriage of convenience.

Her life was worth more than committing it to another without truly loving and trusting him. She wiped a fugitive tear away, swallowing back the rest.

Not even her father, God rest his soul, had ever spoken to her in such a forthright manner.

Had he?

When you marry, I would see you equally yoked, my Little Heart-Full.

Her breath caught, remembering her father's pet name for her, a play on their last name—Little Heart-Full. Papa said he called her that because his heart was full of overwhelming joy the day she was born.

As I've always said, a lady should have options, Belle.

Options . . .

She had taken that to mean she could choose *whom* she married. Her father had educated her in the ways of business so she could relate to her future husband, meet him as more of an equal. But after Lord Blake's words today . . .

Had that truly been her father's aim?

"Come, my Little Heart-Full. I have matters to discuss with you." Her father slid a comforting hand under her elbow, steering her away from her mother. "You cannot talk ribbons and embroidery all day—"

"Bother, John!" Her mother pulled three more ribbon samples out of her basket.

"However will she ensnare a husband if you keep dragging her off to talk shares and investments?"

"Snare a husband? My dear wife, young ladies are hardly poachers, slipping through the dark night, laying ribbon traps for unsuspecting male game."

"Heavens!" Her mother gasped. "What a vulgar—"

"Besides, Belle has excellent ideas as to how we can better manufacture all this frippery." Her father waved his hand. "Our daughter should have choices, my dear. I am merely ensuring she has her wits about her." He shot a telling glance at her mother. "I would hate for her to make a poor or hasty decision . . ."

An advantageous marriage had been the driving goal of Belle's life for . . . forever. She had thought researching Lord Blake's personal history was what her father meant by avoiding a 'poor or hasty decision.'

But what if that wasn't the truth of his advice? Because the more she thought about it . . .

Her father had never once stated she *must* marry. No. That had always been her mother.

Why *was* she settling for marriage to a man she did not know? The more Belle considered it, the more her reasons escaped her.

So . . . what if?

She stood in her bedroom, arms wrapped around her chest, as if she could somehow physically contain the whirlwind inside.

What *if* she chose to remain a single woman of fortune?

Until Belle reached the age of majority at twenty-one, her mother would have to live with her. Which meant her mother would continue to hound Belle to marry. But after reaching her majority, Belle would control her mother's finances completely. Surely, Belle could use that as leverage to convince her mother to let her be, to accept her wishes.

From there, Belle would be her own woman. Setting up her own household was unusual for an unmarried miss, but not beyond the pale. As Lord Blake had stated, she could keep a companion around her at all times as a chaperone. Mr. Sloan, her solicitor, was a dear friend of her father's and supportive of her involvement in her own finances, so that needn't change. Her mother could even continue to live with her, provided she ceased meddling in Belle's affairs.

And if all that came to pass . . .

Belle would be free. Free of her mother and uncle's guardianship. Free to arrange her life without requiring others' approval.

You are capable of amazing things, Miss Heartstone.

The idea was . . . intriguing.

No. *Revolutionary*, as he had said.

Just the mere thought of it . . .

Abruptly, her future fluttered wide open, brimming with choices and options. Wings unfurling, expanding her vision, soaring into a landscape she had never realized existed.

Oh.

Was this what Lord Blake had meant then?

A revolution in truth.

But such a path . . . it would not be easy. Women who flaunted society's expectations often paid a steep price.

Just look at Lord Blake's reference to Mary Wollstonecraft. She had been cast out from all polite society for her actions and writings.

Belle hugged herself harder, as if her hands were determined to keep the new-found wings from taking flight too quickly and dashing her hopes.

Living such a life would be easier in the country. But Belle would need to continue to attend the Season in London. It was the financial center of the world; she could ill afford to *not* be in London for at least part of the year.

But . . .

Belle didn't have to be flamboyant about her decisions. She simply had to be . . . careful. Cautious and obstinate. Respectably unmoved.

She mentally laid out that future in her mind, mapping all the facets of such a life. If she dressed elegantly but conservatively, if she kept Miss Rutger at her side at all times, if she behaved with the utmost propriety. Yes. Statistically, Belle could see that her chance of failure would be quite low.

Mmmmm.

But probabilities, as usual, did not remove emotions from a decision.

Belle rubbed her arms with her hands.

Did she have the courage to embrace such a life for herself? To decline marriage for five or even ten years until she found genuine love? A gentleman who truly matched her, to whom she could be equally yoked?

Belle paused, biting her lip.

Was she a rebel? An incendiary?

She probed her innermost heart. The organ felt raw and untried. She was a fledgling teetering at the edge of the nest, desperate for flight but terrified of the hard ground below.

I feel you are destined for great things, my Little Heart-Full.

Papa's words from long ago. There *was* something buried deep inside . . . a core of steel. She was her father's daughter after all.

Huh.

She had never considered how revolutions began, but she supposed that most did start with a single person in a quiet room pondering how life *should* be.

How could a single conversation so thoroughly shake the foundations of her life? How could she be reborn so quickly?

But . . . life was like this. Endless monotony and then in a single day, everything changed. She could catalog her life by such days.

The afternoon as a child when her father first showed her how to do chimney sums, unfurling the world of mathematics.

The morning Belle made her first momentous financial purchase—a shipment of raw silk thread because she saw a fashion trend toward silk ribbon that year—and had been unerringly right.

The night her father died.

The day Lord Linwood asked to be released from their betrothal.

And now, this day.

The moment she finally saw herself as her *own* for the first time.

Welcome to being an adult, she thought wryly.

So . . . if she cast off the idea of marriage for now, then what?

Be honest with yourself. What do you desire most?

Belle grabbed a handkerchief and slid into a wingback chair before her fireplace.

What did she desire most?

Her fingers beat a steady tattoo against the arm of the chair as she thought, thought, thought.

Women rarely saw themselves as persons capable of acting, of seizing their own destinies. Instead, women were almost always agents to be acted upon—beholden to parents, guardians, and society as a whole.

It was nearly strange to realize she could think and act for *herself*, too.

If she threw off everyone else's expectations, what was left within her own heart? What *did* she want?

Belle stared into the hearth for nearly an hour, tossing ideas around.

She did hope to marry *someday*. Children and a home—yes, she genuinely wanted all that. But did she desire those things right now? At the cost of her freedom? Her self-respect?

No. She really didn't.

Her talents lay in the realm of men—calculating probabilities, anticipating purchasing trends. Granted, Belle knew she brought a uniquely female perspective to it all. Most men didn't give a snap for bonnet ribbons, but she knew first-hand how to appeal to women as customers.

That said, Belle was not delusional. She knew she was no great beauty. And her clever wit never managed to escape her shy tongue, remaining firmly in her brain and not enlivening her conversation.

Lord Blake, himself, had inadvertently pointed out how utterly forgettable she was . . . visibly invisible. No one remembered her face. All they remembered was her great fortune.

But Lord Blake, at least, had the kindness to point out that she was more than the sum of her fortune. Just as he was more than the sum of his rank.

Of course, in the process of freeing her from the societal expectations of marriage, he had shown himself to be a man who would make a remarkable husband.

Ironic, that.

Her father had been a man similar to Lord Blake. And then spent his life married to her pretty, but frivolous and vain, mother. All those years of advice . . . her father had wanted her to avoid the same fate.

Belle held her father's hand, the room dark and suffocating. A low fire crackled in the grate. Candles flickered from the corners.

No one else remained. Mamma had taken herself off to bed, unequal to the task of keeping vigil over a deathbed.

No power on earth could have torn Belle from her father's side.

She leaned forward in her chair, placing a warm hand on his brow. He turned into her touch.

"I'm here yet, Little Heart-Full," he whispered, eyes closed.

But the weakness of his grasp, the gray pallor of his skin, the chill of his touch . . . all these testified that he would not be long for this world.

He had been the picture of health just a week ago. But he had spent a night in a rainstorm, and a cough had settled deep in his lungs.

The day before, the doctor had listened to Papa's labored breathing before quietly shaking his head, shooting Belle a grimacing look that could only mean one thing—

Belle gritted her teeth, angrily swiping at her damp cheeks.

"Please don't leave me, Papa," she hiccupped. "I can't go on without you—"

"Hush, child." He shook his head, the faintest of movements. Papa managed to turn his face toward her. He lifted his eyes slowly, as if great weights held them down. "You will be well, Little Heart—"

"No, Papa—"

"You will." The barest of smiles. "No father has ever been as proud of his child as I am of you. You are so brilliant and clever. You will care for all that I have built. I have ensured that everything will remain in your capable hands."

"I don't want it, Papa. Not without you by my side—"

"You are *my legacy, Belle. The very best of me. You won't let me down—"*

Belle shook off the memory, blotting her cheeks with her handkerchief.

Oh, Papa. I would give every last cent to have just one more day with you.

Papa's death had shattered her. She was quite sure she had been sleepwalking through the years since then, allowing her frivolous mother to guide her life.

Belle swallowed.

Papa would have wanted more for her.

Her father would have liked Lord Blake. They were cast from the same mold.

Though she knew it was for the best, part of her mourned that she would never know Lord Blake better. His kindness had left an impression. He seemed like he might be a kindred spirit.

No matter.

She rose and moved to the small writing desk situated before her bedroom window.

She was decided then.

She would *not* marry for now.

The decision fluttered through her, a flush of stomach-clenching nervousness. She could almost feel her tiny wings spreading outward, deliriously eager but nearly shaking with fear.

What did she want to do?

The idea blazed through her, brilliantly bright.

Of course.

It was so simple.

The Heartstones had always been focused on banking and manufacturing within Great Britain itself. But what if Belle combined her gift for probabilities and anticipating market demands with Lord Blake's societal connections and his first-hand assessment of current trade routes and procurement of materials?

Well.

Well, well, well.

Even if she never saw Lord Blake again, there was one thing she could do to thank the man who brought her to her senses.

I feel you are destined for great things, my Little Heart-Full . . .

Her father had taught her so much. It was time to pass along what she could.

4

... I would ask you to call upon George and myself tomorrow during at-home hours. We have missed your company so . . .

—*message from Cecily Radcliffe Phalean*
to her younger brother, Lord Blake

I am most sorry, my lord, but I cannot divulge my client's name. It would be a serious breach of confidentiality," Mr. Sloan said.

Colin slapped his hat against his thigh, sternly resisting the urge to continue pressing his case.

The middle-aged man behind the desk regarded him with quiet implacability. "All I can say," Sloan continued, "is that this person is in earnest. I have been this particular client's solicitor for many, many years, and I personally vouch for their trustworthiness. I ask you to respect my client's need for anonymity."

Colin grimaced. "Not quite the answer I was hoping for." He slapped his hat again.

"I am aware of that, my lord." Mr. Sloan shifted in his seat, the only evidence of his discomfort in having to deny information to a peer of the realm.

As well the man should be, blast it all.

Yesterday, a note had been delivered to Colin's rooms with a letter forwarded from one Mr. John Sloan, Solicitor. The letter currently resided in Colin's waistcoat pocket, burning with its weight.

Colin had read it at least thirty times in the past twenty-four hours.

> *To The Most Honorable, The Marquess of Blake*
> *May 2, 1816*
>
> *Dear Lord Blake,*
>
> *It has been brought to my attention that you are searching for a financial backer for your current proposed excursion into the East Indies. The East India Company Act has allowed others to venture into the Indian market, and I have been eager to capitalize on the moment. As someone with considerable financial expertise, I have studied your proposal and find your business scheme has merit.*
>
> *Despite your own inexperience in such matters, a general inquiry into your background shows you to be a man of courage and intellect. Therefore, I wish to invest the requested sum of £5000, payable immediately. In return, I propose a fifty percent profit share in the enterprise, as you can see from the enclosed papers.*
>
> *Please direct all correspondence through my solicitor, Mr. Sloan, as I desire to remain anonymous.*
>
> *I wish you God speed in your endeavors and hope for a fruitful return.*
>
> *Your obedient servant,*
> *LHF*

The letter had become a thorn in Colin's side. It seemed the whole world was aware of his plight.

He still had to shake his head over the audacity of that young Miss

Whatever-her-name from the previous week and her offer of marriage. In the moment, he had been so caught off-guard, he had scarcely known what to think. But with a little distance, he had to wonder at the desperate circumstances that would drive her to actually propose marriage to a man she barely knew. He wished her well.

But because of *that* situation, Colin felt the need to more thoroughly scrutinize any correspondence that proffered assistance.

Therefore, Colin currently sat before Mr. John Sloan himself, intent on ensuring this LHF passed muster. At least this particular letter had come through more formal channels, having gone through a solicitor.

That said, he'd like to know the identity of this mystery financial backer. The anonymity of LHF's proposal was nearly bizarre. Simply put—such behavior was not the done thing. But eccentric behavior had been the theme of his week, it would seem.

Colin stared at Mr. Sloan. The man was fairly unremarkable with brown eyes and silver-shot hair and beard, his shoulders tucked into a serviceable coat. Beyond his study door, Mr. Sloan's office was large and bustling. Clerks and assistants sat at desks, the smell of ink black and musty paper hung in the air.

"Would you do this?" Colin gestured toward the man's desk and the stack of legal papers, setting up a fledgling business between this mysterious LHF and himself.

Mr. Sloan did not hesitate. "I would, my lord. Though I am constrained and cannot discuss the particulars, I can say that my client is one of the most honorable people it has ever been my privilege to know. You will be in good hands."

Sincerity dripped from every word.

Though only twenty-three himself, Colin felt much older. Five years of military service had a way of forcing a young man to grow up quickly.

All to say, Colin was a decent judge of character. He trusted Mr. Sloan's word. This LHF was likely a worthy sort.

Now what to do?

Colin grunted. "I shall ponder it some more. You will have my answer tomorrow."

"As you wish, my lord."

Five minutes later, Colin was in a hackney carriage headed toward Mayfair and his sister's home. He stewed as the sights and sounds of London slowly crept past.

Most of him wanted to accept this LHF's proposition. India called to him with her lure of adventure and opportunity.

Moreover, his estates desperately needed an influx of cash. His land required expensive modernization in order to improve yields and lift the lives of his workers. Many of the tenant farmers who tilled his fields lived in ancient homes that leaked in the rain and provided little warmth in winter. As their landlord, it was Colin's responsibility to see to repairs. Hundreds, possibly thousands, of people depended on Colin doing the right thing.

LHF's proposal was sound, clearly coming from a seasoned mind. But Colin struggled to move past the man's insistence on anonymity. If they went into business together, they would surely be in each other's confidence. If LHF was willing to place thousands of pounds into Colin's care, why not trust Colin with his name? Colin was a man of honor. If this LHF wished his involvement to be kept secret, why not simply tell Colin his identity and request his silence?

LHF's lack of trust grated.

Colin was still struggling to make a decision when the hackney stopped in front of a pillared townhouse. Paying the fare, Colin hopped down and rapped on the front door. He smiled at the butler who promptly greeted him, chatting about the weather as Colin shed his overcoat, gloves, hat, and walking stick. Climbing the central staircase, Colin found his sister, her husband, and at least nine other people waiting for him in the drawing room.

"There you are, Blake." Cecily rose and fondly kissed his cheek. "We had started to wonder if we would see you, brother dear."

Ah, Cecily.

He loved his middle sister dearly, but she had taken to his newly-acquired title more than he had himself. So despite the fact that she had spent the previous twenty-three years calling him Colin, the second he had inherited the marquisate, he had suddenly become Blake to her, and no amount of chiding would get her to budge on that fact. She reveled in being the sister of a newly-minted marquess.

Colin surveyed the room with a combination of exasperation and amusement. Cecily was determined to show him off like some prize pony.

All the more reason to board a boat to India.

"Excellent to see you again, Blake," his brother-in-law chimed in, shaking Colin's hand.

George Phalean was an affable sort, but as his father was the youngest son of a duke, he was not above joining Cecily in social posturing among the *ton*.

"Allow me to make introductions." Cecily proceeded to pull Colin around the room, gleefully forcing him to accept an acquaintanceship with the assorted gentry assembled.

Heaven help him.

The entire situation simply underscored why the life of an idle aristocrat had no appeal for him.

Colin was politely bowing to a giggling debutante and her equally giggly mother when another visitor was announced.

"Lord Halbert Phalean," the butler intoned as a tall, pepper-gray man strode into the room.

"Father." George stood up and crossed to the older man, warmly greeting him.

Colin vaguely remembered meeting the elder Phalean once. Colin had been visiting his mother and sisters while on leave from his regiment; George and his father had called upon them.

Colin remembered Lord Halbert as being like his son, affable but clearly concerned about maintaining appearances. Lord Halbert never allowed acquaintances to forget that he was the younger son of a duke.

George tugged Lord Halbert over to Colin. "Lord Blake, I do believe you remember my father, correct?"

Colin smiled and greeted the man, shaking his hand firmly. Despite being overly prickly about his social status, Lord Halbert brimmed with good humor and politeness to those he viewed as equals, which now included Colin.

Thirty minutes later, Cecily's other guests had departed, having stayed the allotted time for a social visit, leaving only family behind taking tea. Colin found himself seated with George and his father, listening as George bemoaned Colin's imminent departure.

"Must you leave, Blake?" George set his teacup on a table. "The ink is barely dry on your Writ of Summons. Your presence is needed here in Parliament."

Colin smiled, tight and polite. "Parliament has survived without me thus far. I cannot imagine that my absence will be noticed, much less felt. However, I have estates, tenants, and debts that desperately need an infusion of cash."

"But India?" Cecily interjected. "Why must you take yourself off to India?"

"It is the best place of making one's fortune, sister." And far from the superficial social pressures of London and the *ton*.

"It's mad, I say," George said. "It's not the done thing for a marquess to dash off to foreign lands."

Colin bit his tongue, declining to point out that plenty of peers had done just that over the years.

Lord Halbert remained quiet during their exchange but now spoke up. "From what I understand, Blake, you cannot leave until you find a backer for your scheme."

"Yes," Colin agreed. "That has been a sticking point."

"Will no bank grant you credit then?"

"My spendthrift cousin exhausted the good will of the marquisate, and all relevant properties are mortgaged to the hilt. No one will extend me credit."

"So I understand." Lord Halbert turned pensive, brow furrowing. "You are trying to find a private financial backer or two?"

Colin found Lord Halbert's line of questioning somewhat odd. It was rather forward for a man who was barely an acquaintance, even if they were family by marriage.

"Yes," he answered Lord Halbert's question. "But as I never attended Eton or Harrow and have had little interaction with the *ton* and peerage over the years, I have no wealthy friends to approach." He thought of

LHF's offer burning in his pocket. "Though other avenues of assistance have recently opened up."

Lord Halbert continued to frown.

"I still say it's not the done thing," George grumbled.

His father glanced at him, eyebrows raising. "Perhaps not, George, m'boy. But I must say, I admire Blake's tenacity and honor in addressing his debts. It is to his credit."

"But for a marquess to engage in *trade*, Father—"

"Plenty of the nobility own factories and businesses, my son."

"Yes, but they don't *run* them themselves."

"True, most do not." Lord Halbert agreed with a nod. "But in all truthfulness, society's reaction to such behavior has more to do with the peer's station than anything else. Something that would be looked down upon in a mere baronet can be lauded in a duke. A marquess is substantial enough that most would not look askance at Lord Blake taking a hand in resuscitating his personal finances. Many would find it admirable, I think."

George pursed his lips. "Perhaps."

"I speak from experience, son." Lord Halbert shot George a wan smile before turning his head to lock eyes with Colin. "Besides, if the thing were done with dignity and some . . . anonymity, the outcome would be suitable."

Anonymity.

Colin's breath caught.

The older man's gaze felt heavy, weighty. As if laden with secret meaning.

George continued to grumble and his father good-naturedly verbally sparred with him. But every moment or two, Lord Halbert would turn to Colin, giving him what seemed to be a pointed look.

Did Lord Halbert mean what Colin suspected?

Colin's mind scrambled to catch up.

. . . *if the thing were done with dignity and some anonymity* . . .

Was Lord Halbert this LHF who had contacted Colin?

The initials were right, in a way—Lord Halbert Phalean. Phalean obviously started with a 'P,' but the initial sound was that of an 'F.'

Colin's breath snagged. Lord Halbert made sense as LHF. His brother, the current duke, was decidedly top-lofty. Colin imagined the man would not appreciate his brother taking an active interest in a trade venture. Hence the need for anonymity.

Though why he didn't simply say so outright, Colin was hard-pressed to understand. Perhaps Lord Halbert wished to avoid any awkwardness within the family?

It was hard to say.

Regardless, Colin deeply appreciated the man making an appearance today, knowing that Colin would have just received his proposal and likely needed assurances.

So when Lord Halbert met his gaze again, Colin smiled, tight and knowing.

As expected, Lord Halbert returned a look in kind.

That was all the final confirmation Colin needed.

He hesitated to accept money from an anonymous stranger. But a man who was practically a relation?

That was an entirely different matter.

Yes, he would accept LHF's offer and allow the man his anonymity.

He and Lord Halbert would be admirable partners together.

To LHF
May 5, 1816

Dear Sir,

I thank you for your investment. I found your discussion of the textiles market remarkably insightful, particularly your clever mathematical calculations forecasting future market growth.

More importantly, I discern you to be a man of wisdom. I firmly believe that your experience combined with my youth and enthusiasm will result in profitable yields for us both. You honor me with your faith in my abilities. They shall not be misplaced.

Sincerely,
Blake

To The Most Honorable, The Marquess of Blake
May 7, 1816

Dear Lord Blake,

Thank you for your correspondence and ideas. Please find enclosed my predictions for shipping times and market fluctuations. I have calculated the amount of silk needed to supply mills for the next year, but our profits will depend on us securing our own ships for transport once you reach India.

I strongly feel that we shall suit each other well in this endeavor. I understand that you will sail for Calcutta Wednesday next. I wish you safe travel on the long journey. I will send correspondence behind you, as needed.

Sincerely,
LHF

THE CARRIAGE SWAYED as it moved along the uneven cobblestone streets, causing Belle to grasp onto a hanging strap to steady herself. The last gasp of sunlight streamed through the glass to her right, scattering prisms of light throughout the carriage interior. The summer solstice was just past, so though the hour was quite late, the sun was yet aloft.

Belle noticed all this only in passing. Instead, she took in another steadying breath, ordering her racing heart to *Be still*. But the stubborn organ refused to listen and continued to thunder away.

Across from her, Miss Rutger smiled, half pity, half understanding. "You must calm down, my dear. All this nervous fretting will only cause you to become lightheaded and faint."

"I know." Belle swallowed. "But I feel that so much is dependent upon this evening."

Belle was attending an intellectual salon for the first time, with only Miss Rutger at her side. Her mother would not be joining them.

That was all good.

But, as things turned out, the idea of a room swarming with activity and chatter was much simpler than the reality of it—so many new faces to learn, so many intelligent minds to speak with . . .

Belle could already see herself frozen, a wallflower, helplessly tongue-tied.

It had only been a handful of weeks since her encounter with Lord Blake and her resolve to transform her life. She couldn't expect to conquer her shyness and tendency to prefer shadows overnight. Her wings were yet so new and untried.

But look at Blake, she thought. *He has embraced his future and, at this very moment, is sailing for Calcutta. You can do this much.*

Besides, the only way to strengthen her wings was to use them. Belle had longed to participate in Lady Simpson's weekly salons for months now, but her mother had remained obstinate.

Just imagine, Mrs. Heartstone had said, *if people found out. They would assume you were a bluestocking who likes to read and harbors her own . . . her own . . . ideas!*

The horror.

The entire concept sounded perfectly perfect to Belle.

Slowly, Belle had whittled down her mother's resistance, until Mamma had reluctantly allowed her to attend Lady Simpson's salon.

Now . . . she simply had to summon the courage to walk through the front door and talk to someone.

"I have faith in you," Miss Rutger said. "You proposed marriage to a marquess just last month. You run a thriving financial empire and have one of the more brilliant minds I have ever encountered. You are courageous."

Belle shot her friend a grateful smile.

"Besides, I like hearing all the gossip, so we must attend these soirees." Wicked teasing laced Miss Rutger's tone.

Belle chuckled.

Miss Rutger settled back against her seat. She looked very much like the paid companion she was—hair pulled into a tight chignon, her dress a well-cut but modest gray. Tall and angular, Miss Rutger had a look that would politely be called Amazonian. She loomed over most men and easily intimidated would-be trouble-makers. But it was her grounded practicality and sense of humor that endeared her most to Belle.

"It is enough that you are trying," Miss Rutger continued. "Sometimes that is all we can do—place one foot in front of another and keep moving forward."

Miss Rutger knew of what she spoke. The eldest daughter of a vicar, Miss Rutger had been orphaned as a teenager. Separated from her younger siblings, she had then been passed between relatives, earning her keep as an unpaid companion or governess. Along the way, she had met a soldier headed off to Spain and the Pennisular War. They had fallen desperately in love and plighted their troth, but he had been killed in the Battle of Salamanca.

Heartbroken and tired of her relatives' condescending ways, Miss Rutger had responded to Mrs. Heartstone's inquiries for a governess and paid companion for her only daughter. Mrs. Heartstone had thought Miss Rutger too forthright, but Belle found her perfect.

Belle needed a strong personality as a friend, someone who she could trust implicitly. Miss Rutger had been that person for Belle from the very beginning. Even though Miss Rutger was twelve years older than herself, Belle never felt that age gap.

"Besides, think of this evening from a business perspective," Miss Rutger said.

"True," Belle nodded.

"There is no better place than the salons of the *ton* to discover what ladies' fashion will be next year. I don't listen to the gossip sheerly for my own enjoyment."

Belle smiled. She knew she was in a unique position. The tradesmen and factory owners who supplied the ladies of Britain's upper ten thousand—the *ton*—rarely had close access to those they served. Belle, however, moved freely in their circles. Yes, she wasn't admitted to the upper, upper echelons of society, but she did mingle where most of the purchasing power resided—the ladies and their eligible daughters. Even at an intellectual soiree such as this one, women would still make passing comments about bonnet trims and fabric preferences.

And knowledge was money when it came to anticipating and supplying fashion trends.

Their carriage lurched to a stop in front of Lady Simpson's townhouse. Belle exchanged a look with Miss Rutger.

"You can do this," Miss Rutger whispered. "I know you can."

Nodding, Belle took a deep breath.

She could do this.

She *would* do this.

Straightening her shoulders, Belle stepped out and climbed the stairs, knocking on the front door. All too soon, Belle and Miss Rutger were ushered into a crowded drawing room.

It was at that point that Belle's nerve failed her.

Everyone seemed so at home, so comfortable in their own skin. It was one thing to write letters or confront a marquess in desperation.

It was something else entirely to brave a gauntlet of well-read matrons who had opinions on everything from the price of corn shares to Aristotle's relevance in the modern political landscape.

"I should not have come," Belle whispered to Miss Rutger.

"Nonsense. You are right where you should be."

Belle wasn't nearly so confident. Her mind drifted to Blake aboard his ship, headed off into the vast unknown. Was he afraid, too? Did the thought of everything before him in India strike terror into his heart?

Were they explorers together in this grand adventure?

For some reason, picturing the difficulties that Blake surely faced brought her a measure of calm.

She would likely not hear from him more than once or twice a year, at most. But it helped to know that he was out there.

That together, they could take on the world.

Besides, Belle knew quite a lot about corn shares. And though she didn't have opinions about the current political landscape, she had read enough of Socrates to appreciate the complexities of a social contract.

So when Lady Simpson came forward a few minutes later, Belle swallowed her shyness and greeted her warmly.

And when Lady Simpson introduced Lord Stratton and his beautiful wife, Lady Stratton, Belle pasted a smile on her face, found her courage, and said, "Lord Stratton, it is a pleasure to finally meet you. I do believe we are cousins of a sort."

To LHF
November 23, 1816

Dear Sir,

Please excuse the brevity of this missive. It is simply a follow-up to my previous letter regarding the spices I sent on from the coast of Ceylon. I know spices have not been part of our plans to date, but the opportunity arose to purchase them at an extremely reasonable price. We should recoup our investment ten-fold. I have some proposed suggestions regarding spices going forward on the following sheet.

Also, on a personal note, I find the sights and sounds of India fascinating. I have enclosed a sketch I did of a cobra and snake charmer for your enjoyment, though please excuse the ineptness of my drawing skills.

Sincerely,
Blake

COLIN SAT ALONE in his rooms, staring sightlessly into the empty fire grate. Some noise intruded, but as usual, he was left to his own company.

Such was the life of an unmarried man in Calcutta.

Colin's quarters adjoined that of other enterprising bachelors, all housed in the British section of the city. His current apartments were on the third floor of a European-style townhouse. In typical English fashion, his countrymen had arrived in Calcutta over two centuries previously and had immediately begun to recreate London on a smaller scale.

As for the townhouse itself, the upward design worked well in a climate that was cold and rainy—retaining warmth and rebuffing wind— but was ill-suited to the heat and humidity of India.

The tropical sun beat down, warming the room to an unholy temperature, forcing him to strip to his shirtsleeves and leave his boots off. Colin desperately wanted to move into a more traditional space, something with large windows and a courtyard that allowed the air to circulate.

But for now, he had to simply survive this latest bout of homesickness.

Today was Christmas Eve.

Granted, Colin had spent a good number of Christmases away from family and friends. But he had never been quite so far away. And in quite so foreign a place.

And with so few friends.

Of course, as the Marquess of Blake, he had been invited to dine this evening with the Governor-General. But such an evening was more about encouraging business contacts than celebrating a holiday. Just thinking about making small talk with strangers set his head to pounding.

Besides, there were still hours and hours before he needed to dress for dinner.

He rested his elbows on his knees, his hands hanging from the wrists. Now what?

He could read, he supposed. Or visit the taproom of the tavern down the street.

Neither option sounded too appealing.

Instead, he slumped further into his chair, head back, allowing his mind to wander.

What was Lord Halbert doing right now, he wondered? Enjoying a festive dinner with George and Cecily? Laughing in cozy warmth as snow fell outside? Surely, they would light a yule log, servants keeping the enormous log burning through Twelfth Night.

He could see it now. An old-fashioned, wood-lined dining room, snug and welcoming. Candles flickering from sconces and the candelabra on the table. Pine boughs and cut holly decorating the fireplace mantel. Perhaps even some mistletoe hung across the doorway. Cecily would make some remark about missing her brother, Lord Blake, and Lord Halbert would smile—

Colin took several deep breaths, forcing back the painful longing threatening to choke him.

He would have that, he vowed. At some future point, Colin would sit with them together at that table and celebrate Christmas.

But until then, he would have to settle for Lord Halbert's letters. Writing to LHF had become something of a catharsis, Colin realized. A much-needed line of connection to home. Colin appreciated the warmth and kindness that shone through every letter he received from the man. He had come to feel a strong connection to his sister's father-in-law.

Before Colin could consciously make the decision, he was moving toward his small writing desk and pulling a sheet of paper out, beginning yet another letter to LHF.

My Lord Marquess
February 12, 1817

   Dear Lord Blake,

Thank you for your letter last week regarding the on-going purchase of silks in Calcutta. I have enclosed a report on the sale of the spices and tea you sent on.

I appreciate your recent letter detailing your progress with the punjab and silk merchants. As I have repeatedly said, nothing is as effective as looking a seller in the eye as you shake hands on a business transaction.

Per your request, I am enclosing my estimates for purchasing further caches of spices. I propose that the return would be worth the investment.

Also, I am not sure I properly thanked you for the sketch you sent of a monkey eating a banana on your balcony. I could nearly smell the flowers. I will direct my cook to prepare my favorite curry tonight in your honor.

   Sincerely,
   LHF

To LHF

Calcutta

March 28, 1817

Good Sir,

The silks are on their way and I pray the market holds fast. They will be arriving late in the season, but I have faith that their quality will command a high price. I have found another supplier for black tea who promises a stronger rate of return and a more nuanced taste. I will journey three days north of Calcutta next week to ascertain the veracity of this. You hit upon genius to think more of a lady's sensibilities when creating our tea blends. Most men overlook the fact that it is the lady of the house who makes decisions as to tea, not her husband. You are wise to focus more specifically on their wishes and tastes.

I feel compelled to add that your keen business sense combined with philosophical insights make you a most compelling correspondent. I appreciate having a seasoned man of such wisdom as my partner in this endeavor—

Belle shook her head as she read through Lord Blake's most recent report.

The man had proved a much more diligent correspondent than she had ever anticipated. He wrote with shocking regularity and liked to include observations and items unrelated to their business. This letter, in particular, was more personal than most.

Belle was unsure what to do with his comment about having '*a seasoned man of such wisdom as my partner*.' Clearly, she needed to tell him about her gender, but what would happen if she did? Would he dissolve their fledgling business? If things fell apart right now, the results could be disastrous for not only her and Lord Blake, but for the thousands who were relying on them—

The door snicking open jerked Belle's eyes upward, breaking her train of thought.

"Belle, love. Lord Armstrong should be arriving within the hour." Belle's mother appeared in the doorway to the study, her mouth drawing down as she took in Belle's desk strewn with correspondence and business ledgers. Not that her mother knew a thing about Lord Blake or the goings on of Belle's day-to-day business.

More to the point, managing her mother's incessant requests *and* discreetly running a thriving international trading empire was pushing Belle's reserves to the limit.

Some days, it felt like she barely had enough time to breathe.

"You must change your dress," her mother continued, her expression a maternal mix of exasperation and dismay, clearly struggling to understand how she had birthed such a daughter.

Only years of experience kept Belle from rolling her eyes.

She had no interest in Lord Armstrong or any of the legions of men that her mother trotted in front of her. Marriage was far from her thoughts currently. Calculating transportation costs and tea prices was far more pressing and important than balls and routes and slow carriage rides in Hyde Park. Her mother simply didn't understand that getting tea and silks to market when demand was at its highest was the difference between fifty- or one-hundred percent profit. A sizable profit meant being able to secure future work for her factory laborers, instead of cutting back.

Thousands depended on Belle and Lord Blake making sound decisions. Something her mother clearly did not understand.

Worse, lately it seemed the more Belle resisted marriage, the more her mother pressured her to accept it.

Her mother *did* understand her daughter well-enough to read Belle's expression. Mrs. Heartstone bustled into the room, hands fluttering, hair and clothes perfectly styled. Despite her years, Mrs. Heartstone still retained the dainty prettiness that had so attracted Belle's father.

"Belle," she said, heaving an exasperated sigh, "you need to accept *one* of these gentlemen."

"Must I, Mamma?"

"Yes!" Her mother's voice climbed an octave. "You come into your inheritance in only six months' time. I am sure that your father, God rest his soul, would not have wanted you to be a . . . a *spinster*." Mrs. Heartstone said the word as if it were particularly repellent.

Belle, truth be told, was decidedly tired of this conversation. She and her mother had been doing a similar dance for nearly a year now, with Belle avoiding telling her mother the truth.

But today, Belle said the first words that crossed her tongue:

"Mamma, I am quite sure that my father, God rest his soul, would not have cared whether I married or not."

"Not cared?!" Now her mother *did* screech.

Oh dear.

This was why Belle had avoided stating the situation so baldly to her mother. She set down her quill.

Perhaps it was the slew of unanswered correspondence before her—decisions about silk orders for the next few months, questions about investing in a factory outside Paisley, and could she possibly contribute to Lord Wallace's charitable foundation?

Perhaps it was a lack of restful sleep worrying over the little white lie she continued to tell Lord Blake finally catching up with her.

Or, perhaps, Belle was tired of using work as an excuse to avoid this very conversation.

So even though she knew she shouldn't bait her mother further, Belle replied anyway. "Mamma, one must be well beyond the age of *twenty* to be considered a spinster."

Her mother's eyes narrowed to small slits. "You are in definite danger of spinsterhood, young lady. Mark my words. And then who will have you? You'll have to settle for a mere *mister* and all my hard work—No! Your *father's* hard work!—will have been for naught."

Belle bit her tongue. *Heaven forbid! A mere mister.* Gasp. *All the civilized world knows we cannot have that!*

Only six more months, Belle repeated her mother's words to herself. Only six more months until her mother and uncle had no more say over her.

Six more months to complete freedom and independence.

"There is more to life than marrying a title." Belle said the words without carefully considering them.

Her mother blanched, face turning deadly white. "I cannot believe a child of mine would say such a thing. Of course, you must marry a title. I shall speak with your uncle immediately. We cannot force you to marry, but you must rethink your reluctance—"

"You're not listening to me." Belle rose from her chair. "Marriage isn't all that is important—"

"No, daughter. *Nothing* is more important." Her mother's cheeks flushed. "Someday you will understand how the world works and you will see."

"I understand enough, Mother. I don't need—"

"You *need* to marry!"

"No, Mamma! I don't."

"You do!"

"I don't! In fact, I may never marry at all!"

Belle's words landed between them with a loud *splat.*

Mrs. Heartstone gasped, hands clutched to her bosom, all the color draining from her face.

"You *c-cannot* be in earnest, Belle."

Belle straightened her spine. The action had become more and more familiar over the past year.

"I am in dead earnest, Mamma." She jutted out her chin. "I am in no hurry to marry. If I meet a man who sparks my interest, I will consider marriage. Until then, however, I will remain unattached."

Mrs. Heartstone sat down on a chair, face aghast.

"You used to be such a biddable, obedient daughter. What has caused you to change so?"

"Mamma—"

"Why must you abuse me in this fashion?"

"Mamma! This is hardly abuse." Belle gave her mother a mollifying look. "I have merely realized that I do not wish to marry right now. Perhaps in the future, that will change."

Silence rang between them.

Finally, her mother managed to swallow.

"But . . . but what will become of me?" her mother whispered. "Who will manage . . . everything? Where will I even live?"

Ah.

The truth at last.

Belle's heart softened.

Of course. Her mother was concerned about her place in the world. Without a man to oversee things—whether that be a husband or a son-in-law—Mrs. Heartstone was adrift. The woman had been adrift for years and was at loose ends trying to find her way back to surer ground.

Belle understood that feeling well.

Her mother needed something to help her see that life could be lived without a man at her side.

"Mamma, who do you think has been managing our investments since Papa's death?"

Her mother blinked at her, as if slowly attempting to comprehend Belle's words.

"Mr. Sloan, I presume," she replied

Belle nodded. "Mr. Sloan has been helpful. But *I* have been managing it all, Mamma. And I will continue to manage it for myself and for you. You have nothing to fear."

Her mother continued to stare, eyes wide. "I don't think it seemly for you to involved yourself to such a degree—"

She and her mother would never see eye-to-eye on the issue of running a business.

"Mamma, have I told you about the lovely property I found for you just outside Cambridge?" Belle changed the subject.

There was no such property. But Belle would set one of her stewards to finding one immediately.

More paperwork, she sighed.

She would need to hire another clerk. Possibly two.

Yet another task.

But . . . if it gave her mother something else to focus on . . .

"Property?" Her mother frowned clearly trying to follow the change in topic.

"Yes. Remember how I mentioned building you—I mean, *us*—a new house?"

"Oh! Yes!" Her mother's eyes lit with interest. "A new house."

Belle tapped the papers before her. "Give me another fifteen minutes, Mamma, and I will come to meet with Lord Armstrong, and then we can discuss the new house."

And you will have a project to obsess over other than myself, Belle mentally continued.

One more task. One more thing added to her to-do pile.

Belle swallowed a tired sigh.

"A new house," her mother repeated, eyes dreamy and clearly focused on building and furnishing a home.

Worth. It. Belle decided then and there.

Particularly as the reprieve allowed her time to pick up a pen and reply to Lord Blake's letter. She would deal with the issue of her identity and gender later.

For now, she and Lord Blake had business to attend to.

My Lord Marquess
August 27, 1817

My Lord,

I shall jump straight to the good news. The first shipment of silks arrived in London last week and fetched five percent more than we had anticipated. The colors and patterns were spot on for fashions this year. Three of the leading modistes in London snatched up the lion's share of the fabric before it was even taken off the ship. I have sent the details of the transaction to your solicitor, along with your percentage of the profits.

On a personal note, I find your continued descriptions of life in Calcutta to be fascinating. Large tigers, traveling by elephant, the smell of spices in the air. As I have mentioned, my personal circumstances do not permit me to travel. I deeply appreciate your kindness in sharing your experiences with me through your words and drawings. I have often wondered if I would find India fascinating or if homesickness would take me. Though with your words and images to keep me company, I do not have to leave my desk to experience other climes.

And to reply to your posed riddle . . . What grows when it eats, but dies when it drinks?

A fire. (Hah! It took me a moment to think of the answer.)

Here is one of my own: At night, they come without being fetched. By day, they are lost but never stolen. What are they?

Your friend in this journey,
LHF

6

To LHF
Calcutta

June 21, 1818

   Good Sir,

The spice investment has been a thorough success, thankfully offsetting the losses we suffered earlier in the year. I still regret that our last load of silks arrived too late for the first rush of dress orders for the Season. We will do better next year. That said, I deeply appreciated your sage words of advice in dealing with the tribesmen conflict. Without your guidance, I don't know that we would have gotten the silks to market at all.

Like in Homer's Odyssey, you have truly been Mentor to my Telemachus. Though in Hindi, they use the word guru more often to describe a trusted teacher. I bow to you in humble gratitude, my guru.

Please note my attached predictions if we continue to import spices at our current rate. Also, please thank Mr. Sloan for securing the mortgage on my family seat in Dorset, as well as my townhouse in London. It is a relief to usher the marquisate back from the brink of ruin.

Also, thank you for forwarding the latest volume of poems from Mr. Coleridge. I find his descriptions of the Far East in Kubla Khan to be evocative. Though he describes China not India, his words do indeed remind me of my time here in Calcutta. I have included several pages of my scribbled thoughts as I read the volume.

I must admit to enjoying literature that explores the exotic and phantom more than I should. The works of Sir Walter Scott are a particular delight. A guilty pleasure perhaps, but one I am not ashamed to admit to among friends.

You are kind to continue to enjoy my drawings, inept as they are. I will never make my living as an artist. But I wish you to feel fully a part of the experience here in India.

As for your last riddle: What always runs but never walks; always murmurs but never talks; has a bed but never sleeps; has a mouth but never eats?

Hah! A river.

And now one for you: Four days start with the letter 'T.' One is Tuesday. The other, Thursday. Can you name the other two?

> *Your friend,*
> *Blake*

COLIN REMOVED HIS hat, using a handkerchief to mop the sweat dripping down his face.

Damn and blast but India was hotter than Hades on a good day.

A train of pack mules and wagons stretched ahead of him, circling toward a small village. Hired guards rode the perimeter, their colorful silk robes collecting dust, rifles glinting in the bright sun.

Shoving his hat back onto his head, Colin drank deep from his water flask.

Colin wouldn't breathe a sigh of relief until this shipment was safely loaded aboard ship. Only two more days until they reached port. He would be damned if he was late getting silks and tea to market in London this year. He had spent the last several months forging stronger bonds along trade routes, moving deeper into India.

Fortunately, the tribesmen Colin had hired to protect his wares had done their job. There had been the occasional skirmish over the past week—an enterprising group of teens had tried to run off some of their horses one night, a small band of would-be thieves had fired at them from a distance before racing off—but never a pitched battle.

Granted, Colin had laid his plans carefully. He needed the locals to see him as a force to be reckoned with. So Colin had hired several "drunkards" to spread word of his fearsome reputation as a former captain in His Majesty's Army through the taverns and streets of Calcutta.

Colin was quite sure that his actual ferocity did not match the rumors he had spread, but that was entirely the point of the rumors.

It was LHF who had suggested laying the initial groundwork of rumors.

The man was a bit of a tactical genius, to be honest. Where others would use more traditional methods of brute force, LHF always suggested employing the sections of society that Colin would never have considered—widows, orphans, injured veterans, etc.— to carry out more stealthy, emotional attacks. LHF's thinking was always unexpected and cleverly cunning.

All of which partially explained why Colin had made this journey himself. He surely could have hired an overseer to do it for him. But he wanted to touch the silks and spices with his own hands. He wanted to ensure that the products were as promised.

And perhaps even more importantly, he didn't want to let Lord Halbert down. The man trusted Colin to see things through properly.

"Nearly there, my lord." The leader of his hired guards, Arjun, pulled to a stop beside Colin. "Just another day and then we will be in the city proper."

"How great is our current risk of trouble?" Colin asked.

Arjun shrugged. "Most of the danger left when we passed through the mountains. Villages like these"—he motioned toward the small houses ahead—"pose little threat to us. The people are too busy worrying about their next meal. They won't pick a fight that they would surely lose." Arjun hefted his rifle, punctuating his point.

Colin nodded. "Carry on, then. I'd like to reach an inn before sundown. Sleeping in a real bed tonight would be nice."

Arjun saluted and rode off to communicate with his men.

Colin took another swig of water.

Only two more days and then he could report success to LHF.

Now he simply had to think up a riddle to include in his letter.

"REALLY, MY DEAR, I fear I must insist that you cease accompanying me on these . . . excursions." Mr. Sloan placed a steadying hand underneath Belle's elbow, helping her tiptoe across the filthy street to their waiting carriage.

"I need to assess the conditions in my factories, Mr. Sloan. I like seeing my workers' faces and reading the stories their eyes tell. I've said this repeatedly."

"Yes, but, it is hardly seemly—"

"The managers think I am your niece. Miss Rutger"—Belle waved a hand toward Anne at her side—"is here as chaperone. It is perfectly respectable."

Mr. Sloan darted his eyes up and down the street. They were in a decidedly grimy section of Bristol. Dung and refuse turned the paving stones into a river of muck. The factory gates behind them dripped with humidity; chimney-smoke clung to the gray stones.

Belle regretted nothing. The factory visit had been enlightening. She did not adhere to the belief that workers should be kept tired and hungry and desperate in order to be profitable. If anything, she felt the opposite to be true. The drawn faces of the men, women, and children on the factory floor, spinning cotton into fabric, had told her all she needed to know.

She had long suspected that her manager might be hiding secrets.

She was not wrong.

The money she had allocated for providing for her workers had not, in fact, trickled down to them. Worse, she was quite sure she had seen some extremely young children, definitely under the legal age of nine, which Belle already felt to be obscenely young to be working in a factory.

She would correct the problem immediately. As soon as she could sit down and draft a few letters.

Mr. Sloan looked around again. "This is no place for two ladies."

Belle barely bit back her sigh.

Yes, she knew this wasn't precisely 'proper.'

Oof! She was so tired of *proper* and *polite* and . . . *clean*. She longed to get her hands even dirtier. To delve and dive into the everyday management of her business, correct the wrongs she saw going on even within her own properties—

But as a woman, this was all denied her. The best she could do were these occasional visits with Mr. Sloan and vigorous letter writing.

For all intents and purposes, Mr. Sloan was part advisor, part father-figure. He had been loyal to her father and now was devoted to her. More to the point, he was the man who acted on Belle's behalf in the business world.

For example, when she needed to visit a factory to assess a situation, Mr. Sloan would accompany her and Anne. Or when she wished to inspect a new property. Or, well, anything at all. He was her mask and her protector.

Belle had to trust someone with all her secrets; Anne Rutger as her companion turned best friend and Mr. Sloan as her solicitor were the only two who knew the true identity of LHF.

Blake still did not know the truth of Miss Belle Heartstone.

For possibly the millionth time, she pondered how she had arrived in this place with Blake. She had never meant for their correspondence—their relationship, such as it was—to reach this point. She had just intended to send him the money as a thank-you and then go their separate ways.

But he had replied and she had replied, and she had found herself in the middle of their friendship before really meaning to.

And now, nearly three years later . . . things had traveled too far. Too many people depended on her and Blake making wise decisions. Too many depended on them together as partners.

This factory visit was an excellent case in point.

They stopped beside the carriage, Mr. Sloan lowering the steps and lifting a hand to help Belle inside, because heaven forfend that she should step into a carriage unassisted—

But just as she placed her hand into Mr. Sloan's, a dark shape leaped from the shadows, pushing Belle with one hand and reaching for the reticule dangling from her wrist with the other. Startled, Belle screamed and reflexively jerked her arm away, staggering sideways into Mr. Sloan.

Mr. Sloan caught her, holding her upright, but his hands were tangled in her pelisse.

Sensing his moment, the thief reached for her reticule again, clearly intent on what he thought might be money inside.

He wasn't wrong.

The man had just wrapped his hand around Belle's wrist, when Anne smashed her umbrella across the thief's head. The momentary distraction was long enough for the coachman to leap down and restrain the man in a headlock.

The sound of a gun cocking froze them all in place. The thief stilled in the coachman's hold, though his hand still held Belle's wrist. Anne panted beside them.

"Hold there!" Mr. Sloan had a pistol pointed at the would-be thief.

Belle blinked in surprise, eyes darting between the gun and Mr. Sloan. She hadn't even realized that he had anything like that on his person. She yanked her arm from the thief's grip.

Fear and surprise chose that moment to catch up with her. Energy flooded her body, followed quickly by horror. How would this situation have gone if their would-be assailant had a pistol instead of Mr. Sloan? All of Mr. Sloan's prior warnings tumbled through her brain.

Hands shaking, Belle hugged her arms, rubbing warmth back into them. Without Mr. Sloan's preparation . . .

She lifted her eyes, meeting those of the man in her coachman's grasp.

The man panted, face muddy, eyes wild. A ragged scar cut across his left cheek and nose, and he seemed to be missing his left ear. His clothing, Belle noted, was little more than rags. More to the point, his left hand was only a stump. Though he couldn't be much older than herself, his blue eyes held a lifetime of struggle.

Belle could not remove her gaze from him. Emotions winged through her, so chaotic she could scarcely catch them.

"Hold him, Mr. Reynolds, until I can fetch a constable." Mr. Sloan's tone was brisk.

There was something about the thief's eyes. A sense of terrible desperation.

"No!" She held out a staying hand.

Everyone stilled.

"My dear," Mr. Sloan began, "this man is a law-breaking thief—"

Belle didn't hear the rest of his words; the sound of her own heartbeat drowned out all else. She finally put together what the man's clothing had once been—a soldier's uniform.

Oh!

His obvious injuries suddenly made more sense. Swallowing back her fear and righteous anger, Belle continued to hold the soldier's gaze.

"What is your name?" she asked him.

He licked his lips, his head still at an awkward angle from Mr. Reynold's tight hold.

Mr. Reynolds rattled the man. "Answer the lady," he growled.

"Thomas Kincady," the man rasped.

"Formerly of his Majesty's army?" Belle asked.

After a brief hesitation, Thomas nodded. "Lost me 'and and ear at Waterloo. Got caught in a saber charge." He waved the stump of his missing hand at her.

Any remaining righteous anger drained from her. So much suffering was held in those simple facts. This man had been gravely wounded defending Britain against French aggression.

And society repaid him with poverty and desperation.

"Why do you need my purse?" Belle lifted her wrist, the reticule dangling from it. Thomas' eyes followed the motion.

"Miss Heartstone—" Mr. Sloan began again. "—this man tried to rob you. There are a thousand like him in just this part of the city—"

"Let him speak, please, Mr. Sloan." Belle kept her tone firm.

She nodded toward Thomas.

A long pause.

"Me family 'asn't eaten in three days," Thomas finally said. "M' wife and children need food."

The words *could* be a lie. Belle had no way of knowing.

But . . . somehow she doubted it.

Though subtle, Thomas reminded her of Blake. They didn't look much alike, she supposed, but the sense of underlying strength was the same. Thomas would do what he must to provide for his own.

And so Belle asked herself the same question she always did: What would Blake do if he were here?

Honestly, she had no real idea.

But she'd like to think that Blake would talk to the man. That he would understand why Thomas Kincady had landed here, snatching reticules from seemingly helpless women. His crime would probably have him transported at best. At worst, he would face a hangman's noose.

"We will not call the constable," Belle said.

Mr. Sloan bristled. Mr. Reynolds frowned. Thomas sagged in relief.

Belle ignored them all, tugging her rumpled pelisse back into place, righting her skewed bonnet.

"Tell me your story, Thomas," she said.

To My Lord Marquess
May 12, 1819

Dear Blake,

I have attached a separate letter for you with the details of your latest shipment. I do believe you will have enough to clear the rest of the debts left to you by the previous marquess. Also, I understand congratulations are in order for your appointment as counsel to the Governor-General. Well done, my friend.

Your description of the plight of the poor in India has lingered with me. Particularly, as you rightly observed, such desperation exists everywhere, even in Britain.

Unable to purge your thoughts from my head, I have spoken with Mr. Sloan about establishing a charity to help soldiers reduced to poverty after Napoleon's defeat. Though it has been four years, many still do not have gainful employment, having lost limbs in the war. As a former soldier yourself, I hoped you would have insight as to what would be best. I want to do more than simply feed or house these people; I want former soldiers to feel a sense of purpose again.

To that end, I have my eye on an estate in Dorset of around five thousand acres that is currently empty of tenants. I have been thinking of creating a working farm, of sorts. A place where soldiers and their families could build a new life and tend to the land without the weight of a heavy rent. Your thoughts, good sir?

As per your repeated requests for me to tell you more about myself, I would plead for your forbearance. I know you value honesty, and I do not wish you to doubt my integrity. There are reasons for my silence on this matter, none of which would impact yourself. Consider me eccentric. I can, however, provide an answer to your request for a description. I am neither tall, nor short in stature. Neither thin nor stout. My hair and eyes are simply brown. In summation, I am utterly unremarkable.

In an attempt to remind you of home (and perhaps indulge in your taste for things gothic and ghostly), I have included a recently published novel. It is titled The Vampyre *and is all the rage in London at present. Lord Byron insists he is not its author, but regardless, it is a guilty pleasure to read. I hope it shivers your spine.*

And I have an answer to your latest riddle—I know of a house where one enters it blind and comes out seeing. What is this house?

A school

And one for you: You answer me, but I never ask you a question. What am I?

Your friend,
LHF

Colin set LHF's letter down on his desk, glancing at the book he had just unwrapped, before shaking his head.

He pondered the riddle for only a moment—*You answer me, but I never ask you a question. What am I?*—but as he held correspondence in his hand at the moment, the answer was obvious: A stamp.

But the riddle wasn't the phrase that puzzled Colin.

In summation, I am utterly unremarkable.

This from a man who had compassion on the poverty-stricken soldiers from the conflict with Napoleon. His Majesty's government had treated the men so poorly after their sacrifice and service. That Lord Halbert would see this need and try to help in any small way . . .

LHF had surprising depths of humility.

Colin added it to the column of Things He Admired about Lord Halbert. His business partner had a brilliant mind for business (and riddles, truth be told), in addition to his clever correspondence. It was a pity that he hid it from his family.

As their friendship had matured from mere business associates to true friends, he had to wonder why Lord Halbert insisted on the charade. Colin had been trying to coax the older man into revealing himself, but to no avail.

Colin respected his friend's wish for privacy. But that didn't mean that he hadn't drafted more than one letter announcing that he knew LHF's true identity, that he wished to bring their correspondence into the light. The letters remained unsent in his writing desk.

A letter would be well enough, but most of him wanted to thank the man in person. It was enough, for now, that Colin knew his identity.

"Shall we continue, my lord?" Colin's secretary lifted his head from the desk opposite where he sat.

Nearly a year ago, Colin had finally managed to put together sufficient funds to let a proper house with light-filled rooms and a fountain to cool the air.

Sounds drifted in. The buzz of insects, the distant chatter of monkeys, the incessant clatter of wagons and shouting of travelers beyond his garden wall.

Colin slipped LHF's letter inside the book, nodding his head.

"Yes. Where was I in my dictation?"

"You had just asked the Governor to forward on the shipping reports, my lord."

"Yes. Allow me to continue."

Colin rattled off numbers, his secretary dutifully writing down the words. But Colin's mind was far away, thinking of home. England with its cool rain and fresh winds.

And his friend whom he would someday greet and converse with in person.

To LHF
Calcutta

March 24, 1820

My dear friend,

I appreciate your concern for my safety. Cholera has claimed a great many lives here in Calcutta, but I have remained well. It is perhaps due to your sending me that novel, Frankenstein, or The Modern Prometheus. Once I had absorbed the horror of Dr. Frankenstein's monster, I daresay even pestilence itself decided to keep its distance. I appreciate you keeping me well-stocked with gothic literature. It has often, ironically, lifted my spirits.

Mr. Sloan has apprised me of the continued progress being made with Hopewell Manor. I was moved as I read stories of the soldiers who have found hope within its bounds. You have done well and give me far too much credit. I merely matched your own generous donations. Those who fought against the French Terror need my assistance more than do my own coffers. I have instructed Mr. Sloan that I wish to assist in the purchase of the adjacent two thousand acres you mentioned. It will allow us to help so many more.

I agree with your latest assessment of our trade. I intend to remain here another year or two, at minimum. I have strong contacts within and without the British community. 'Twould be a shame to leave when there is so much yet to build.

I greatly enjoyed your last riddle: The more I dry, the wetter I become. What am I?

A towel, of course.

And now one for you, which I greatly hope will stump you most thoroughly—

What is so delicate that even saying its name will break it?

In friendship,
Blake

To My Lord Marquess
December 28, 1820

   Dear Blake,

My good friend, I cannot express my abiding sympathy at the passing
of your dear mother. I know the depths of your affection for her. Please
accept the condolences of a true kindred heart. I find it fitting that your
last letter described your journey to a glorious tomb which you called the
Taj Mahal. I am still captivated by your description of the place and
the drawing you sent. The expanse of inlaid white marble, the spires
that soar to heaven. I shall think of your mother resting in a place such
as that, surrounded by angels and those she loved.

   Your friend in grief,
   LHF

Belle swiped at her wet cheeks as she sanded the ink on the letter she
had just written.

Ah, Blake. She knew he would feel his mother's loss keenly. They
appeared to have had a close relationship. She regretted that her letter
would take so long to reach him.

A discreet knock sounded on her study door.

Sucking in a steadying breath, Belle glanced quickly in the mirror
above the fireplace, assuring that all signs of her emotion were tucked
away.

"Come," she called.

The door to her study opened.

"Mr. Sloan to see you, madam," her butler intoned.

Her solicitor strolled into the room, a smile peeking out of his beard.
"Belle, my dear, it is always a delight to see you."

"Mr. Sloan." Belle rose to greet him, placing a fond kiss on his cheek. They had long ago abandoned any formality with each other. "How are Mary and your boys?"

"Well. The boys are thriving and Mary keeps us all sorted. How is your mother?"

"She is in good spirits, though she is already hinting at wanting to redecorate her new home." Belle barely suppressed an undignified eye roll. "But she writes endlessly about a handsome widower who has recently taken a house near hers, so she appears well-entertained."

"That is good to hear," Mr. Sloan chuckled.

Belle motioned for Mr. Sloan to be seated in the chairs before the fireplace. "To what do I owe the pleasure of your visit?"

"I have some papers for you to look over, m'dear." Mr. Sloan sat down, bending to retrieve some paperwork from his satchel. "You had inquired into creating an orphanage for children left parentless due to the conflict with Napoleon."

"Oh, yes. I have so been wanting to create a sister project to Hopewell Manor." Belle instantly perked up. "I had thought you too busy just now to set your mind to it—"

"I had an ambitious clerk begin the research. The challenge will be finding an appropriate property, as we've been saying. But I am tracing some leads and these initial reports are most interesting. I wished to get your thoughts on them before continuing."

"Wonderful."

Mr. Sloan spread the papers before her—several properties that could function as the basis of an orphanage. They discussed each estate in detail, pointing out the advantages and disadvantages.

"I would love to find a property that has an old church we could use as a school," Belle concluded. "The children must receive a proper education."

"Agreed. But a greater problem might be getting a local magistrate to authorize our project. Many do not like the idea of a large orphanage in their midst."

Belle grimaced. "Well, we shall keep looking. Do you remember Thomas?"

"The veteran who accosted you in Bristol?" Mr. Sloan snorted. "I shan't ever forget that moment. I am quite sure my heart stopped."

Belle narrowed her eyebrows. "That was hardly the only incident, Mr. Sloan—"

"True, but part of me heartily hopes that there will come a time when I will see the last of such things. The risks you take, Belle dear—"

"—are my own. I will not allow my sex to relegate me to a gilded cage, Mr. Sloan. You know this."

"I know." Mr. Sloan sat back. "But that doesn't mean I don't worry for your safety."

"We were perfectly safe visiting Hopewell Manor last month. England is hardly the wilds of India."

"Hopewell Manor is safe, I agree. But your visit to the factory in Manchester, however—"

"I had to confirm, in person, if there was any truth to the allegations against our factor there. Mrs. White's report was quite specific," Belle's voice rose. "You know I keep a midwife on call for each of my factories, and they keep me apprised of *situations* as they arise. Particularly if those situations involve one of my managers."

For example, Mrs. White had written her with some decidedly disturbing news. Belle knew that having a midwife see to the needs of her female workers was unusual, but she could not leave the women in her employ without help. Many employers cared less if their female workers had children or not, as long as the women showed up to work. But as most workers were married, pregnancy and children inevitably followed. Many expectant mothers labored on the factory floor until the hour they delivered their babes.

Belle simply wished to ensure that all the women were properly cared for. And that meant tasking the midwives with keeping their eyes out for *other* problems.

"You should have waited for me to accompany you." Mr. Sloan said his words carefully, but the reproach in them couldn't be ignored. "A lady shouldn't have to sully her mind with such . . . things."

Belle bit back the retort that hovered on her lips. *Well, someone needed to investigate if our man was accosting girls, as Mrs. White stated.*

It was *her* factory, in the end. She was responsible for what occurred inside it.

She had taken two footmen and her man-of-affairs with her.

Of course, that hadn't stopped the factor from launching himself at her man-of-affairs when the man fired him. It had taken the constable and a letter from Mr. Sloan to finalize the manager's removal.

She loved John Sloan as a beloved uncle-figure. But he would forever see her as a young lady. Yes, she took risks, but she always made sure her behavior was discreet. She was careful.

"Regardless, back to my first question," Belle said, "you remember Thomas? I visited with him and his wife when I visited Hopewell. Their two older ones are making tremendous progress with both their reading and their sums. I love the idea that our schools could one day produce the managers and other workers we need to run our various enterprises."

"I agree with your assessment. I will continue the hunt for the perfect property." Mr. Sloan nodded, gathering up his papers.

"Give my love to Mary and your boys, please."

"Of course. We shall have to organize a leisurely dinner party some evening."

"I would enjoy that, but I would enjoy it even more if your boys could join us."

Mr. Sloan gave a wry laugh. "They are scamps, but I do love them." He paused, meeting her gaze. "Does any of this create an ache in you, my dear?"

Belle tilted her head, a quizzical expression on her face.

"All this discussion of children?" Mr. Sloan clarified. "Does it make you long for one or two of your own?"

Belle drew back slightly.

Mr. Sloan rarely commented on her most private life, but when he did, it was with fatherly concern, like now.

Children? A family? She *had* been giving it some thought as of late, but she was in no hurry. She was barely four and twenty. "I should like to have children one day."

That was her truth. Someday, she would like to have a child. Someone to pass along her insights and knowledge, just as her father had done for her. Someone to love and be loved in return.

What was it Blake had said to her that morning so very long ago? *What do you desire most?*

For the longest time, her dream had been prospering her business, becoming the independent woman she currently was.

But without someone to share it all . . .

Children would require a husband, and Belle had yet to meet a gentleman who captured her interest.

Sometimes in the dark of night when sleep was fleeting, she would ponder this future life. A home, a husband, the patter of a child's feet, the squeal of giggling laughter. Usually, her husband was a shadowy figure, a source of calm.

But lately, the fantasy husband had begun speaking with Blake's words. She would often wake with a sense of laughing blue eyes and wavy chestnut hair.

Belle had only seen Blake a handful of times so many years ago, the last time being that fateful morning in Hyde Park. Clearly, her mind remembered his coloring and general physical appearance: taller, brown-red hair that curled at the ends, blue eyes sparking with life and good humor.

But she didn't recall the timbre of voice. The exact set of his head, the shape of his face.

How could he be invading her dreams now?

It was as if Blake were seeping through cracks and crevices to inhabit her very soul.

Worse, Belle wasn't entirely sure she found his presence there unwelcome.

She constantly felt his kinship. They were partners. Sometimes Belle felt as if she didn't make a single decision without thinking of him and considering what he would like her to do.

It was no real surprise, she supposed, that she would think of Blake as the partner in her personal life, too.

COLIN SHOOK HIS head, smiling politely, before taking a small sip of wine.

Another year. Another Epiphany spent with the Governor-General. Another winter away from home.

As usual, the Governor's large dining room danced with light from chandeliers and reflected crystal. Servants in traditional Indian attire moved silently in and out, removing dishes, replenishing drinks. The ladies had left the gentleman to their conversation and port. Even half a world away from England, the Governor still imported the traditional wine from Duoro in northern Portugal.

The Governor-General was deep in conversation at one end of the table. Several of the other gentlemen were arguing over the outcome of a horse race earlier in the week.

"Have you been enjoying your time in Calcutta, Lord Blake?" The question came at him from a gentleman across the table—a Mr. Smith, was it? Colin could scarcely recall. People arrived and departed with such regularity, he struggled to remember them.

Besides, how many times had he been asked this very question?

"Yes, as much as one can when away from home," Colin cordially answered, as he always did.

Mr. Smith cocked his head. Colin could nearly predict what he would ask next.

First, it was a question about his time in India.

Then . . .

"Devilish hot here. Do you ever get used to the heat?" Mr. Smith asked.

Yes, the weather.

Time-honored English topics of conversation.

Colin smiled, spinning his port on the table. "No, I'm not sure anyone ever gets used to this heat. You simply learn to tolerate it, I suppose."

Mr. Smith grimaced. "That's a pity."

Silence.

And . . . they had exhausted all topics of conversation, it appeared.

Dash it all, Colin was tired of these inane evenings, where everyone said the same things and asked the same questions, but no one ever bothered to truly *know* the other person, to truly see them.

Loneliness, and its close friend, Self-Pity, were mental traps Colin valiantly tried to avoid. But as his time in India passed the five-year mark, his mind kept turning toward home. Often he wondered if it was England itself that he missed, or more just the companionship of true friends. The casual friends he had in Calcutta had teased him about it one night, pointing out that if Colin would just marry, he would solve most of his problems.

But even marriage was hardly a simple matter. Certainly there were women in Calcutta who would be delighted to fill the role of Lady Blake. But Colin wanted so much more than a marriage of convenience. He longed for a soul-mate, a marriage of the deepest love and respect and admiration—

He stopped right there.

Pondering too long on the topic was liable to lead him right into the mental mire he sought to avoid. He could do nothing to make the perfect woman magically appear. He simply needed to be patient. He would find her eventually.

Until then, he would be content with what he did have. Like his relationship with LHF, for example.

Damn, but Colin admired the man. Sensible. Good-natured. Honest nearly to a fault. His correspondence remained one of the highlights of Colin's week.

Did Lord Halbert have a circle of close friends? Did they gather for evenings of laughter and lively discussion? Or did he favor family more?

Memories washed over Colin. His parent's cozy home in Surrey as a child. Cecily and his sisters laughing over Christmas punch, exchanging stories. His father, home on leave, voice booming and warm. His mother arguing a philosophical point until they all had jumped into the fray.

Loss swamped him. His parents were gone, now. His sisters scattered to the winds with their husbands.

Sometimes in his more maudlin moments of homesickness, Colin imagined Cecily and George sitting with Lord Halbert after dinner. Perhaps Lord Halbert had confided in them about Colin. Perhaps they would read snippets of his letters together—

Colin shook his head.

Such mawkish sentimentality was unlike him. The holiday season brought it out, he supposed. Or maybe it was LHF's insistence on maintaining the facade of anonymity that rankled more today.

Someday, Colin vowed, someday he would sit down for dinner with Lord Halbert and hear everything directly from the man himself.

A thought occurred to him:

Perhaps if he mentioned Cecily more in his letters—and by extension Lord Halbert's son, George—Lord Halbert would get the hint and say something in return.

Hmmmm.

The idea was worth a try.

7

To LHF
Calcutta
April 14, 1821

My dear friend,

Thank you again for addressing my concerns over the fall off in silk prices. I've enclosed a detailed plan for our purchases continuing forward.

In other news, I have recently commissioned a portrait of myself. Yes, it is as vain as it sounds, though sitting still for hours on end is sufficient punishment for my vanity. My sister, Mrs. George Phalean, is endlessly pestering me for a current likeness, and I have decided to indulge her requests in this. It will take nearly a year to complete and reach her, but I hope she will be satisfied.

As for your proposed scheme of an orphanage, I am eager to help where I can. I understand that finding the correct location has been a challenge, but I trust in your abilities to secure us a suitable property.

Sincerely, Blake

BELLE TRACED THE lines of Blake's latest letter with a finger. His handwriting was distinctive. The commanding swoop of his capital letters, the gentle slope of his sentences. The lettering a microcosm of the man himself. Strong, self-sufficient, but possessed of unexpected depths of gentleness—

"If you stare at his letter too long, you are liable to burn a hole through it, dear. And you would be sad if you damaged any of Lord Blake's fine scribblings." Anne's voice cut through Belle's daydreaming.

Afternoon sun streamed through the floor-to-ceiling windows of Belle's study, flooding the room with light. Anne sat opposite Belle's desk, calmly doing needlepoint before the popping fire. Even though Belle would reach her twenty-fifth birthday this year, she knew that as long as she remained unmarried, she would never outgrow the propriety of a chaperone and companion.

Not that Belle minded. Anne was a dear friend and Belle was always glad of her company. Despite Belle's urging her to marry, Anne had no desire to leave Belle's employ. She had lost her love in the conflict with Napoleon and had no intention of ever marrying.

"Will this be the year you tell him?" Anne interrupted her musings. "You are bolder than you were years ago."

Belle stared into the fire, not missing Anne's meaning. *Will you tell Lord Blake who you are? Inform him that he has been writing a young lady of fortune all these years, not a middle-aged gentleman of some means?*

"I have lost my shyness and hesitancy, that is true," Belle sighed. "He continually calls himself Telemachus and me, Mentor—"

Anne snorted. "Without realizing that you are actually Penelope to his Odysseus? The woman patiently weaving at home, waiting for her other half to finish wandering the world and return to her?"

Belle nodded, managing a tired smile. "Though instead of weaving, I calculate probabilities and fashion trends."

Anne chuckled.

They were in London for the Season. Again. Belle continued to attend, year after year. Not for the bevy of suitors and admirers who hunted her for her fortune (though there was no shortage of those, either), but more to keep her fingers on the pulse of modern fashions.

She was content to remain unmarried.

Besides, no suitor had captured her attention.

Worse, the more she came to know Blake himself, the more she compared every other man of her acquaintance with him.

And, thus far, every other man had come up short. If only she could find a man as principled and intelligent as Blake.

It had been over five years. Five years of letters written and sent. Initially only every couple of months, but during the last two years, they had been corresponding nearly every week. Granted, their letters took upwards of six months to reach each other, requiring nearly a year to ask a question and receive an answer.

But the straggling nature of their correspondence did nothing to dim the excitement of it. Ideas and drawings exchanged. The endless riddles. Their shared interests in dreadful gothic novels and societal reform, which really were not as far apart as one might think.

Lord Blake had become one of her closest friends.

"Most of me wants Blake to know my identity, and surely I could summon the courage to tell him. But . . ."

"But he is a gentleman of honor." Anne snorted. "The sort of man who clearly understands that an unmarried lady and eligible peer of the realm should not carry on a private correspondence. Were it to become known, 'twould dishonor him and ruin you."

"Yes," Belle slumped in her chair. "And I've come to realize that Blake prizes honor and honesty."

She and Anne had this conversation with such regularity, Belle could recite their words before it began.

Anne: You could be ruined if you say anything.

Her: Possibly, but only if he is indiscreet. He never breathed a word about my behavior five years ago.

Anne: Granted. But neither has he ever spoken another word to Miss Heartstone.

Her: He has been in India for the past five years. How could he contact me?

Anne: Hrmph. Were he to discover your subterfuge, you risk losing your friend and business partner.

Her: Perhaps LHF could die, and I could introduce myself as his daughter? Arrive on his doorstep in black mourning—

Anne: You read too many gothic novels, my dear. They are starting to addle your brain. Besides, you have far too much honor yourself to engage in such an elaborate deception.

And that's where the argument always landed.

Belle had never meant to take the charade this far. But, like so many things in life, she was in the midst of it before realizing it had begun. She hadn't meant to keep writing him.

But when Blake had struggled with bickering tribes attacking their shipments, how could she not offer him advice and unconventional solutions? How could she not provide him with calculations of probabilities and predictions based on fashion trends she saw in London? To say nothing would have been cruel, too.

Ugh. She was in an impossible situation.

Belle comforted her conscience, knowing she had never specifically lied to Blake. She had never deliberately told a falsehood. Blake had assumed her to be a man. She had merely declined to correct his misperception.

Admittedly, a *very* fine line, but one she did not intend to cross.

The real problem was simple: she didn't want to lose Blake's friendship. She valued his good opinion above all others.

Not since her father's death had anyone occupied such a place in her affections. Like with her father, she and Blake understood each other, seeing eye-to-eye on nearly everything.

To be clear, Blake certainly hadn't replaced her father—her feelings toward Lord Blake were decidedly not filial in nature—but the feeling of respect and trust was similar.

Belle found herself thinking of her father more and more. As a child, he took her to see a hot air balloon fly. She had watched, hands clasped under her chin, as barrel after barrel was positioned under the rising cloth, releasing a gas—hydrogen, her father called it—into the silk fabric. Before long, the enormous ball rose high in the sky, two people standing in a basket underneath it.

Belle had bounced on her tiptoes, hands clasped in worry.

"What will happen to the men inside the basket, Papa? Won't they be dashed to the ground?" she asked.

"No, Little Heart-Full. See the ropes there?" Papa pointed to the ropes, stretched and straining to Belle's eyes. "See how strong and thick they are? The ropes tether the balloon to the ground. It can't fly away."

"Oh! How clever!" Belle laughed and clapped. "So the men can fly into the sky, but still be safely held to the ground?"

"Exactly. The wind can blow hither and yon, but the balloon won't be able to fly away. When they are done, the ropes will bring them safely down."

Belle stared up, eyes round. "I wonder what they can see from up there?"

Papa chuckled. "I imagine they have a view for miles and miles from that height. The higher you are, the farther you can see."

Belle had come to consider it a metaphor for her life. Blake had been the one to set her aloft—allowing her to soar on thrilling winds, to see and understand things she had never even considered—all the while keeping her tethered to the ground. To become a person she had never thought possible.

Would she ever tell him thank you face-to-face? Help him understand how in a mere fifteen minutes of time, he had utterly altered the trajectory of her life, allowing her to soar to new heights?

Yes . . . someday, she would tell him.

Someday.

To LHF
Calcutta

June 14, 1822

 My good friend,

Thank you for your report about the orphanage. You were wise to purchase Fyfe Hall outside Swindon. The estate looks to be an excellent place for children to be raised, though as you noted, the property will take nearly a year of renovation to make it habitable once more.

I also appreciated your idea to place the children in small family units and hire a veteran and his wife to act as de facto parents to them. It is a brilliant stroke of genius to give both veterans and children a sense of family. I have enclosed instructions to Mr. Sloan to dispatch funds as needed.

I have also been thinking much lately about the idea you posed in your last letter, that quote from Sir Francis Bacon, "Nothing is terrible except fear itself." You then stated, "My father used to say that our greatest fears are what they are because they describe what will happen to us." I was moved by the tale of your friend—whose greatest fear was the death of his son and heir—and who subsequently buried all his children.

So what is my greatest fear?

Mine is akin to yours. You fear being left alone in the world, of losing the trust and friendship of those you hold most dear. I am afraid I will never find the other half of me; I fear I will never have that "marriage of true minds," as Shakespeare describes it . . .

Colin broke off writing his letter to LHF, eyes raising to the rain pattering against the window pane. The summer monsoon had settled in with a vengeance, rain falling almost incessantly. Servants moved through his house, completing their tasks, the sounds clinking outside his door.

He had longed to marry for several years now. But he wished to raise a family in his native land, on the estates he had inherited. He was ready to build a legacy.

Did he truly fear he would never find true love? Perhaps once.

But recent events had changed everything.

He smiled thinking of a pair of vivid hazel eyes and lush smile that was rapidly becoming dear to him. Miss Sarah Forrester had definitely captured his interest.

His fear might soon be laid to rest.

Briefly, he contemplated writing as much to Lord Halbert. But his relationship with Miss Forrester was new enough that he hesitated. Perhaps in his next letter, he would say something.

He continued writing.

> *. . . I know not for myself. But as for you, I must say, my good friend, you should never fear on my account. You will always have my trust and friendship. On that score, you may be certain . . .*

"MISS HEARTSTONE, I am so pleased you could attend my little soiree this evening."

Belle smiled. "The pleasure is all mine, Mrs. Phalean. Allow me to introduce my friend, Miss Rutger."

Belle exchanged a few more pleasantries with Mrs. George Phalean before passing into the Phalean's drawing room.

"You are quite shameless," Anne murmured in her ear.

Belle did not disagree.

She felt a bit like a spy, invading Blake's homeland, surveying the countryside, as it were.

But . . . he had sent his sister, Cecily, a portrait. A *current* portrait. Surely it had arrived by now. How could Belle hope to resist seeing such a thing?

Belle had known for years that Blake's sister came to London for the Season. For the past five years, Belle had deliberately not sought a friendship with the woman. To befriend Cecily Phalean, without ever mentioning a word of it to Blake, felt like crossing an invisible threshold from misunderstanding to brazen deception.

But . . .

Fate had intervened. Belle had happened to meet Mrs. Phalean at the opera one evening. The slight acquaintance had then led to an invitation to attend a dinner party hosted by Mrs. Phalean.

What else was Belle to do? She couldn't outright refuse to attend. Besides, Belle had a purpose beyond simple curiosity tonight.

She *needed* to see Blake. And as the man himself was still in India, his portrait would have to do.

The reason?

Somewhere amidst their letters about *Frankenstein* and the Taj Mahal, Belle suspected she might have given Blake her heart.

Like the letters themselves, she was in the middle of it before realizing it had even begun. But she thought about him at least twenty times a day, and oh, the rapturous thundering of her heart whenever a letter arrived.

This was not normally how Belle felt about correspondence from other friends.

How horrid to have a best friend who didn't even *know* he was her best friend. A love who didn't know he was her love.

Poor Blake.

Poor *her*.

A cordial friendship with the fictional LHF was all well and good. But enthusiastic discussion of philosophy and literature was hardly the same thing as romantic interest.

In her most fanciful moments, Belle had imagined writing the words:

Do you recall that forgettable woman who proposed marriage to you one spring morning in Hyde Park? Allow me to relate a humorous anecdote . . .

She would tell him the truth behind LHF, and he would rush to her side, overcome with emotion. Sweep her into his arms, professing a deep and profound love, begging her to always be his—

She stopped herself.

Enough, she whispered. *You don't know for sure if you feel anything for him beyond brotherly respect and friendship.*

In fact, this overwhelming attachment was a large part of why she had accepted Mrs. Phalean's invitation this evening.

Was her infatuation with Blake a genuine thing? Or was it more likely a case of absence-makes-the-heart-grow-fonder?

Her mind seemed to think that seeing his likeness would sort the issue for her.

So she smiled and nodded at a few acquaintances, all the while surreptitiously scanning the walls, trying to see if one of the many portraits belonged to Lord Blake.

Would she recognize his likeness? Or had India changed him too thoroughly? Certainly, his skin would be bronzed from the sun, perhaps taking his hair a shade or two lighter.

It was hard to say.

She and Anne continued to move around the drawing room, talking with friends. Part of Belle marveled that she had ever found this sort of social interaction difficult. It all seemed so normal now. She would never have a spirited demeanor, but her shyness had settled into a graceful sense of confidence and poise.

She and Anne passed onto the music room, still greeting the bevy of guests. Belle accepted a glass of sherry from a passing servant. It was only as she sipped that she felt all the fine hairs on her neck stand in attention.

Later, she would relive the moment over and over, pondering its significance.

Slowly, Belle turned her head, staring at the wall behind her.

Oh.

Oh!

There he was.

His eyes gazed at her, quiet, intent. Soul-piercing.

It was a bust portrait, showing him from the chest up, body slightly angled. His cravat fell in precise folds, tucked against a bottle-green coat. The green caught the reddish highlights in his hair, which was indeed a shade lighter than she remembered. A hint of a smile tugged at his lips.

But it was the intensity of his blue eyes that held her. They saw through her, challenging, calling to her innermost soul.

His likeness was achingly familiar and utterly new all at once.

I see you, he seemed to say. *We are similar creatures, you and I.*

Belle's foolish heart choked her, aching with so much . . . feeling.

Oh, Blake.

My heart.

Heavens, *now* what was she to do—

"I see you've been captured by my brother, Miss Heartstone," a chipper voice sounded at her ear.

Belle only barely stopped herself from startling.

She turned with a strained smile to Mrs. Phalean.

"Pardon?" Belle managed to say.

Did Cecily know? Was Belle's attachment written plain upon her face?

And given the depth of her emotion, how could she *not* show it?

"My brother, Lord Blake." Mrs. Phalean gestured toward the portrait, fortunately appearing oblivious to Belle's emotional crisis.

"Yes," Belle eked out, voice still breathy.

"'Tis a pity he has spent so long in India. He would be quite the favorite, I am sure, were he in London this Season."

"Yes," Belle repeated, dragging her brain back to the moment at hand.

Cecily Phalean was truly Blake's sister. The resemblance was certainly there, in the color of her eyes, the shape of her nose. And a sister would know so much . . .

Belle forcibly held back the thousand questions about Blake that clung to her tongue. Such overeager interest would not be seemly so early in a friendship. And, more importantly, delving deep into Blake's personal life certainly crossed a line into gross deception and betrayal.

So despite the cacophony of her thoughts, Belle gave a polite smile. "Is it an accurate likeness of Lord Blake, do you think?"

"Oh yes, most definitely. I know I am his sister, but Blake has always had a dashing air about him. The ladies quite swoon when he enters a room." Mrs. Phalean laughed at her own wit. "But he has never allowed the attention to go to his head. He has always been a most attentive brother."

That's when Belle realized that Blake was Cecily's favorite topic of conversation.

Hallelujah!

Belle didn't have to say a word. All she did was smile and nod, and Mrs. Phalean monologued on and on about her brother.

His kindness and concern for their late mother.

His attentiveness to Cecily in sending her a portrait of himself.

The brilliance of his career in India and his well-read mind.

Belle listened, nearly entranced. But the more she heard, the more her suspicions were confirmed.

Blake owned her heart. Thoroughly. Utterly.

Worse, she had no hope that he would ever offer his in return.

To LHF
September 23, 1822

My dear friend,

I hope this letter finds you well. I am inspired by your last words regarding the potential for reform at home. The success of Hopewell shall merely be our starting point. In fact, I anticipate returning in a year's time and taking up my seat in the House of Lords during the parliamentary session beginning in January of 1824. Hone your ideas, my friend, as I intend to utilize your keen insight when drafting my bills.

You might well be surprised at this decision. It was precipitated by another happy event. Please congratulate me. By the time you receive this letter, I will be a married man. My betrothed, Miss Sarah Forrester, is anxious to rejoin family in London, and I am only too eager to see England again.

Though we have never broached the subject, I would dearly love to finally meet you in person. Thus far, I have respected your right to privacy, but to be very honest, I know your identity, my friend. I have known since the beginning of our venture.

Fair warning, I intend to call upon you when I arrive in London. I wish to express, in person, my gratitude for your faith in a penniless peer so many years ago.

Another riddle for you: What occurs once in every minute, twice in every moment, but never in a thousand years? I long to best you at something!

I hope this riddle truly stumps you.

Your true friend,
Blake

8

. . . My dearest Blake, though you insist that I should not fear losing your trust and friendship, I worry that it will come to pass. You see, there is one small detail about myself that I have not mentioned . . .

—excerpt from the fifth draft of a letter from Miss Heartstone to Lord Blake, written but never sent

*B*y the time you receive this letter, I will be a married man.

The words fairly stole Belle's breath away, their impact not any softer even a week after the letter had been delivered to her London townhouse.

She held Blake's letter in trembling fingers. Phrases and words jumped off the page, sinking into her skin, painful thorns.

. . . *my betrothed, Miss Sarah Forrester* . . .

. . . *love to finally meet you in person* . . .

. . . *I know your identity, my friend* . . .

. . . I long to best you at something!

Best her?

If only he knew.

He had defeated her in every way.

She lowered the letter, breathing slowly. Despite this being precisely the fifty-third time she had read it, the pain refused to abate. Particularly on evenings like this one, when she and Anne sat alone before the fire, occasionally talking, but mostly listening to silence. Silence which rendered her thinking too loud.

Belle's heart had shattered at his words. She could still scarcely speak of it without tears.

He was married.

Blake

Her Blake.

But he was not her Blake. He would never be her Blake now. He was a married man and that was that.

She glanced at the letter, sternly telling herself to let it be. She did not need to read it again. Its contents would not change. Besides, she had memorized its brief lines days ago.

. . . I know your identity, my friend. I have known since the beginning of our venture . . .

Hah!

Those two lines had nearly stopped her heart when she first read them.

But, no, it couldn't be true.

Blake had more than once referred to her as a 'man of seasoned wisdom.'

So . . . he clearly did *not* know who she was.

Which begged two questions—

Who did he think LHF to be?

And, more to the point, what was she to do about his return?

He had written this letter last autumn. He had likely been married for months now, as England was awash in March rain at present. If he hadn't already, Blake would shortly set sail, arriving in England in less that than six months.

She would see him. It was only a matter of time now. Her friendship with Cecily Phalean had naturally progressed over the past year. Belle had been careful not to actively pursue a friendship with her, despite liking Mrs. Phalean quite thoroughly. Blake was already going to feel betrayed once he learned of LHF's identity. No need to add 'consorting with his sister' to her list of crimes. So though Belle did not claim Cecily as a bosom friend, they called upon each other and occasionally dined together.

Cecily would certainly welcome her brother home like a returning hero. And Belle, as a tolerably close acquaintance, would be included in the festivities. She would have to greet Blake and the new Lady Blake. Would he smile when he saw her? Would he remember that morning so many years ago—

"Really, Belle dearest, you must give that letter a rest." Anne's voice broke into Belle's internal monologuing, as it was wont to do.

Belle bit her lip, blinking furiously.

"My poor friend." Empathy tinged Anne's voice as she bent over her embroidery. "This situation is most difficult."

"Yes," Belle whispered, digging a handkerchief out of her pocket. "I just wish I knew what to do."

"There isn't much to do. He is a married man now, Belle."

"I know."

"You must tell him the truth of LHF. That point is not up for debate."

"I know. But he will be significantly betrayed. I didn't realize until receiving this letter that he thought he knew LHF."

It only underscored how little she knew about Blake. It was odd. Knowing someone so well, and yet, not at all.

"Will you write to tell him? Or are you still set on waiting and doing the deed in person?"

Sucking in a deep breath, Belle dabbed at her eyes.

"I am unsure," she whispered. "He will likely be angry. It is a most difficult matter. Our lives are so thoroughly entangled. He's at sea at the moment, so any letter won't reach him until he lands in England regard-less. I could contact his solicitor and arrange a meeting . . ." Her voice drifted off. Just the mere thought of seeing Blake, face-to-face, and telling him . . .

She swallowed. Perhaps if they continued to exchange necessary business correspondence through Mr. Sloan, all would be well—

"Belle." Warning in Anne's tone. Her friend clearly read Belle's vacillation. "This situation with Lord Blake was problematic before. Now that he is married and returning to England, it is most unseemly. It would utterly ruin you if it were made known. You *cannot* avoid telling him."

"I will tell him, Anne." Belle finished drying her tears. "I simply need several weeks to let the initial sting of this disappointment fade. Then I will map a course of action."

Seeing Anne's disapproving look, Belle rushed to add, "There is no urgent rush. Any letter I write will not reach him now. Blake is on a ship somewhere between here and India at present; correspondence with him is nearly impossible. I must think through what to do with our joint business ventures, and what I would like the rest of my life to be."

Silence. The clock ticked on the mantelpiece. Traffic clattered outside. Somewhere in the house, footmen polished silver, metal clinking.

"Will you marry, do you think?" Anne asked into the quiet.

Belle asked herself that question quite frequently.

Unbidden, Blake's words from all those years ago fluttered through her:

If you reach a point where you want a permanent companion or children, then seek out a man to share your life with you. But only marry because it is your heart's desire.

Yes, marriage was her heart's desire currently. She longed for it. After years of channeling all her energy into her business, she was more-than-ready for the next phase of her life: a husband and children.

She ached to build a family with someone. For quite some time, that *someone* had been Lord Blake. Belle closed her eyes, anguished tightness clenching her chest. She swallowed back the lump burning in her throat.

Any possibility of that dream was now shattered.

His marriage aside, had she honestly entertained the idea that Blake would forgive her trespasses? Her small white lies?

He was a good man, but even Blake's warm heart had bounds.

Her only choice now was to plot a course for her own life without Blake.

"I can nearly see my children. I hear their laughter sometimes in my dreams." Belle met Anne's gaze.

"Children require a husband," Anne said.

"Yes." Belle looked out the window, forcing herself to think past her current heartbreak. She was not so naive as to believe she would meet another man such as Blake. "I . . . I will have to put this disappointment behind me . . . somehow . . ." Her voice ended on a whisper.

Silence hung in the room.

Both she and Anne knew that would prove a long road.

Belle waved a hand toward Blake's letter. "There is nothing more to do. I must move on. I am six and twenty. Any longer, and there may be no children for me."

Though Belle wanted to bury herself in the country for a solid decade, mourning the loss of what would never be, such a thing simply was not possible. Not if she wished for a family of her own.

More silence.

Anne smiled, a little wanly. "Shall I draw up a list of potential suitors for you?"

Belle barely avoided a grimace.

But . . . Anne had the right of it.

"You know that you will have your pick of men, Belle dear," Anne continued.

Though it sounded arrogant, Anne spoke truth.

As the wealthiest unmarried woman in all of England, Belle was a highly-sought prize. Though she had not actively pursued marriage up to this point, she most certainly hadn't hidden away as a recluse either. Attending social functions of any sort meant inviting the acquaintance of unmarried gentleman.

She knew that most potential suitors—particularly the penniless ones—viewed her as a challenge. To them, Belle was the proverbial sword in the stone. Like crusaders of old, they would throw themselves against her walls, knowing that winning her hand guaranteed them a king's ransom. The man who succeeded in fixing her affections ensured for himself a life of ease and luxury.

Consequently, nearly every eligible gentleman in London would first try his luck with Miss Heartstone before proposing marriage to another woman. Such was the lure of her . . . assets.

Belle nearly snorted at her own cleverness.

No one ever praised her person, her wit, her beauty . . .

Well, they did, she supposed. But only as a way to her fortune. Such compliments were usually too extravagant to be taken seriously. What was it Mr. Carleton had said over the pianoforte four evenings ago?

"We should carve you a pedestal, so all can admire your exquisite beauty."

Though Belle supposed she should be grateful. Mr. Carleton's fawning manner was not nearly as ridiculous as some. Sir Reginald Spears had been particularly absurd. What had he said?

"We should change your name to Helen, dearest Miss Heartstone, because I am quite certain your radiant beauty could launch a thousand ships."

After that particular incident, Belle had taken to preemptively declining many a gentleman to avoid such preposterous lip service. Otherwise, she feared her eyes would be permanently strained from the effort to stop them rolling entirely out of her head.

Honestly.

She was so much more than a mere ornament, even if she *were* a great beauty to be admired. Though it would be lovely to be known and admired for something beyond her vast wealth. Or, at least, to have a suitor who recognized the intellect and hard work that created it.

The passage of years had been kind to her, she supposed. Anne insisted that Belle was even more handsome at twenty-six than she had been at nineteen; her lingering baby fat had melted away, leaving her face regally sculpted.

Belle wasn't quite sure she agreed.

Thanks to Blake's friendship, she knew her own worth. She would never be wallpaper to decorate a man's life—some polite, all-but-invisible bauble. Belle wondered if that sense of confidence was more her allure than anything else.

The problem remained, however. How to separate fortune-hunters from other genuinely eligible men? And, more importantly, would interest in another man help heal her shattered heart?

"Yes, Anne," Belle conceded. "I suppose it's time to create a serious list of potential suitors."

Anne nodded. "Consider it done. I will look through your list of current invitations and see if there are one or two that will help us narrow the field down more quickly."

Belle nodded.

In the meantime . . .

Six months. She had six months before Blake would return. Time enough to shutter her wayward heart, sort out her own life, and decide how to address the wrongs she had inflicted on her business partner and best friend.

As with everything else she faced, Belle simply needed a plan.

PART II

April, 1823

BETRAYALS

9

. . . I would be honored to attend the balloon ascension with yourself and Lord Stratton, Monday next.

And in reply to your other question, you quite have the right of my situation at present. I have decided that this is the year in which I will finally seek a husband in earnest. You and Stratton have inspired me. So, yes, I am content to have Lord Odysseus included in our small outing . . .

—excerpt of a letter from Miss Heartstone to her friend, Georgiana Carew, Lady Stratton, dated April 14, 1823

Belle stretched on her tiptoes, trying to see over the heads of those around her.

"Oh, heavens!" She gave a startled gasp, clutching a hand to her chest.

An enormous, round balloon rose slowly into the air, its bright red and blue stripes glinting in the early morning light. The thousands of gathered spectators cheered and whistled.

"How marvelous!" That bit came from Georgiana, Lady Stratton, at Belle's side. "This was a brilliant idea, even if it did require rising at such an appallingly-early hour."

"Of course, it was a brilliant idea. I thought of it." Lord Stratton chuckled at his wife's side.

"They say Mr. Green took his horse up with him last year." Lord Odysseus shook his head in wonder, leaning in closer to Belle. "I should desperately like to try my hand at such a thing."

Belle smiled, exchanging a glance with Anne beside her.

They made a merry band—Lord and Lady Stratton, Belle with Anne as her companion, and Lord Odysseus Camthon. They had all risen early, trekking to Hyde Park to watch a balloon ascension. Mr. Charles Green, a noted balloonist, planned to fly in his balloon this morning.

Lord Stratton and Belle shared the same great-great grandfather, making them distant cousins. As such, they had consistently been thrown into each other's orbits. Lord Stratton had been most helpful from time to time when Belle needed advice on dealing with parliament and assisting veterans.

More to the point, Belle had seized on the loose family connection as an excuse to claim Lady Stratton as a friend. Georgiana was close to Belle's age and sparked with good humor. So naturally, Georgiana had instantly gone into matchmaking mode once she learned that her dear friend was officially seeking a husband.

"At last!" had been her precise words.

Granted, Belle was still reeling from Blake's letter announcing his impending nuptials. Only four weeks had passed and her heart was still raw and sore. She had yet to receive a follow-up letter announcing that his nuptials had indeed occurred. Had he and his new bride decided to take a wedding trip? The wait for Blake's next letter was proving positively criminal in its cruelty.

Worse, Belle didn't really have time to properly nurse her dashed hopes. The London Season was in full swing. And all the civilized world knew that the height of the London Season was the place to see and be seen.

So if Belle wished to survey prospective husbands, this was the time to do it. She simply needed to summon the proper enthusiasm for the task.

All of which explained Lord Odysseus's presence. Lord Odysseus was Belle's most devoted suitor at the moment. Georgiana had introduced them and was convinced that Lord Odysseus would be the perfect match for Belle.

Belle was still undecided on that score.

More to the point, as the fifth son of a duke, Lord Odysseus Camthon was rich in impeccable aristocratic breeding and decidedly poor in everything else. He needed a wealthy wife.

His father apparently had a fascination with Homer and named each of his children after a different character. Lord Odysseus' elder brother—Agamemnon Camthon, Lord Hentley (or Aggie to his closest friends)—was the current heir to the dukedom. But should something happen to Aggie, Lords Hector, Paris, Achilles, and Odysseus waited in the wings.

Belle shot Lord Odysseus a sideways glance.

To be sure, Lord Odysseus Camthon certainly took his heroic name to heart. Draped in a fashionable caped greatcoat, Lord Odysseus was danger and mystery personified. Darkly handsome with striking blue eyes and plenty of devil-may-care swagger, he had recently returned to England after years abroad. His charm and stunning good looks had cut a wide swath through the hearts of every lady in his path. No one quite knew how he had passed his time abroad, but rumor stated Lord Odysseus had been, at times, a privateer for His Majesty, an advisor to the Sultan of Bhutan, a marooned pirate, and a crowned chieftain among the people of Bligh.

Georgiana had her fingers crossed that Lord Odysseus had truly been a chieftain.

Belle hoped he proved slightly more stable than his name and reputation would suggest.

She could not, however, fault his flawless manners and dashing persona. Dressed in the first stare of fashion—long overcoat draping elegantly down to his polished boots, starched collar points high and extending above his chin—he oozed charisma. Lord Odysseus truly did appear to have stepped straight from the pages of a swoon-worthy gothic novel.

More importantly, Belle believed his interest in her to be genuine. Underneath his panache, she caught glimpses of an empathic heart. They had common interests and were able to talk with ease. And if sometimes Belle wondered if things would have been similarly easy with Blake, well . . .

Belle refused to contemplate what Blake would make of all this. Blake was lost to her and she needed to move on to the next phase of her life.

The balloon rose higher and tentatively reached toward the sky. Cables and rope stretched outward, as the small basket underneath peaked out from beneath the immense balloon.

Belle vividly remembered attending the balloon ascension as a child with her father. But that was years ago, and it appeared the entire process had been modernized since then.

"So how does it work again?" Anne asked Lord Stratton.

"It's quite simple." Stratton flashed a boyish smile. "The air inside the balloon must simply be lighter than the air outside. Typically, balloonists have used casks of hydrogen, but the cost is prohibitive. Mr. Green is the first to employ coal gas to fill a balloon—"

"Coal gas? Like that which lights street lamps?"

"The very same. You can see there—" Stratton pointed to several men who held a long tube stretching from what appeared to be a gas-light main. "—they have stretched a connection and have nearly finished filling the balloon with it."

"But how will Mr. Green return to earth?" Belle asked.

Stratton shrugged. "He will ride the air currents until the gas in the balloon dissipates and the balloon descends."

"That sounds . . . less safe." Belle frowned.

"Yes," Lord Odysseus grinned, "but infinitely more exciting."

Belle and Anne exchanged a look.

Ah, men.

Forever boys.

The balloon rose upward, eliciting gasps and exclamations from the gathered crowd. The men pulled away the gas main hose and tightened the ropes tethering the balloon to the earth.

"Hurrah!" Lord Odysseus cheered, waving his hat high over his head. "Have you ever seen a sight so glorious?!" He smiled down at her, his eyes suspiciously bright.

Belle repressed a smile.

Lord Odysseus was a bit of a crier. He had wept for a solid fifteen minutes earlier in the week over the painful beauty of a fallen sparrow. On a less handsome man, such behavior would surely appear comical. But Lord Odysseus was so heart-achingly beautiful and pulled the entire affect off with such verve, one couldn't help but be charmed.

The balloon rose higher and higher until the wicker basket became airborne, the form of Mr. Green and a few friends visible, waving to the massed crowd below. The crowd obligingly hooted and clamored as the balloon sailed above the nearby trees.

Lord Odysseus shamelessly wiped a tear away.

Belle was quite sure Lord Blake, were he here, would be too enamored of the scientific aspects behind the balloon's rise to become emotional. Blake was always looking to use mechanics to improve any aspect of their business. Perhaps she could include a description in her next letter to him—

Stop.

You are done with your letters to him.

Belle swallowed. The next time she interacted with Blake would likely be her last. It would be to tell him the full truth and swallow whatever bitter pill he saw fit to give her. The most favorable outcome would be for Blake to slowly disentangle their business ventures. The worst scenario? *That* one likely involved Blake denouncing her perfidy to the entire known world. Belle shrank from even contemplating it.

How ironic, she thought. For so many years, she had considered Blake to be the one who had tethered her to the ground, allowing her to fly free from the narrow constraints of society's expectations but still create a space for herself. She had adored her freedom.

But as she watched the balloon before her lift upward—it's vibrant blue and red stripes filling her vision—she wondered if that metaphor had shifted.

Men moved into place, intent on removing the mooring ropes. After which, the balloon would be at the mercy of the air currents, carrying it off into an uncertain future.

Was this her life at the moment? Had Blake cut her tether loose? And now she found herself to be a lost balloon floundering through the sky, sailing undirected into an unknown destiny?

She shook her head.

Enough.

These metaphors needed to stop.

Blake was lost to her. She might feel adrift, but the sensation was momentary. Soon she would set her life to rights—

Heavens, such melodrama.

Lord Odysseus would certainly approve.

The men released the first of the mooring ropes, sending an enthusiastic roar through the crowd. The balloon lurched higher, straining on the remaining ropes.

Abruptly, an errant draft caught the balloon, tugging it sideways and hurling it directly toward Belle's group. The loose mooring rope swung wildly out, arching over the crowd.

The area around Belle erupted into chaos.

People screamed and ducked, frantic to get out of harm's path, dashing every which way. Lord Stratton instantly wrapped his large body around Georgiana, protecting her. Lord Odysseus and Anne were swallowed up in the surging crowd.

Belle struggled to stay upright, but in the ensuing melee, she was viciously pushed. Staggering sideways, her foot caught on the hem of her pelisse, sending her arms windmilling. The ground rose up as she fell. She tensed, bracing for impact.

Instead, powerful arms banded around her waist at the last second, catching her. Belle was pulled upright and twisted around until all of her was pressed against a manly chest. Her hands fluttered to clutch a pair of powerful shoulders as she fought to right her feet. The smell of wool, starched linen, and Eastern spices assaulted her.

Time hung for the space of two heartbeats. And in that brief hiccup in reality, Belle felt . . . treasured. Protected. As if all the world had been wrapped in soft cotton, absorbing the edges of life.

Yes. *This* was the metaphor she had been seeking. At times, life was chaotic and haphazard and one might feel adrift. But when you were paired with another, they would strengthen and support you, saving you when you were helpless to save yourself.

She lifted her gaze and met eyes of smoky blue looking down at her, a shot of unexpected color in her rescuer's tanned face. Dark chestnut hair waved in loose curls across his forehead. Strong jaw, straight nose. His expression reassuringly concerned.

Belle froze, her apology dying on her lips.

Be still my heart, was her first thought.

Dashing, was her second.

You. I'll take you, was her third.

And then . . .

. . . recognition sank in.

OH!

Belle reeled back from the man's chest, shock and surprise blasting every thought other than *huhnnnnn* from her brain.

Impossible!

How could *he* be here?

He kept gloved hands on her elbows, steadying her.

"Are you quite all right, madam?" he asked dropping his hands from her elbows, aristocratic vowels crisp, gaze concerned. He bent to snatch up his hat which had fallen to the ground. "It appears the momentary panic has settled."

Indeed, it had.

But Belle barely noticed.

A cheer went up from the crowd as the balloon righted itself, soaring into the sky. Or perhaps it was simply the roar of her heart.

He glanced up toward the balloon.

Belle continued to stare at him.

This was inconceivable! Blake was on a ship in the vast ocean somewhere.

Surely her memory was faulty. She wished to see him everywhere and so she saw him in this man. She would have heard if he had returned. He would have written. Or, at the very least, set society abuzz.

Six months. She still had *six months* to plan.

Because, heaven knew, she was going to need a plan of Napoleonic proportions to deal with *his* return—

Belle had to be wrong. This man was not Blake.

She was mistaken.

Something.

"I say, Miss Heartstone, are you feeling ill?" Lord Odysseus's voice sounded near her ear. "You nearly took quite the tumble."

Belle began to shake her head. Then nodded. Then shrugged. Unable to tear her gaze from this stranger with Blake's eyes.

"Miss Heartstone?" Lord Odysseus said again.

The man-who-surely-was-not-Lord-Blake raised an eyebrow. The motion was at once darling and charming and . . . and . . .

Belle managed to gulp in a breath, darting a glance at Lord Odysseus. "Thank you. I am quite well."

No. This man could not be Blake. It was impossible. Besides, he hadn't reacted at all to her name. Was is possible that Blake could have so utterly forgotten the woman who proposed marriage to him all those years ago?

"You are quick on your feet, sir. I thank you for your assistance." Stratton appeared at her other side, extending a hand to her rescuer. "Stratton, at your service."

The man extended his hand, clasping Stratton's in a firm grasp, smile pleasant.

"Blake," he said.

Oh!

Belle's heart took a flying leap into her throat, choking with its force. She felt more than heard Anne's similar gasp behind her.

Blake settled his hat back atop his head. His gaze flitted back to her, smiling, teeth white against his tanned cheeks, before he looked away.

Not a flicker of recognition in his eyes.

Belle swallowed.

Well. That settled that, didn't it?

Blake had returned.

He did *not* remember her.

Belle took in a breath. Then another.

Don't stare. Don't gape.

Don't throw yourself into his arms a second time.

All three were a difficult challenge.

The portrait he had sent Cecily Phalean was a faint imitation of the real man.

He was just so . . . *him.* The same, perhaps, but utterly changed. Older, obviously. Broader than her memory. More knowing in his eyes. A caped greatcoat hung from his shoulders, the dark-blue wool of his tailcoat peeking through.

More importantly, an air of command clung to him. A confidence. A sureness. He wore authority like a second skin. A lord who gave orders, and others fell over themselves to follow him.

He's a married man, she reminded herself, though no woman accompanied him at present.

With just a handful of words so many years ago, he had altered the course of her life for the better. That pivotal fulcrum where everything had veered in a different direction. Her friendship with him had evolved into the most precious thing in her life.

He owned her very soul.

But for him . . .

Miss Heartstone did not exist.

COLIN SMILED AT the group before him, his mind still churning on the jolting shock of catching an unknown lady in his arms.

The moment had been . . . unexpected. But not unwelcome. A man would have to be dead before feeling nothing when holding a beautiful woman in his arms.

"Lord Blake?" Stratton asked.

"In the flesh," Colin replied.

"This is indeed a pleasure, sir," Stratton grinned. "I heard someone mention in the House of Lords yesterday that you had just returned."

"Yes. My boat docked only two days ago."

"Welcome home."

Stratton seemed a good sort: tall, smartly dressed, and affable. Colin took an instant liking to him. Now that he thought about it, he remembered LHF mentioning Stratton on occasion in his letters. Lord Stratton was a power to be reckoned with in Parliament.

What a relief to be back in England. Colin knew he had missed home, but he hadn't realized to what depth until he had landed in London. A man was in a bad way when the filthy docks of south London looked like paradise. Even riding up the Thames had been the finest pleasure—seeing the lush rolling hills of England, breathing the cool spring air.

He had shown up on Cecily's doorstep the day before, sending his sister into whooping hysterics at his unexpected arrival.

It was all certainly welcome. The reward after so many years spent toiling and working and fighting to restore the marquisate, to forge a solid place for himself.

Colin's only disappointment had been to learn that Lord Halbert was not in London currently. The man resided in Bath, coming to London for only a month or two of the Season, or so Cecily had informed him. But this year, Lord Halbert had apparently decided against coming to London at all. Which meant that Colin would have to wait to confront his closest friend and business partner.

Unfortunately, the duties of a marquess newly-returned to England took precedence over tracking down reluctant business partners. The King himself had sent word last night, demanding Colin make an appearance at Carlton House later in the week.

Stratton turned to his wife. "Pardon my manners, my dear," he said. "Permit me to make introductions."

Colin smiled at Lady Stratton, strikingly pretty with her blond curls, before bowing over her hand. He dutifully shook hands with Lord Odysseus, murmuring a greeting and listening as his lordship effusively thanked him for saving 'precious Miss Heartstone' from a nasty tumble.

Lord Odysseus certainly made an impression. Colin was yet unsure what, precisely, that impression was.

"Lord Blake, may I present Miss Arabella Heartstone?" Stratton turned to the woman Colin had caught before she fell to the ground.

Miss Heartstone.

She appeared slightly stunned, which struck Colin as somewhat unexpected as she had the general appearance of a woman not given to hysterics. The incident with the balloon must have truly overset her.

Lovely had been his first assessment. With her wide brown eyes and oval face, Miss Heartstone was decidedly beautiful.

Mature was now his second. An eligible miss, perhaps, but the more sophisticated end of the species. No fresh-from-the-schoolroom girlishness from Miss Heartstone.

Thank goodness.

He had suffered enough of that for a lifetime.

"Miss Heartstone, a pleasure." He bowed, precise and polite.

"Lord Blake." She dipped a curtsy.

He angled his head. Did she suddenly seem vaguely familiar to him?

The thought was lost as Stratton continued to ask questions. "Your family name is Radcliffe, is it not, my lord?"

"Yes."

"I remember hearing tales of a Captain Radcliffe who served in the 23rd Dragoons."

Delight washed Colin. He chuckled.

"That would be my father, sir. He had a way of making a legend of himself." Though Colin had rarely seen his father as a child, he had followed the man's prolific military career with intense dedication.

Stratton frowned. "Are you sure it was your father? The stories I heard were of a younger man who performed some heroic deeds during '15 . . ."

Heat touched Colin's cheeks. He felt the weight of Miss Heartstone's gaze. Odd that she should make his skin prickle with awareness.

"I think you are being too modest," Stratton continued. "Were you really on the front lines of Waterloo?"

Colin narrowly avoided wincing. He preferred not to think about his short but intense career as soldier in His Majesty's army. Seven years in India had helped dim the horror of the battlefield, but only just.

"Yes, I was," he replied.

"Do you happen to know Major Alexander Fraser then?"

"Major Fraser? Of course. I've wondered what that rascal was up to lately."

Stratton chuckled. "I hear he has settled in Plymouth with a lovely widow . . ."

Colin and Stratton talked for several minutes. Like himself, Lord Stratton had been a captain in His Majesty's army before being raised to the peerage as the Earl of Stratton. Better yet, they held a number of friends in common. Within moments, Colin and Stratton were reminiscing about camp pranks and outrageous stories.

Though the ladies listened politely, Lord Odysseus kept interjecting with a grumbling, "Humph," followed by a bored nod, and ending with a judgmental, "Certainly soldiers in His Majesty's Army have better things to do with their time than chase goats?"

Colin had it on good authority that the soldiers did not, in fact, have anything better to do with their time. War was best described as endless stretches of mind-numbing boredom punctuated by moments of abject terror.

Finally, Lord Odysseus seemed to have heard enough of Colin's exploits.

"Have I told you about the skirmish I experienced with a highway-man in Virginia?" Lord Odysseus asked and then, before receiving any sort of reply, launched into his tale, weeping tears over a friend whose life had been lost.

As he spoke, Lord Odysseus edged closer and closer to Miss

Heartstone's elbow until Colin worried the man would finish his tale by pulling Miss Heartstone into his arms and gazing into her eyes as he declared, "and that's how I knew John was gone forever."

Colin struggled to decide if he was amused or annoyed.

Miss Heartstone, however, did not appear to take as thorough a notice of Lord Odysseus and his dramatic flair. She simply smiled, politely nodded, and took a step back, darting a quick glance at Colin.

Interesting.

She had kind eyes, he decided, chocolate brown pools that promised to be sweet and warm.

"We are glad you are returned, Blake." Lady Stratton drew his attention back once Lord Odysseus finished. "Will you settle in London then? Will we be seeing you about town?"

Colin managed a small smile. "Alas, I am in Town mostly to meet with my solicitors. I have much that needs to be seen to before I can lose myself in social niceties."

"What a pity, my lord." Lady Stratton angled her head. "I take it your answer means that there is no Lady Blake, at present? As surely if you had a wife, she would not be content to be left alone as you tend to business?"

The words were not gauche or even unexpected.

Even so, Colin barely stopped a grimace.

"No, my lady, I am not married," he said.

No, there was no Lady Blake at present. The last woman he had considered for the position had behaved in such a manner—

Colin stopped himself right there. Even nearly seven months on, the reminder stung.

He would not think about Sarah. Six months aboard a ship had left him ample time to contemplate all his mistakes and Sarah's clever machinations.

She had played him well.

But Sarah was his past. Some other woman would be his future.

NO. I AM *not married*. Blake's words lingered in Belle's ears.

She was quite sure her heart was attempting to climb out her throat. Anne let out a gust of air behind her. Lord Odysseus crowded closer.

None of this filtered through to Belle.

She was fixated on Blake's handsome face, trying to piece the last few minutes together.

Blake was here.

He was *not* married.

How?

What had occurred? Why had she received *no* letter about this? Would he tell LHF what had happened with Miss Sarah Forrester?

Belle's mind was a buzzing hive.

What happened if he said nothing to LHF? What other items of this magnitude did he keep from LHF? And, even if he did, she could hardly begrudge him his privacy.

Oh!

And worse—

He would surely be calling on the man he assumed to be LHF—whoever that was—and then come looking for the real LHF.

How was she to even numerate it all?

But one point was crystal clear—

Her days of anonymity were numbered.

She needed to tell him. No more disassembling.

But . . .

Her foolish heart sat up, springing to life with violent force.

What if? it whispered.

He was here. He was *unmarried*.

She was here. She was unmarried.

Both of them.

Not married!!!

(She mentally added a mountain of exclamation points to that thought.)

There was still *hope*. Hope that he would see her. That he might accept her as LHF.

But Reality—ever at the ready to silence her mental celebrations—spoke up.

When she had asked him to marry her so many years ago, she had played every card in her hand. Laid them all out on the table. And he had still easily walked away.

Why did she think that the passage of seven years and one enormous white lie would pave the way toward a happily-ever-after?

If anything, Belle was in a runaway carriage, headed straight for a cliff.

Ugh.

Enough with the metaphors!

She *had* to tell him and take her punishment.

She would name a time and place to meet him. She would.

She would write him a letter as soon as she arrived home. She would.

And this time . . . she would post it.

She told herself that, over and over.

Now she just needed her heart and hands to act.

10

. . . I hardly know how to begin this letter, so I will be succinct. I am returned to England. I am not married nor betrothed. Perhaps someday I will tell you the entire sordid tale of Sarah Forrester. I should have solicited your advice, as surely your guidance would have saved me much heartache. Unfortunately, I have learned that you are not in London at present. My heart's desire is to set out for Bath immediately and thank you in person. But I have too many pressing obligations at the moment. The King himself has requested my presence in London for a while yet. It is with bitter regret that I will have to wait to call upon you, but I hope to do so in four weeks' time . . .

—letter from Lord Blake to LHF, dated April 21, 1823

The King has released you from further duties, I hear," Stratton sat back in his chair, taking a sip of brandy before raising his eyebrows at Colin.

"Yes." Colin nodded. "I had to ride out to Windsor earlier this week, as His Majesty was too ill to travel and desired my presence—"

"Again?"

"Again. But now I am free for the time being." Colin glanced about before continuing in a quiet voice. "And between you and me, it's about damned time. I have far too many other issues to sort. I leave tomorrow for several of my estates to the west. Too much has been left unaddressed for too long."

Including a much-needed, long-anticipated visit to one anonymous business partner, Colin finished mentally.

This evening, he and Stratton were chatting over drinks at White's, the exclusive gentleman's club. Colin had been elected into White's years before but had visited for the first time only a week previously. It had been a mere three weeks since meeting Stratton in Hyde Park, but he and Stratton had become close. Colin already felt he had a friend for life.

Some relationships were like that, he pondered. And, heaven knew, he needed the help of a gentleman like Stratton at the moment.

Colin had not anticipated the giddy rush of excitement his return would send through polite society. Like Agamemnon of old, the *ton* wasted no time in rolling out a red carpet in welcome. Invitations had poured in as soon as the knocker on his London townhouse had been affixed last week, indicating he was in residence.

How everyone had learned of his arrival was still a mystery. The marriage-age misses and their eager mammas had swarmed him almost immediately.

He and Stratton had chatted for hours upon hours about it. After endless tales of their years in the army, they had moved on to shared stories of eager women trying to trap unsuspecting lords into marriage. Lord Stratton had come into his earldom unexpectedly and, like Colin, found himself in the middle of a whirlwind of eligible misses, all desperate to secure his money and title for themselves.

Before leaving for India, Colin had been too new to high society and too poor to garner such attention.

Well, not much.

There had been the one strange incident all those years ago with that heiress, hungry for his title. He had nearly forgotten about it. What had been her name? Miss Liverock? Miss Rockhearth? He was truly terrible with names and faces.

But, now, with his fortunes restored tenfold, he was the prize of all prizes. So many young misses, fresh from the schoolroom, had already been paraded before him like cattle up for auction. Why would a man such as himself wish to marry a girl who was barely considered an adult? He had no desire to wed a child. The very idea was nauseating.

It had been less than a month, and he was already infinitely weary of the whole mess. Just another reminder of how things had ended with Sarah—

He stopped himself right there. Enough. The past was the past and needed to stay there.

"Did a young woman really hide herself in your carriage last week?" Stratton asked, amusement lacing his tone.

"Yes." Colin sighed. "And then had the audacity to request I escort her home."

"Did you?"

"Of course." Another sigh. "After insisting my footmen sit in the carriage with us."

"I heard Lady Tyson tried four times to leave you alone with one of her girls."

"That too. I was practically chased from room to room at her musicale."

"But I would wager you still bowed politely on your way out the door." Stratton chuckled.

"That is the ultimate problem here. They know I am a gentleman of honor. My life would be much simpler were I a scoundrel. I could simply toss them all aside without a care for their reputation or my own. But as it is . . ."

Colin sipped his tea.

"You *do* plan to marry at some point, however," Stratton pointed out.

"Naturally. But I have this decidedly old-fashioned notion that I should be permitted to choose the bride myself."

Stratton chuckled.

Obviously, marriage had been on Colin's mind for years now. The appalling mess with Sarah had been a set-back, for sure. He had vowed never again to court a young girl over a decade his junior. He had already tried that—

No. If and when he married, it would be to someone closer to his own age. A more mature sort of woman who matched him.

Hence the draw of Miss Heartstone. Colin found himself thinking about her over and over. Her kind eyes, the husky softness of her voice. He had even seen her in passing at Stratton House, climbing into a carriage as he alighted from his own. She appeared to be a woman of breadth and intellect. After Sarah's betrayal, Colin was ready for someone steady and straightforward.

"What was that about Blake and a wife?" A loud voice interrupted their conversation.

Colin turned with Stratton as a group of gentlemen walked over to them. Colin had quickly realized that White's was the best place to meet the gentlemen of the *ton*. All he had to do was ensconce himself in a leather wingback chair, and every man who passed him by would stop to introduce himself.

Which also explained why the seven other men felt comfortable taking up chairs around Stratton and himself.

"Once you have a wife, Blake, you won't be able to leave town until the last ball of the Season," one of the men chuckled.

"Hear, hear." Another man raised his glass.

"I have three sisters. You may have your pick of the litter," a particularly ruddy-faced man said with a wink.

Heaven help him.

Colin merely managed a small grimace and took a healthy sip of brandy.

Stratton gave a knowing laugh. "I don't wish to pry, Blake, but it does seem that you have been somewhat taken with Miss Heartstone."

The words caught Colin unawares, causing him to choke slightly on his next sip of brandy.

"Hah!" Stratton chuckled more loudly. "Lady Stratton was correct. You *were* taken with her."

Blast. He had walked right into that trap, hadn't he?

His social manners were somewhat rusty.

The mention of Miss Heartstone caused quite a reaction from the gathered men.

"You mean Blake was taken with her fortune, correct?"

"Who hasn't been taken with Miss Heartstone? The bigger question—will she take you?"

Colin paused, as if pondering, but he was curious.

"Why *should* I consider Miss Heartstone?" Colin asked.

The group of men laughed.

And then stopped as they realized he was in earnest.

"I think we sometimes forget that you haven't been in London the past several years." Stratton replied. "Why Miss Heartstone, then?"

Colin nodded.

Stratton shrugged. "In addition to her obvious physical charms, she is intelligent and most sensible. Furthermore, she is wealthy in her own right. You would not have to worry about her chasing you for your money or title. She has had her pick of the aristocracy for years now and has chosen not to marry." Stratton gestured toward the men around him. "She attracts men like flies to honey, but year after year, she resists their advances. It has become something of a rite of passage, has it not?"

"Aye," one of the men agreed, "none of us can move on to other pastures until Miss Heartstone has refused our suit."

Interesting. Miss Heartstone chose to remain single. A woman like himself—feted and courted and, as a consequence, always suspicious of others and their true intentions.

"What says the betting book currently?" a third man asked.

The betting book at White's was notorious. Gentlemen would record wagers with one another, betting on everything from when a certain lord would marry to which raindrop would reach the bottom of a window pane first.

The bloods of the *ton* were a thrill-seeking bunch.

"The odds are twenty-to-one that Miss Heartstone will marry this year," a voice called from the group.

The announcement was met with loud guffaws.

"What are the odds that Lord Blake will finally be the man to get her before a vicar?"

"Not if Lord Odysseus gets there first."

That particular statement was deemed even more hilarious.

Mentally, Colin frowned. Vividly he remembered how Lord Odysseus had stood close to Miss Heartstone, clearly claiming her as his territory.

"Am I such an unsightly specimen, then?" Colin asked.

"Hardly," Stratton said, "but Miss Heartstone has a definite reputation."

"It is said she truly has a heart of stone. None can win her approval."

Colin sagged into his chair. "She seemed delightfully affable and perfectly lovely."

"Oh, she is," came a reply.

"Particularly when she rejects your marked attentions."

"You would know!"

"We *all* know."

Colin's frown deepened. "Pardon? You have all been rejected by Miss Heartstone?"

A chorus of *ayes* and *yes* greeted his ears.

Stratton alone stayed silent, as he had been married before Miss Heartstone made her debut.

"Her reputation for giving a polished rejection is legendary," he said.

"Very true, Stratton. Miss Heartstone has the entire procedure down to an art form. The past several years, she has taken to no longer waiting for the gentleman to pop the question to her. She takes a stand before things reach that point."

"She does?" Colin swirled the brandy in his sifter. "That seems . . . unusual."

"I gather she abhors leading a gentleman to think that she favors him in any way," Stratton explained.

"Truly?" Colin asked.

Stratton nodded.

"How does she go about doing that?" Colin had to ask it.

Several of the men sat forward.

A young buck spoke first, "Well, first she will loll her head to the side, her eyes going soft-like—" He mimicked the motion. "—before saying, in her kindest tone—"

"—'My lord, I have something I wish to speak with you about'." His friend spoke in a high, breathy voice. "'I must tell you how much I enjoy your company'—"

"And then she gives a compliment." Another man said. "Mine was the cut of my coat."

"Mine was the kind way I speak to my mother."

"My dancing skill."

"Riding seat."

"Friendly manner."

Stratton chuckled.

"Miss Heartstone truly does this?" Colin had to ask.

Every man in the room nodded.

"And then after the compliment she says—"

" 'But after much pondering, I am afraid that we are not suited—'"

" '—though I thank you for the honor you do me in your attention.'"

A pause.

"That is how she does it?" Colin asked.

"Yes."

"Every gentleman."

"Every time."

"I do believe it has become a rite of passage, in all honesty," Stratton said.

"And she somehow becomes lovelier with every passing year."

"Yes. How does she manage that?"

"It must be a woman-ish thing. They have their ways."

"Do you wish to enter in on the betting?" A voice asked.

No, Colin certainly did not wish to do that.

One of the men downed his drink in one hearty gulp. "I have heard she earnestly intends to marry this year."

Dead silence greeted his statement.

"You don't say?"

"Lord Odysseus would like to think that."

"She has tolerated him longer than most—"

"With looks like his, how can we mere mortals compete?"

The men continued to chatter on about Miss Heartstone. Her grace. Her kindness. Her beauty.

The largess of her fortune.

For his part, Colin could care less about her fortune.

Now he was even more curious to better know the woman herself. He felt a sense of kinship with her. Who was the woman beyond the facade she presented to the world?

That jolt of initial contact lingered. He wouldn't mind, indeed, exploring it more.

Besides, Lord Odysseus needed a little competition.

11

. . . my lord, this letter has been years in the making. Sometimes small misunderstandings grow into enormous mountains until one doesn't know where to begin to surmount them . . .

—excerpt of letter from Miss Heartstone to Lord Blake;
written, signed, and sealed but not sent

Colin looked out his carriage window at the row house, his brows drawing down.

His brow wrinkled further, glancing down at the address his sister had given him for Lord Halbert Phalean. He stared back at the house.

Mmmm. This *was* the correct place.

But it didn't seem quite . . . right.

The house itself wasn't necessarily a problem. Like nearly all houses in Bath, this one was clad in honey-colored stone with triangular pediments above the central windows.

The street was quiet. Not the most fashionable address in Bath, but not poor either. *Genteelly shabby*, he'd label it. The sort of place that a younger son of a less-than-wealthy duke might land later in life.

His frown deepened. Colin alighted from the carriage, looking left and right.

LHF had to be one of the wealthiest men in all of England. His pockets were vast. Why would he choose to live in this place? More of his desire for anonymity? Or was he truly that modest of a person?

It only served to underscore how little Colin actually knew about LHF. How odd to know a person's innermost thoughts about the human condition but nothing about the reality of their day-to-day living.

Well, Colin was determined to change that.

He had been forced to wait upon the King in London for almost three weeks before being able to politely leave the city. But once he was free to leave, Colin had traveled straight to Bath and Lord Halbert.

Problems and issues had piled up in the meantime, the demands of running a vast financial empire never ending. After this critical meeting with LHF, Colin would spend weeks traveling around to his various estates in southern England, meeting with his stewards, addressing in person the needs of each property.

LHF had sent precisely three letters since Colin's arrival—a polite one congratulating him on his return to England, as well as two others detailing pressing business issues. Decisions needed to be made about an investment opportunity in Massachusetts. Their factory in Perth needed to hire more laborers, and Colin wanted the new workers to be veterans, not child labor. All things he hoped to discuss with Lord Halbert in person today.

So much to be done. At the very least, if he and Lord Halbert could just talk about these issues, it would save Colin precious time. Surely LHF could see that.

Shrugging off his thoughts, Colin mounted the steps, rapping on the door. The seconds ticked before shuffling sounds came from the hallway beyond. Finally, the door creaked open revealing a butler just as genteelly shabby as the house. The elderly man blinked, taking in Colin's smart appearance and the gleaming, newly-purchased carriage behind him.

"Lord Blake to see Lord Halbert, please." Colin extended his card to the man.

The butler gave a flustered nod and hastily ushered Colin into a sparsely furnished entrance hall.

"I shall inform his lordship at once, my lord," the butler said in a rush before climbing the stairs to the second floor with as much alacrity as the old man could muster.

It was telling that the butler didn't remotely insinuate that his lordship might not be home to visitors. Even more telling was the fact that the butler returned in less than three minutes to escort Colin upstairs, showing him into a drawing room, murmuring that Lord Halbert would be down shortly.

Left alone in the room, Colin turned in a circle. His eyes quickly scanned the aging furniture, the threadbare carpets, the clock that had to be at least a century old if it was a day.

The house was deathly quiet.

For the first time, misgivings settled in with a vengeance. How could Lord Halbert be running an international empire from this place? Colin would have expected to see at least a secretary or an official man of business. Or, at a minimum, hear the far-off murmur of voices discussing business matters. Something.

Instead, the entire house felt tired and worn down. Everything overused and underpaid and ready to be sent to pasture.

Before Colin could get far in his assessment, however, the door snicked open.

Lord Halbert bustled in, somewhat out of breath, as if he had raced to prepare to greet his guest.

"Lord Blake!" The older man exclaimed. "You honor my humble abode with your presence. I received a letter from George just yesterday stating that you had returned to England. Welcome home, my lord."

Colin smiled, strained and tight, as the older man shook his hand with emphatic vigor. Lord Halbert was just as he remembered, though older now: tall, gray hair tending toward white, clothing neat and well-cut but showing its age.

Worse, not a flicker of anything beyond polite inanities gleamed in Lord Halbert's eyes. No wariness. No recognition. Not an oblique reference to Colin's repeated requests for an audience.

Most certainly not an admittance to being LHF.

All of which left Colin with a sinking stomach and rising sense of what? Panic? Disbelief?

Had he been wrong all those years ago? Was Lord Halbert *not* LHF then? Or was his old friend putting on a good show, still intent on protecting his secret identity?

Both possibilities were nauseating.

"Won't you please be seated?" Lord Halbert swept a hand over a sagging sofa.

Colin eased himself down.

Lord Halbert sat, bristling with excitement. "To what do I owe the honor of this visit, my lord?"

Colin cleared his throat. He sorted through his barrage of feelings and settled on *irritation* as his preferred state.

Enough of this cat-and-mouse.

"With all due respect, Lord Halbert, do you truthfully not know why I have come?" Colin asked, emotion making his voice sharper than the situation warranted. "I would assume that a man of your intelligence would be beyond playing this game."

Colin fixed the older man with his commanding look. The drilling stare that had caused more than one subordinate over the years to quake in his boots.

To his credit, Lord Halbert withstood it better than most. But the man was clearly not . . . unaffected. He squirmed slightly, frowning.

"I . . . uh . . ." Lord Halbert licked his lips. His eyes darted to the side, assuring the door was closed. He leaned forward. "I assume George has taken it upon himself to talk to you about my current . . . problems."

Colin barely avoided flinching.

Problems?

"Problems?" Colin repeated, voice wooden. *Not* where he saw this conversation going. What did George have to do with this?

Lord Halbert sagged, shoulders slumping. He rubbed a weary hand across his forehead. "'Tis nothing, my lord. George worries needlessly. Only a few gambling debts that some economy and retrenching will correct soon enough. I should know better than to play five-card loo when deep in my cups, particularly when a beautiful widow is present. Never the combination to create a steady head." He gave a self-deprecating laugh, color tinging his cheeks. "Though I confess chagrin that George felt the need to run to you over it. I didn't think that George understood the severity of the situation."

Colin's frozen brain struggled to catch up with the reality facing him.

The older man took Colin's silence as permission to continue speaking. "I fear I have allowed pride to overcome my better sense. But I am, at present, willing to accept whatever assistance you deem fit to provide, my lord. The Good Lord will humble us for our sins, will he not?" Lord Halbert grimaced before offering Colin another strained smile.

Colin returned the expression, mind humming in stunned shock.

How could—

What the—

His heart thundered, drowning out anything else Lord Halbert said.

Colin surged to his feet, hands clasped behind his back. He walked to the large window overlooking the street.

He swallowed. Once. Twice.

Lord Halbert assumed Colin had come at George's request to settle some gambling debts.

And more to the point—

Lord Halbert was clearly *not* LHF.

How could that be?

How could Colin have been *so* wrong?

Nausea clawed at his throat.

He paced back and forth, the weight of Lord Halbert's frazzled gaze heavy on him.

"Are you quite all right, my lord?" Lord Halbert's eyes widened. "Do my sins sit so heavily upon you?"

Colin paused and pinched the bridge of his nose, shaking his head.

"No," he managed to say.

He wasn't ready to admit defeat quite yet. He stopped and met the older man's gaze with intense directness.

The time for subtly was long past.

"I will happily render whatever aid is needed in exchange for your absolute discretion and brutal honesty," Colin said.

"Of course, my lord." Lord Halbert straightened in his chair. "My word is my bond. I am the soul of discretion."

Colin nodded. "Do the initials LHF mean anything to you?"

There. He had said it.

Lord Halbert froze. But it wasn't the hesitation of a caught animal. Instead, it was a pause of confusion, of dismay.

"You asked for my honesty and, I must admit, the initials LHF mean nothing to me." Lord Halbert frowned, clearly rattling through his memory. Abruptly, his expression brightened. "Oh! LHF could be *my* initials—Lord Halbert Phalean, assuming an 'F' to mimic the beginning sound of Phalean."

See?! Colin wanted to shout. *This is why I assumed this man was LHF. He is clearly clever.*

"Has someone misled you, my lord?" Lord Halbert continued. "Has someone done something, and you assumed it was me?"

Colin could do nothing more than clench his jaw and nod with one sharp up-down motion.

Lord Halbert looked suitably outraged. "Heavens! What a dastardly thing—"

"Again, I would ask for your absolute discretion with this matter," Colin reiterated. "To clarify, on your honor as a gentleman, you have no understanding to what I refer?"

Lord Halbert met his gaze with forthright directness. "Upon my honor, my lord, I know not of what you speak."

Lord Halbert's words lashed across the room, shredding any trace of doubt that might have lingered.

Colin closed his eyes for a few moments against the onslaught of emotions, letting the sensations flow through him—shock, anger, betrayal, frustration. Only a lifetime of breeding allowed him to keep most of it off his expression.

That was that, then.

Lord Halbert was definitively *not* LHF.

Now what?

He swallowed noisily and opened his eyes.

He would soldier on. He always did.

His father died, and Colin enlisted in the Army to provide for his mother and sisters.

He inherited a tarnished title and bankrupt estates, and Colin immediately set out for India to earn his fortunes.

Sarah betrayed him, and he swallowed his pain and grief and moved on.

His best friend and business partner mislead him—

Colin stopped there. He would deal with the emotional and possibly financial repercussions later.

First things first. He couldn't show up on Lord Halbert's doorstep unannounced and not offer help.

Fifteen minutes later, Colin stepped back into his waiting carriage, leaving Lord Halbert a happier man than he had found him. Colin had pledged to clear some of Lord Halbert's debt, provided the man never breathe a word of his help to another soul. As before, Colin did like the older man. He was reserved and proud but also grounded in good sense.

That wasn't what had Colin clenching his jaw and tapping his fingers against his thigh, however.

If Lord Halbert wasn't his man, then . . .

. . . who the hell was LHF?

Who was the brilliant mind behind their business ventures? Who had been the man to mentor him? Who had Colin claimed as a best friend all these years?

Who had he trusted with his innermost secrets? And what was he to do about it?

The feeling of betrayal sank deep.

Though logically, Colin knew LHF hadn't betrayed him specifically, he was hard-pressed to not feel like a deceived fool.

Colin had long thought LHF to be a man of honor and integrity. The man's actions over the years had proven this time and again.

But now? LHF had to know that Colin was mistaken in his identity. How could LHF claim to be a friend but treat Colin's trust so cavalierly?

More to the point, how could LHF, in good conscience, have allowed this farce to go on so long?

Sarah's betrayal had stung.

But this?

This scorched his very soul.

As you may have deduced by now, I have been mistaken as to your identity. My dear sir, permit me to be frank. We have been friends and business partners for seven years this month. You know much about my life. However, I do not even know your name. I am troubled by your continued insistence on anonymity. Initially, before becoming friends and confidants, I could understand your reluctance. But now, why do you deny me your trust?

You once asked what I fear most. I had answered at the time that I feared not finding the other half of myself. I have since amended that statement. My greatest fear is discovering that those whom I trust are not worthy of that trust.

I am a man of honor. I had taken you to be a man of honor, as well. I ask you directly—meet me, face-to-face.

—*letter from Lord Blake to LHF, dated May 17, 1823*

B elle read Blake's letter, a grimace on her face.

Anger and hurt laced every word.

I am a man of honor. I had taken you to be a man of honor, as well. I ask you directly—meet me, face-to-face—

Belle set the paper down with trembling fingers, struggling to gather her thoughts.

Yes, she had known that he was mistaken.

Yes, she was the worst scoundrel for not having told him the truth before now.

His subtle accusation only underscored the problem: *I had taken you to be a* man *of honor . . .*

Yes, this day of reckoning had long been coming.

The letter was dated over two weeks ago but had only just arrived. Blake had been traveling, and Mr. Sloan had enclosed an apologetic letter, stating he had a spell of ill health as of late, causing the delay.

Clearly, Belle had to tell Blake the truth about LHF. She just didn't know how to go about doing it.

No, that wasn't quite correct. Belle needed to be more honest with herself.

She knew *how* to tell him; that wasn't difficult to ascertain.

It was more the timing of it all. Once he knew, Blake would be honor bound to sever their working and personal relationship. Disentangling their business interests would be messy and would inevitably hurt some people.

But Belle knew that was more of a reflexive excuse at this point.

The real reason? She did not want lose Blake in truth.

Her wayward heart lurched and howled at the thought.

Her greatest fear realized.

There had been a small part of her that still held out hope . . . if Blake chose to court her . . .

Her pulse raced at the thought.

He had not shown a single spark of interest in her seven years ago, even with the enormous carrot of her plump dowry and the need of his extreme poverty.

And now . . . the man was wealthy. No heiresses required. Young, handsome, titled. He had been welcomed home like a conquering hero. In short, he could have his pick of any eligible woman in the British Isles.

Her mind flashed back to that breathless moment at the balloon ascension, the surprise of meeting Blake's gaze, the startled sense of something . . . *more* from him.

Her heart hitched in her chest. She ached to see that look in his eyes again: surprise, warmth, tenderness.

But Blake had been caught up in a whirlwind of meetings with Parliament and the King as soon as he arrived. And then he had left London for Bath, she assumed, and an ill-fated meeting with whomever he had assumed to be LHF.

She cringed at the very mention of that meeting. It must have been horrifically awkward and embarrassing. How he must detest her.

Yes, any hope she had of engaging with him socially before telling him the truth had rapidly evaporated.

But Belle scarcely had time at the moment to chase down Blake in person. He was still traveling around to his various estates, she assumed. And she and Anne were busily readying for a house party at Stratton Hall in Warwickshire. They were to leave in just two days' time. Georgiana had practically begged Belle to join them.

Belle was eager to escape London for Stratton Hall. Two weeks of country air and tranquility would be the perfect respite. Georgiana was a kind, undemanding hostess, and invitations to her house parties were always a coveted commodity. When she had first issued the invitation, Georgiana had assured Belle that Lord Odysseus would be in attendance, though he would arrive a day late. And as Belle had been considering Lord Odysseus as a potential husband, the house party would be an ideal locale to continue their courtship.

Of course, Blake's unexpected arrival in England—unmarried, unattached, and impossible to ignore—had put a wrinkle in Belle's matrimony plans.

A wrinkle? Hah! More like Blake had upset the entire clothes' press, and Belle was at sixes and sevens trying to decide how to smooth everything out again.

She wasn't sure what she wanted anymore.

But one thing was certain—any hope of Blake forgiving her was gone. She had thoroughly abused his good-will and trust. She deserved his scorn.

There would be no graceful exit from this. She had created this mess; it was now her time to clean it up.

Belle faced the gallows of her own making.

And if the thought of losing the friendship of the man who mattered most created large cracks in her heart threatening to drag her down into a sea of tears?

Well, that was the price of her deception.

Biting her lip, she pulled a fresh sheet of paper from her desk. She would send off the letter asking him to name a date and place to meet, await his reply, and take the two weeks at Stratton Hall to collect her thoughts.

She had once asked the man to marry her. How could telling him this truth be any more frightening?

And yet, somehow, she felt that it would be.

13

. . . My lord, I am sympathetic to your anger and frustration. It is most understandable. Forgive me. Please know that I have *always* been your true friend. The reason I have kept my identity hidden from you is breathtakingly simple. If you would do me the honor of setting a time and place of your choosing, I will meet you there, in person, to explain all—

—*letter from LHF to Lord Blake, dated June 5, 1823*

Belle descended the central staircase of Stratton Hall, the demi-train of her sky-blue satin dress sweeping behind her, hair curled and amassed atop her head. Pearls glowed softly at her wrist and neck, others peeked out from her hair. Long white gloves encased her hands and arms, while a soft cashmere shawl looped through her elbows provided extra warmth should the evening weather turn chilly. Anne walked sedately at her side.

Three days. It had been three days since she sent off her letter to Blake, asking him to name a time and place to meet. He would receive it in a day or two more, write his reply, and then . . .

Belle clasped an arm around her stomach, sternly telling all the swirling butterflies to be still.

She had at least two weeks of reprieve. Two weeks to formulate her response, to concoct a mix of words that would somehow not end her friendship with Blake entirely. Two weeks of Lord Odysseus' company to decide if she wanted to continue to encourage his attentions. Georgiana's house party would be the perfect place of calm to do so.

Stratton Hall was a more modern building, built in the neoclassical style of the previous century, with pedimented doorways and rooms that led one into another, the entire effect harmonious and elegant. They passed through the entrance hall, through the music room, and into the green drawing room.

Belle paused in the doorway, somewhat taken aback. She and Anne had arrived earlier in the day and retired to their rooms, eager to rest after their journey. Consequently, she had not witnessed the arrival of the other guests.

She had expected the usual assortment of acquaintances from Georgiana—married MPs, older friends with refined tastes, perhaps a poet or artist to round out the company. In other words, a small, intimate group of like-minded people.

But, instead, Belle faced a room of . . . not that.

Two matrons stood to one side with five fluttering charges between them. Belle recognized one of the women as Mrs. Jones-Button, a mother known for her ruthless determination to see her three daughters married. Belle did not know the other woman, but given that the woman surveyed the room like a general preparing for battle, her intentions were obvious. The girls ranged in age from young to younger and cast longing looks across the room to the bucks gathered around a brandy decanter.

For their part, the group of men ignored the young ladies, preferring instead to pass around the brandy and laugh at each other's jests. Belle recognized most of the men, a group of friends she collectively thought of as the Gold Miners. They each sought a wealthy wife for one reason or another—some out of necessity, others out of greed. In either case, Belle preferred to skirt their company.

Why this odd group of people? It was so unlike Georgiana.

Granted, Lord Stratton's stepfather and mother were in attendance—most likely invited from the nearby vicarage. And Belle also recognized two other gentlemen and their wives, known for their reformist views on labor which aligned with Lord Stratton's own. A widow and her nephew, both heralded for their wit.

But why the host of unmarried young ladies and gentlemen?

Anne noticed Belle's pause and said, *sotto voce,* "From speaking with the housekeeper, I understand Lady Stratton owed a favor to Mrs. Jones-Button who is a niece to her ladyship's aunt. Mrs. Jones-Button brought along her own three daughters, as well as invited her sister and her two girls. Hence the need for more eligible bachelors. Though we are to stay for two weeks, as close friends of the Strattons, most of the other guests will be leaving after only a week. So it won't be two weeks of this."

Anne motioned toward the Gold Miners with her eyes. One of the gentlemen was now attempting to balance a deck of cards on his nose. Another took bets. A third was pouring generous glasses of Lord Stratton's finest brandy.

Charming.

All of Belle's hopes for a relaxing house party sailed rapidly away, balloons ascending into the sky, no tethers or hope of alighting anywhere pleasant. Belle simply wished to avoid a disastrous landing.

It was going to be a long week, even with Lord Odysseus's arrival tomorrow. She was relieved he would be in attendance to help dissuade the attentions of other men.

If only she didn't like Georgiana quite so much . . .

Belle lifted her chin. She was being unfair. The presence of fortune-hunting men and marriage-chasing women need not affect her. She would still have a week of quiet once they left.

Belle's eyes focused on Georgiana herself. Standing before the fireplace, Georgiana looked elegant in an ivory silk dress with small, puffed sleeves, her golden hair glinting in the early evening light. Belle smiled as she recognized the silk ribbon on Georgiana's dress—the very ribbon Belle had insisted would be all the rage this year.

She had not been wrong.

Georgiana stood speaking with the vicar and another man who had his back to Belle. A wide smile broke across Georgiana's face as Lord Stratton crossed the room to stand at his wife's side—the love in Georgiana's eyes as she looked at her husband, his returning look of intense affection.

Belle firmly beat down the pang that kicked in her chest.

Why did she have to *want* such a relationship so fiercely? The one thing that no amount of money could purchase—she, of all people, would know.

Why did love have to be so elusive? Or, in her case, so pathetically one-sided?

She should simply be content with her life. She had money enough for multiple lifetimes. Charities that needed her. Friends who shared her sense of humor and who had children she could dote upon.

Her life was full. It was enough.

And maybe if she continued to remind herself of that fact every other minute, she could finally believe it.

Catching Georgiana's eye, Belle swept across the room, intent on greeting her hostess. Georgiana smiled and said something to the man before her and then walked forward, greeting Belle with an affectionate kiss on the check.

"Belle, dear, how delightful you look this evening. You are always the epitome of fashion."

"Georgiana, you are too kind, as ever." Belle embraced her friend.

"I must apologize for not giving you advanced warning about my guests," Georgiana whispered in her ear. "I owed my aunt a favor but was still selfish enough to want your company."

"Think nothing of it, Georgiana."

Georgiana pulled back and, snagging Belle's hand, tugged her forward. "Well, as recompense, I have a small surprise for you."

Belle smiled politely and walked with Georgiana, finally getting a solid look of the profile of the man standing beside the vicar, listening attentively to the older man.

She froze.

No!

A few inches taller than herself, curling sun-kissed chestnut hair, golden skin, dancing blue eyes sparking with intelligence. Bottle green cutaway jacket over a beautiful silk-embroidered waistcoat.

He was here.

Blake was here. Georgiana had invited him.

Blood thundered in her ears.

Wait. Georgiana was still speaking to her, holding her hand, leaning in to her ear like the good friends they were.

". . . so sorry to have caught you off guard. I am sure you assumed you would know all my guests, but this house party is somewhat different than usual. So I thought I would give Lord Odysseus a little competition." Georgiana paused, surely noting Belle's wide-eyed stare. "Did I do wrong?"

"No," Belle tore her eyes away from Blake's shoulders and gave her friend a strained smile. "Not at all."

Georgiana narrowed her gaze, clearly not convinced, but too polite to say anything else. "I do not wish to misspeak, but I sensed that Lord Blake might have taken some interest in you after our encounter in Hyde Park. I know you are more actively looking for a husband this year. Why not add Lord Blake to your list?"

Hah!

Blake had been the sole occupant of that list for more years than Belle could quickly recall. That wasn't quite the problem.

She had really been looking forward to procrastinating the day of her reckoning for at least another couple weeks. But as the man was now standing six feet from her, she was only damning herself further if she stayed silent. She had no excuse other than cowardice. Which, as an excuse, had served her well up until now—

Laughter from the gaggle of girls across the room drifted over to them. Of course. They were here for *him* more than the Gold Miners.

Belle turned her head away.

Georgiana noticed, of course.

"Come." She threaded her hand through Belle's elbow. "You are doing nothing more than bettering your acquaintance with Lord Blake."

Belle allowed herself to be dragged over to where Blake and Stratton chatted amiably with Stratton's stepfather. She swallowed, sternly telling her racing heart to slow down.

He's just a man. He doesn't know that you love him.

"Lord Blake, you remember Miss Heartstone from our encounter in Hyde Park last month?" Georgiana smiled, keeping Belle at her side.

Later, Belle would spend hours wondering if Blake's response was the most wonderful thing possible or an absolute catastrophe.

He turned toward her, head swinging around.

He locked his eyes with hers.

And . . . his face lit up. A candle bursting to life. Delighted and charmed.

"Miss Heartstone. Of course. A pleasure to meet you again, madam." He bowed over her hand, that smile firmly planted on his face.

My heart.

Belle quite forgot how to breathe. She knew that air was supposed to go into her lungs—the breath of life and all that—but she couldn't pull air in for all the tea in China.

How was she supposed to tell him the truth about LHF when he looked at her like *that?*

How was she supposed to shatter her longing, *hopeful* heart?

And how could she continue on *without* telling him?

COLIN'S HEART LURCHED at the sight of Miss Heartstone.

In fact, he had accepted Lord Stratton's invitation to this house party solely because Stratton had not-so-subtly told him that she would be present.

Miss Heartstone was every bit as elegant as he remembered. Yes, elegant. That word best captured her. Graceful and poised in a pale blue dress he knew his sisters would collectively drool over, her hair artfully curled and studded with pearls. Her face held the sharper edges of true womanhood.

As he remembered, she exuded the quiet confidence of a woman secure in herself and her surroundings. Intelligent and polished without being brash or pushy. Granted, the speculative gleam in Lady Stratton's eye indicated Stratton had likely taken his wife into his confidence.

Regardless, Miss Heartstone was a welcome relief from the younger misses giggling in the room. He christened them the Desperate Debutantes. They shot hungry looks in Colin's direction until he felt like the mangy tiger in the Tower of London menagerie. Lauded and admired while gazing wistfully out of an iron cage—utterly trapped.

After Sarah, Colin was quite sure he was done with flighty, spirited women for good.

This country party was supposed to have been a respite. But as with everything else, it was not quite as it should have been.

When Colin had set out from London weeks ago, he had done so with high hopes.

He would meet with Lord Halbert in Bath and thank his business partner. He would visit his estates and take stock of things.

Nothing had gone as he had planned.

He had discovered that a steward of one of his properties in Cornwall had been siphoning money off the estate. Another farm had suffered catastrophic flooding due to malignant tampering with a nearby canal, wiping out thirty tenant homes that now needed to be rebuilt.

And then there had been Lord Halbert himself. *That* particular episode had been the sharpest cut of all—to learn that his business partner was not the man he thought him to be.

Who had he been corresponding with all this time? Obviously, LHF was wealthy and well-educated. They had discussed nearly every topic imaginable over the years. It seemed almost impossible that Colin could know the man down to his soul and yet remain ignorant of his name.

And more to the point, why did LHF insist on hiding behind a cloak of anonymity? It made no sense. How could LHF call himself a man of honor when he behaved in this fashion?

And still the sense of betrayal sat raw in his breast. Colin knew it was irrational. LHF had never pretended to be Lord Halbert. The erroneous assumption had been Colin's mistake entirely.

But that didn't stop the jittery ache that banded his chest every time he thought about his friend.

Colin had sent off his first letter nearly three weeks ago, demanding a face-to-face meeting. He had yet to receive a reply. Colin knew that he had been traveling. That any letter from LHF would take a week or more to catch up with him.

But that didn't lessen his frustration.

And the longer LHF took to respond, the more Colin's hope for an amicable resolution faded. *All* correspondence from LHF had dried up, as a matter of fact, even those related to business matters. Colin had sent another letter just four days past. If he heard nothing from LHF, he would have to chase up Mr. Sloan when he returned to London and ascertain what was to be done. Most likely, he would need to hire a Runner to unearth LHF's identity and confront the man in person. One of the smart gentlemen from Bow Street could get to the bottom of this LHF mess easily enough.

How had he and LHF come to this?

Colin mentally shook his head.

Enough of these maudlin thoughts . . . he had a house party to enjoy. Or, at the very least, the pleasure of furthering his acquaintance with Miss Heartstone.

". . . trust you had an uneventful journey from India, my lord?" Miss Heartstone was saying.

Colin admired how the fading sunlight turned her satin gown into shimmery patches of light, highlighting the soft curves of her body.

Heavens but she was lovely.

"Yes. Quite placid, actually," he replied. "We had feared to encounter pirates outside Cape Town, but remained unchallenged."

"Pirates?" Lady Stratton's expression brightened considerably. "How tragic you did not encounter any."

"You are incorrigible, my love." Lord Stratton leaned into his wife. "Pirates are not, as a general rule, a good thing. They tend to be quite bloodthirsty—"

"Oooh, do not tease me so. It has been ages since I had a proper adventure—"

"Georgiana!" Stratton's reproof half serious, half laugh.

Colin caught Miss Heartstone's eye. She looked almost wistfully at the earl and his wife.

She quickly smoothed her expression. "Lady Stratton has quite the vivid imagination."

"Of course, I do!" Lady Stratton looked at her friend. "It is why you so enjoy my company."

"I am found out." Miss Heartstone gave a soft laugh.

Lady Stratton leaned toward Colin, lifting her hand as if to impart a secret. "Miss Heartstone and I share a shocking love of dreadful gothic novels. We read them out loud to each other and shiver in delight when dastardly deeds are done."

"You wrong me, Georgiana. What shall Lord Blake think of such behavior?"

Colin gave a warm chuckle. Here was a topic he knew well.

"Perhaps I share the ladies' taste in novels," he said with a lift of his eyebrows.

Stratton groaned. "Say it isn't so, Blake."

"I hope it is no jest, my lord." Lady Stratton quirked her lips. "Miss Heartstone and I would welcome a third party to our readings. We wish to read *Ivanhoe* again, and a male voice would be appreciated."

Colin smiled as Miss Heartstone looked demurely away.

Charming. She was utterly charming.

He found himself fascinated by the conundrum she presented.

Why had she chosen not to marry? If the gentleman from his evening at White's were to be believed, she had her pick of men. She could marry practically anyone she wished.

And yet, she did not.

Was there a tragedy in her past? Some long-lost love?

Was there truth behind the rumor that she was now entertaining the idea of marriage?

And, why the devil after his disastrous mess with Sarah last fall, was he even asking the question at all?

A FEW HOURS later, Belle slowly fanned herself, only partially listening to the conversation buzzing around her. The Gold Miners were in fine form, jesting and jostling for position next to her. She wondered if one, or all, of them would offer for her hand—again—before the week was out.

The heat from the fire had gone from pleasant to stifling. Or was it her own sense of inner conflict that caused the walls to close in?

Blake was more attractive every time she met him. His confident charm during dinner, his polite manners . . . the goodness she knew lay within his soul . . .

She fanned herself a little harder.

Somewhere between the soup and fish course, admiration and respect had merged with his warm smile and kind comments, pushing her feelings off the cliff into heart-stopping, soul-altering love.

That would not do.

How to proceed?

She had thought to have time in which to plan. To decide how to tell Blake the truth about LHF.

But now . . .

The longer she put it off, the worse things would be, the more betrayed he would feel. She had to *tell* him.

The gentlemen surrounding her—and they *always* surrounded her, eager to make a bid for her enormous fortune—were now giving a point-by-point recap of a curricle race from London to Brighton.

"You are quieter than usual this evening." Georgiana leaned in closer.

Belle shot a glance at the men around them. "Just the usual fatigue of pleasantly keeping . . . people . . . at bay."

"You and Lord Blake alike."

Belle stiffened at the mention of Lord Blake on Georgiana's lips, instantly shooting her friend a questioning look.

"Sebastian has been telling tales all week of the shocking lengths enterprising misses have gone to in order to trap him into marriage. The poor man can scarcely venture from his own home."

"Indeed." Belle hated the faintness of her voice.

"Blake has declared he will have none of them and rightly so. A woman who shows no reservation in trapping a man into marriage— what other deceptive things will she do once she *is* married? Such forward behavior is not to be tolerated. Blake is wise to steer clear of all of them."

Belle swallowed. "Yes. Most wise."

She risked a glance at Blake standing in the corner with Stratton.

Why hadn't she realized Blake would be the target of every fortune-and-title hungry woman in Britain? Of course, he would be. And knowing him as she did—his sense of honor, his innate kindness—he would instantly reject any woman he perceived as being dishonest with him.

Say . . . for example . . . a woman who proposed marriage, was refused, and then allowed him to erroneously assume she was a man throughout seven years of lengthy correspondence.

Someone like that.

Belle swallowed.

She *had* to tell him. Somehow she would get him alone this week and do the deed.

And take whatever outcome would fall.

14

. . . you are wise to encourage me to continue to hold out hope of finding a suitable wife. After having my affections so sorely abused by Sarah last fall, I had thought to avoid pursuing any other lady for some time. But when a lady of charm and elegance crosses one's path, one has no other choice but to act. Do not ask me for more details about the lady in question, sister dear. I shall say no more on the subject. For if it all comes to naught, I will not have a peal rung over my head . . .

—*Lord Blake to his sister, Mrs. George Phalean, dated June 2, 1823*

Hurry. I am quite sure I saw him duck around the edge of the house."

The young lady's voice carried to Colin, followed by a titter of girlish laughter.

The Desperate Debutantes on the hunt.

A pack of hungry lionesses was less persistent. And, like lions, the debutantes had a keen nose for male English blood.

Glancing around, Colin refused to panic. They were just women after all. And more than one of them, which was a blessing. They could hardly entrap him as a group.

Could they?

The morning had dawned bright and clear, beckoning him outside for a brisk morning walk. He should have thought to bring along a footman.

The giggles grew louder. Now what?

A large window near him stood ajar. Without thinking, he pushed the window farther open and climbed inside, darting to the side, pressing himself against the wall just in time. Footsteps sounded on the gravel outside.

"I could have sworn he came this way." Muted voices carried inside and then faded.

He peeked cautiously out the window.

"Gracious, Lord Blake. Have you come to burgle the breakfast silver?" a calm, feminine voice asked. "Or is Stratton Hall being invaded?"

Suppressing a yelp of surprise, Colin whirled to face the room. He took in the large oval dining table. The sideboard laden with covered dishes. The smell of freshly brewed coffee. The sunlight flooding the room from two large windows.

Ah. He was, indeed, in the breakfast room. Two women sat at the table.

Miss Heartstone sipped her morning tea, amusement evident in her warm brown eyes.

Her companion—Miss Rouger? Miss Ruster? No, no. Miss Rutger! Hah!—merely glanced up from the newspaper she was perusing and then went back to reading.

Colin tugged down on his waistcoat and cleared his throat. "Given that I am a man of integrity and not taken to thievery, I believe I will go with latter, Miss Heartstone. Invasion it is, I am afraid."

Amusement moved from her eyes to pull at her lips. "Yes. The wilds of Warwickshire have ever been treacherous."

A particularly loud burst of laughter drifted through the window. Colin ducked back, almost involuntarily.

Miss Heartstone glanced toward the window, not missing Colin's flinch.

Sympathy edged into her gaze. "I do believe there was report of marauding widows recently," she continued, voice warm. "They arm themselves with fruitcake and platitudes."

"I daresay it is more the *daughters* of such women who concern Lord Blake," Miss Rutger said without looking up from her reading as she stirred more sugar into her teacup.

"Mmm." Miss Heartstone leaned closer to her companion. "I hear they travel in vicious packs."

"Yes. I believe they took down an unsuspecting baronet just two days ago near Charlecote. They had the poor man trussed and carried before the local vicar before he could raise the alarm. 'Tis most dreadful." Miss Rutger nodded, matronly mobcap bobbing up and down.

"Lord Blake cannot be too careful."

Colin chuckled, relaxing. "True enough." He chanced a glance through the window. He thought he saw a flash of muslin retreating down the drive, but he couldn't be sure.

"Feel free to take refuge as long as you would like. We shan't betray you." Miss Heartstone neatly spread strawberry preserves on a toast triangle. "Have you breakfasted yet, my lord?"

He had. But when faced with the choice of leaving the breakfast room to wander the estate, dodging the pack of Desperate Debutantes, or staying put and enjoying Miss Heartstone's charming company—

Well, that was hardly a choice now, was it?

He had been able to speak with her at length the previous evening, and he was more-than-ready to stake a claim when it came to courting her. Lord Odysseus, when he did arrive, was not the only eligible bachelor she should consider.

"I believe some coffee would serve me well." He strode over to the sideboard and poured himself a cup. And then added a crumpet and a rasher of bacon to a plate.

He sat down at the table with his back to the windows, facing Miss Heartstone. The soft morning sun streamed through behind him, bathing her in light.

She looked every inch the wealthy heiress. Gleaming chestnut hair meticulously styled, a wide green ribbon threaded through her curls. Her sprigged muslin morning dress perfectly cut to her figure, a generous fichu of Venetian lace tucked into the bodice. Elegant and strikingly pretty.

More importantly, Miss Heartstone looked *sensible*.

He was sure if he told her such, she would take it as an insult. Most women would, he supposed. But given how few people—men or women—truly were, being deemed sensible could only be a rare compliment.

Again, that same recognition washed over him. Had they met before at some *ton* function?

He spread honey on his crumpet before taking a bite, enjoying how the two ladies didn't feel the need to fill the room with chatter.

"Did you enjoy your evening last night, Miss Heartstone?" he asked after a moment.

"Certainly." Miss Heartstone fixed him with her warm brown eyes, stirring her coffee. "Lord and Lady Stratton are always accommodating hosts. Are *you* enjoying *your* stay, my lord? Or have the marauding misses spoiled it for you?"

Colin gave a reluctant chuckle. "I am far too much a gentleman to offer an opinion on that score, Miss Heartstone."

"Portraying yourself as kindhearted will only encourage them, my lord. Set their hearts aflutter."

"Are you suggesting a campaign of cold, ruthless behavior?"

"It would serve you well."

"Adopt a cruel persona?" he replied. "Like Lord Ruthven from *The Vampyre*?"

A slow, delighted smile lit her face. "I do appreciate a gentleman who has a thorough grounding in the, uhmm, great *classics* of modern literature. However, I fear being thought a vampire will most likely only *heighten* the ladies' interest."

"I concede your point."

"You simply must assure them you are neither a gothic creature nor a hero from a novel by Sir Walter Scott."

"Perhaps more like a bumbling fool from a Shakespearean comedy?"

"Precisely. Less Ivanhoe, more Bottom, if you will forgive me." Her eyes lit with mischief.

He laughed in earnest.

Sensible *and* clever. Yes, indeed.

His heart sped up. A bubbly sense of *rightness* fluttered through him. It was that tingling sense he got just before making a large business deal. The sensation that he was on the correct path. That this decision was momentous.

Perhaps his phantom sense of recognition was simply one kindred soul meeting another.

"And what about yourself, Miss Heartstone? I understand you have had your own share of . . . pursuers."

"Do you refer to the Gold Miners?" Miss Rutger interrupted, raising her head from her newspaper.

Colin lifted his eyebrows, catching Miss Heartstone's spreading blush. "Heavens, Miss Rutger, what will his lordship think?"

His lordship would think you are absolutely charming, Colin wished to reply.

But such extravagant compliments were not his style.

Instead, he said, "I perceive that you and I are birds of a feather, Miss Heartstone. I call my own group of—shall we say, *admirers?*—the Desperate Debutantes."

"Desperate Debutantes. I quite like that." An impish smile danced across her face.

"Gold Miners is clever."

"Thank you. I had also considered Treasure Trappers."

"Also excellent. Mob of Marriageable Misses—that was one I rejected."

She tapped her chin with a finger. "Yes. I can see why."

"You *can* take alliteration too far."

"Agreed."

She shot him a delighted grin, gold hints popping in her warm eyes.

By Jove, she was lovely. Colin quite forgot how to breathe.

The giddiness rushing through him was decidedly welcome. After everything with Sarah, part of him had worried that his trust in women had been forever tainted. But that was proving unfounded. Distance and eight months of allowing his heart to heal had done the deed.

And now, Miss Belle Heartstone's presence had him wondering why he had ever considered marrying someone like Sarah Forrester.

They chatted about pleasantries after that. Yes, Lord and Lady Stratton were amiable hosts. The weather was delightful as of late. Naturally he would be joining everyone tomorrow to picnic amongst the bluebells in full bloom in the south fields. Miss Heartstone enjoyed being outdoors.

Through it all, she gave warm, clever answers, wit and humor showing through each reply.

A footman entered midway through their conversation, carrying letters on a silver platter. He presented them to Miss Heartstone.

"Thank you, Thomas." She took the letters and flipped through them, noting each address before tucking them away in a pocket.

Colin still couldn't shake the nagging feeling they had met before Miss Heartstone stumbled into him in Hyde Park the month previously. But where?

"I must say, Miss Heartstone. Have we met?"

Was it just his imagination, or did she freeze momentarily?

BREATHE. BELLE FIRMLY reminded herself. *Do* not *overreact*.

It was a simple question. And, given their past interactions, a reasonable one.

How to respond? She had already told him so many white lies; she hated adding another.

So was this the moment then? She would tell Blake now?

Panic choked her. Thoughts scattered.

She wasn't prepared for this conversation.

Not at this moment. Not this morning.

She had been up half the night, concocting one scenario after another, trying to work out *how* to get Lord Blake alone to tell him the truth about LHF.

Though as Anne shifted beside her, she realized that the present moment might be her only chance. The entire scenario had been ceremoniously handed to her on a platter.

"Why do you ask, my lord?" she asked, hedging, collecting herself.

She could do this. She could tell him.

"You seem somewhat familiar, that is all."

She pasted her brightest smile on her face.

"I am sure all young women look alike. We just blend together into a blurry mass—"

"No. 'Tis something else. I'm not quite able to place a finger upon it."

There was her opening.

Well, you see, my lord, we have met in the past. In fact, we know a shocking amount about one another—

Heart clogging her throat, Belle opened her mouth, willing the words to come out.

"You are too generous, my lord. Perhaps the sense of familiarity comes from—"

A rumble of loud voices outside the breakfast room interrupted her words. Blake turned his head toward the sound.

The door *snicked* open. Lord Odysseus walked in, clearly having just arrived. The scent of wind and sun whisked in with him, his hair and jacket slightly rumpled. The sight did nothing to detract from his stunning attractiveness. Did Lord Odysseus spend hours simply staring at himself in mute amazement?

Belle's nerves were strung so taut, she gave a hiccupping sigh at the abrupt reprieve.

Unfortunately, her sigh was not lost on Blake.

He most likely interpreted her reaction much differently.

But . . . the tenuousness of her situation came home. Imagine if she had been in the middle of telling Blake about LHF and Lord Odysseus had walked in? Or anyone else for that matter?

Clearly, she needed a strategy.

Strategy would require some time to organize.

And why did that thought produce such profound *relief?*

She was a coward of the worst sort.

"Miss Heartstone." Lord Odysseus beamed at her, motioning for her to remain seated. "It is a pleasure to see you again."

"Thank you, my lord. Did you have a good journey?" Unfortunately, Belle realized too late that her sense of reprieve caused her answering smile to be absurdly delighted.

Lord Odysseus, however, eagerly basked in it, his own smile stretching wider.

"My journey was as tolerable as could be expected. Though much better for seeing you at the end of it, madam. I truly feel like Odysseus of old, returning home to find my fair Penelope by the fire, awaiting me." He punctuated his statement with another deep bow and a heated gaze.

Oh dear. Belle was quite torn between giggling and fanning herself. Lord Odysseus certainly knew how to deliver a flattering line.

Blake, however, was not so torn. He hastily changed his inadvertent snicker into a cough.

Which meant that Lord Odysseus finally registered Lord Blake's presence.

His smile freezing in place, Lord Odysseus looked back and forth between Belle and Blake, taking in Anne's polite expression.

Lord Odysseus was no fool, Belle would grant him that. He immediately understood that Blake had become his competition.

The greatest irony, of course, was that she *had* actually played Penelope to one of the men in the room, tending to his lands in his absence and deterring would-be suitors.

Just not Lord Odysseus.

Smile still wooden, Lord Odysseus extended a hand, tone polite. "Blake. A pleasure to see you again, my lord."

Blake shook the other man's hand, the men exchanging a *look.* Was it her imagination, or were the gentlemen's knuckles turning white from the tightness of their mutual grasp? Belle wasn't sure if the emotion bubbling in her chest was hysteria, hilarity, or genuine alarm.

Fortunately, Georgiana chose that moment to bustle into the

breakfast room. "Lord Odysseus. How dreadful of Stratton to not tell me you had arrived."

Georgiana proceeded to ask a mountain of questions, drawing Lord Odysseus's attention.

Blake shot Belle an amused smile and took a chair closer to her, ostensibly to resume their previous conversation.

Heaven help her.

Luckily, Blake moved on to discussing the state of the roads between Cambridge and Warwick, making droll observations that set her laughing.

But the tension that had galloped into the room with Lord Odysseus did not dissipate. It didn't help that Lord Odysseus kept sending furtive glances her way as he spoke with Georgiana, clearly trying to understand the dynamic between her and Blake.

You and me, both.

But Belle had Blake's full attention and felt no pressure at the moment to confess everything, not with so many others in the room. So she indulged in the sheer delight of his company.

"What are your current plans, now that you have returned to England?" Belle asked Blake.

"I have over seven years of news and problems to sort through." Blake folded his arms across his chest, his blue eyes meeting hers with charming intensity.

It was all Belle could do to keep stars off her expression. She wanted to devour him with her gaze. Hardly a ladylike thought, but nevertheless true.

"That sounds onerous," she replied.

Could Blake hear her breathlessness?

From across the room, Lord Odysseus laughed loudly.

Both Belle and Blake hardly noticed.

Instead, Blake smiled. "After I settle my estates and deal with some pressing business issues, I shall be at my leisure."

His words were straightforward, but the lingering heat in his eyes said that he would love nothing more than to spend his leisure with her.

Belle mentally fanned herself.

She was not slow to pick up the baton he had just handed her.

"What leisure activities do you enjoy, my lord?" She leaned closer to him. "Aside from debutante dodging and gothic novels?"

The question earned her a delicious, low chuckle.

Was it her imagination, or did his eyes flick to her lips?

Heaven help her.

"I say, Blake," Lord Odysseus' voice boomed from across the table, "how did you find the roads from Oxford?"

The words worked as Lord Odysseus intended, breaking the spell between Belle and Blake.

Smile turning strained, Blake turned to Lord Odysseus. "The roads were fine if a little rutted in places. And you?"

The men continued their conversation. As Blake spoke, Belle forced herself not to catalog every little thing about him.

The way his elegant long fingers moved as he talked.

The rumbling timbre of his voice, edged with something faintly foreign—evidence of his time spent in India.

How the morning light behind him amplified the gold highlights in his chestnut hair.

Or how his blue eyes animated as he recalled a humorous anecdote from his travels.

Or the weight of his letter—forwarded from Mr. Sloan—burning in her pocket.

Most importantly, she most studiously ignored the painful ache spreading out from her heart again. Stupid hopeful thing.

It was just . . . he was *here*. Speaking. Talking. Laughing. A voice speaking with the same words and cadence she had long recognized from his letters.

Part of her wanted to clasp her hands at her breast in rapturous wonder, hearts floating across her eyes.

But another part frantically hoisted a flag of distress, knowing she was a floundering ship in dangerous waters.

Yes, unbeknownst to him, Blake was one of her best friends.

Yes, when she told him the truth about LHF, he would assume she had played him. And, perhaps, in a sense she had.

But telling him would surely shatter her. Was such emotional devastation worth the price of his friendship?

She didn't even have to pause before answering herself:

It was.

Heaven help her, it was.

15

. . . Your continued silence puzzles me. I have called you a friend, and you have always dealt honorably with me. However, it has been nearly weeks without a word from you. I grow weary and frustrated with this dance. I ask you, one last time, to please reveal yourself to me. I will learn your identity one way or another. Stand up and be the man of honor I know you to be . . .

—*letter from Lord Blake to LHF, dated June 14, 1823*

The bedroom door cracked open behind Belle, causing her to hurriedly stuff Blake's latest letter into her reticule. His words were already seared into her memory:

I grow weary and frustrated with this dance.

Mr. Sloan's illness and Blake's travels over the past few weeks had apparently delayed all of Blake's correspondence—both coming and going—as letters were slowly catching up with them both. Had Blake received her letter asking him to name a time and place? Or had that been delayed too?

Blake's opinion of LHF had surely sunk even lower, if that were possible.

She needed to tell him. But even that was proving difficult.

Blake was understandably paranoid about being alone with any of the young, single women attending the house party. He was vigilant in always having someone else at his side.

In general, Belle approved of such caution. However, it had made speaking to him alone in any surreptitious fashion nearly impossible.

She didn't think that Blake lumped her in the same category as the Desperate Debutantes (she still mentally chuckled over the moniker), but any request for a private audience would certainly appear . . . odd.

Though Belle was honest enough to admit she hadn't tried *too* hard.

Turns out . . . it was quite difficult to summon the courage to willingly shatter your own heart.

Particularly when Blake smiled at her.

Or talked.

Or walked.

Or, honestly, simply breathed.

Yes, Belle was sure she could happily pass an hour or two watching him sleep—

Mmmmm.

Perhaps she did consume too much gothic literature—

"Are you ready?" Anne stepped into the room, pulling on her gloves, her abrupt arrival causing Belle to jump.

"Of course." Belle took a steadying breath, adjusted her reticule, and turned to face her friend.

Anne raised her eyebrows, shooting a cautious glance through the still open door behind her.

"Re-reading that letter, I see." Anne missed nothing. It was what made her such a dear friend . . . most of the time. "I understand that the *sender* of your letter wishes a quick reply."

Belle bit back a sigh.

Ah, my conscience.

"We will discuss it later, you and I," Belle said, tone cautious and mindful of the open door.

Footsteps echoed down the hall, followed by eager voices. A bonneted head poked into Belle's room.

"Are you coming, Miss Heartstone? Miss Rutger? We don't want the gentlemen to start without us." With a giggle, the young ladies continued on down the hall.

Anne turned back to Belle, a smirk on her face. "And by gentlemen, I think they mean Lord Blake."

"Poor man. Though Lord Odysseus has also been . . ." Belle trailed off, searching for a proper word.

"Pursued?" Anne supplied on a whisper.

Belle angled toward her. "I was leaning more toward *harried*."

Anne laughed lowly. "*Tormented*, even?"

"Shall we go save them both?" With an evil grin, Belle snatched up her bonnet and hurried out of the room.

COLIN HURRIED DOWN the front steps of Stratton Hall, boots tapping, walking stick swinging broadly, his long overcoat lapping at his heels.

The morning post had arrived just as everyone gathered in the large entry hall, intent on their walk and picnic. Two items from his solicitor required his immediate attention, delaying him from attending the picnic.

There was also a letter from Mr. Sloan's clerk, firstly informing him that Mr. Sloan had been ill, and, secondly, apologizing for several items that had been misdirected to Colin's estate in Cornwall. The clerk felt confident that the post would find its way to him shortly, if it hadn't already arrived.

The man neglected to mention if any of the misdirected correspondence was from LHF. More than enough time had passed for his friend to pen a reply. Colin had nearly run his mind to exhaustion, trying to figure out who LHF might be. But he had arrived at no real answers.

Learning of Mr. Sloan's illness had taken some of the sting out of Colin's frustration.

Perhaps LHF *had* written.

But . . . was Colin's luck truly so bad that *all* LHF's letters had gone astray?

Or was something more afoot?

Why LHF's reluctance? Why the secrecy? Was his business partner the man Colin had taken him to be?

Or was the matter simpler than that? Perhaps his friend was not a prompt correspondent? When in India, it had taken nearly a year to send a question and receive a reply. Who knew how long LHF contemplated his questions before taking pen to paper?

But, no. LHF's letters had always come with regularity over the years. Besides, the man had responded quite quickly to Colin's first letter after returning to London, so why was he taking so long—

Patience.

For now . . . Colin just needed to trust and be patient.

He kept repeating the mantra to himself.

He knew LHF. He did.

He might not know the man's face or name, but he did know LHF's heart. The man who shared money so charitably, who dealt with Colin so honestly, could not possibly have played Colin for a fool all these years.

He had to be a man of honor. A gentleman.

There had to be a logical explanation.

Though given the strange turn of events, Colin wasn't sure he believed his own words anymore.

How long could he remain so optimistic? How long before LHF's odd silence created a permanent wedge between them, if it hadn't already?

Colin strode across the broad front lawn and into the grove of trees beyond. The butler had given him detailed directions for reaching the field of bluebells and the picnic.

And, indeed, a well-worn path cut through the trees. Birds fluttered among the branches. A cool wind rustled the bare bushes, brisk and invigorating. Colin inhaled deeply.

Walking deeper into the woods, he wondered how far behind he was, part of him wishing he had brought along a footman, anyone, to act as a chaperone. This was the last place he wanted to encounter a pack of Desperate Debutantes. Or, worse, a solitary one.

They had become more and more ridiculous. Colin had taken to locking his room whenever he left to dissuade the bolder women.

He picked up his pace.

As he rounded a bend, a scrap of white fluttering on the ground caught his attention, stark and bright against the damp earth.

Later, he decided Fate had led him to that moment. To turn his head in just the right direction. To see the folded paper nestled on top of brown leaves and fallen branches.

He picked it up and turned it over.

Every last bit of air left his lungs in a shocked *whoosh*.

The direction was clear.

To LHF
Care of Mr. John Sloan
Solicitor
London, England

Blake signed in bold letters across the bottom right corner supplied the postage. Fingers shaking, Colin opened the letter. The date and first lines jumped out at him:

London, England
June 14, 1823

   Dear sir,

   I yet await a response. Your continued silence puzzles me. I have called you a friend, and you have always dealt honorably with me . . .

Colin read the entire thing. The lines he had written just days before. Nothing more or less.

How—?!

He stood in statuesque silence for far longer than was manly.

His first thought was simple. Had he not sent the letter after all? Had it just been resting in his pocket all this time and fluttered free?

Colin pondered that for a moment, studiously recalling his actions.

He had penned the letter at the desk in his London townhouse. Sanded the ink. Folded and sealed it with a thick glob of red wax. Franked the front with his signature. Placed it in the stack of other letters to go out with the evening post.

Another quick glance at the front revealed an inked postal date, another point of proof.

Yes. He was positive he had sent the letter.

His mind raced, struggling to put the sequence of events into proper order.

But nothing settled into place.

Only two facts stood out to him:

This letter *had* originated with him.

But its presence in Lord Stratton's wood was *not* his doing.

Colin neatly refolded the letter and carefully tucked it into the inner pocket of his tail coat. He walked up the path, more briskly this time, mind churning through the logical possibilities.

How had his letter ended here? Had it gone astray? Had LHF never received it? Had it been returned to Colin due to the muddle of Mr. Sloan's illness? And then somehow escaped to roam free in Stratton's forest?

That last seemed . . . less likely.

Perhaps?

Or . . . someone had stolen the letter and planted it here for Colin to find, knowing he would be coming up the path to catch up with the rest of his party?

That seemed needlessly melodramatic, not to mention, completely pointless. There was nothing to be gained or lost through the discovery of the letter. Besides, aside from Mr. Sloan, his own solicitor, his man-of-affairs, and several secretaries, no one knew about LHF. Their relationship was anything but common knowledge.

No.

The farther Colin walked, the more he kept circling back to the idea of *Occam's razor*—the simplest solution to a problem was the most likely one.

The most straight-forward explanation for the presence of Colin's letter?

LHF himself had been or still was at Stratton Hall.

LHF had received the letter and then accidentally dropped it himself while out walking, which could explain why LHF's reply had been delayed.

But the letter was quite crisp. Unspotted from rain, which given that it had rained just two nights past . . .

LHF had been in the vicinity quite recently.

The very thought made Colin's heart speed up.

Who was he? A local man who liked to walk the earl's garden paths? Or was he a guest of Stratton's house party?

The latter seemed the most likely scenario. *Occam's razor* again.

To think, he might have been talking with LHF over dinner the previous evening without even knowing it.

The air around him suddenly felt too heavy to breathe. Obviously, LHF knew who Colin was, so why not reveal himself?

His stomach gave a painful lurch.

The longer this situation stretched on, the more Colin worried that their friendship was not what he had thought it to be, that LHF was not a man of honor.

The thought . . . burned.

Betrayal tasted acrid and sour in his mouth.

Why would LHF behave in such a fashion? The man *knew* Colin wished to meet him. He knew how much Colin trusted him, valued his friendship.

So . . . why?

Colin's heart pounded in his chest, thoughts intent on the path before him.

He blundered into something soft and warm. The smell of lavender swirled around him.

His hands automatically extended in an attempt to hold himself and whatever he had bumped into upright, fighting to keep them both stable.

Which is how Colin found himself embracing Miss Heartstone in the middle of the Earl of Stratton's forest.

BELLE HAD LOST her letter. She had fallen behind everyone else, intent on reading it one more time, trying to compose a reply in her head.

But one of the Gold Miners had decided to fall back, hoping to catch her alone, no doubt. Fortunately, Anne was on to him. They both converged on Belle, who had hastily folded the letter and returned it to her reticule.

Only now the letter was not there. She must not have secured it properly. The wind or some errant movement had dislodged it.

She had been scouring the sides of the path, searching for a telltale flash of white, when she bumped into something hard and unyielding.

Blake.

Who was now holding her, her face buried in his cravat.

The *shock* of his arms around her. That sense of strength and gentleness that was uniquely his. The smell of wool and sandalwood that engulfed her.

The sheer stunned joy of being in the one place she had dreamed of being for more years than was wise . . .

"I *do* beg your pardon, Miss Heartstone." He instantly set his hands to her shoulders, burning her like firebrands, and peeled her off of him.

Did his hands linger? Or was it simply her excited imagination wishing for more?

He bent to pick up his top hat that had tumbled off.

"I was not looking where I was going," he said. "Again, I am most sorry. Are you quite all right?"

Belle used the opportunity to glance up the path behind him.

No flash of white anywhere.

Where had her letter gone? Though thank the heavens it wasn't fluttering around here for Blake to see.

He was brushing his hat and fussing with his walking stick.

All his normally cool composure gone.

Belle figured now was *not* the time to mention he was adorable when he was flustered. Men didn't appreciate being referred to as adorable. Or flustered, for that matter.

"I am quite fine, my lord." Belle righted her bonnet, shook out her skirts. "See, no harm done."

He paused and really studied her, raking her from top to bottom with his blue gaze, taking in her rose-colored pelisse with its row of pearl buttons and fashionably-ruffled edges. The matching bonnet perched on her head, curls escaping in an artful mass.

"Uh, you are quite alone, I see." He glanced behind her.

He didn't appear concerned, but Blake was excessively polite.

And what if he asked her why she was on the path? Would she tell him the truth?

Well, my lord, I seem to have lost the letter you sent to LHF—who is actually myself, surprise!—I don't suppose you've seen it?

Oh dear.

Her stomach churned at the thought.

And Belle, who prided herself on her cool, level head, did the last thing she expected herself to do.

She panicked.

So instead of confessing all as her conscience urged her to do, she pasted a bright smile on her face. "Never fear, my lord. The Mob of Marriageable Misses isn't far behind." She waved a hand up the path. "I am merely the initial scout. They sent me ahead to assess the lay of the land. Get a sense of how best to confound the enemy. Though be warned, you have rarely seen debutantes quite so desperate."

He at least had the decency to flush. Again, looking adorable in the process. Blushing also being top on the list of Things Never to Bring to a Gentleman's Attention.

"Th-that is not what I meant."

"Is it not?" She fixed him with her sauciest eyebrow.

His blush deepened. Still adorable. Drat the man.

"I promise to make no attempts upon your virtue," she continued. "But once the Desperate Debutantes arrive, all promises become void."

His shoulders relaxed. He gave a soft chuckle. The wind kicked up again, further ruffling his mussed hair, swirling his greatcoat around his legs. With a sigh, he settled his hat back atop his head.

"I am afraid you quite terrify me, Miss Heartstone. I feel I should raise the white flag of surrender." He extended his gloved hand. "Truce?"

"Truce."

With a smile, Belle took his hand, shaking firmly. Forcing herself not to shiver at the sensation of his fingers engulfing hers. At the strength of him. What wouldn't she give for a lifetime of holding his hand?

To tell him that she loved him. Utterly. Completely. Wholly.

To hear him say those words in return.

She swallowed, tight and sharp.

He offered her his arm and gestured for them to continue up the path. She readily wrapped her gloved fingers around his elbow, reveling in the flexing muscles she felt in his arm.

The trees creaked and cracked in the slight breeze. Ravens cawed overhead.

Belle's panic had faded in a steady sense of dread.

She had to tell him.

She cared too much about him to continue this charade. And she was not this timid person who shied away from doing what must be done.

Blake had taught her that much.

Just do it. Open your mouth and tell him.

You can do this.

You owe him your honesty.

Sucking in a fortifying breath, she began, "My lord, there is something I wish to speak with you about—"

"Oh?" Was it her imagination or did Blake stiffen somewhat? "Must we discuss something?"

Uhmmm.

Not quite the response she had been anticipating.

"Well, yes, my lord, I am afraid I must." Her hand surely trembled where she held his arm. Did he feel the depth of her emotions? "Before I say what I must, please know how deeply I admire you—"

"Have I told you about the weather in India?" Blake's loud question caused Belle to jump.

What on earth?

The weather?

In India?

Why ever would Blake wish to speak of such a thing?

But hallelujah!

YespleaseletustalkabouttheweatherinIndia!

Would she have the fortitude to bring up the question again?

COLIN BLAMED ASTONISHMENT for his outburst.

Was Miss Heartstone honestly launching into her vaunted speech so soon, politely telling him that she was not interested in his attentions? Had his gaff of insinuating that she was trying to get him alone, like one of the Desperate Debutantes, really offset her so much? She had looked panicked there for a moment or two.

Would she summarily dismiss him before even giving him a chance?

He was half-amused, half-appalled. First LHF's letter, and now this?

He and Miss Heartstone had just formed a *truce*, for heaven's sake. A truce signaled the *beginning* of a relationship, not its end.

He had only begun to pay attention to Miss Heartstone. And more to the point, she hadn't seemed to be averse to his attention.

"The weather in India is quite different from that of England," Colin continued, wincing at the inanity of his own voice.

"Indeed." The puzzled humor of her tone indicated Miss Heartstone likely saw his interruption for what it was. "With a truce in place, have we decided to talk about the weather?"

"It seemed a safe topic."

Miss Heartstone walked calmly at Colin's side. Her skirts brushing against his overcoat. The lovely smell of her lavender perfume hanging in the air.

A cool breeze kicked up in earnest.

Miss Heartstone cleared her throat. "Do you miss the heat of India, my lord?"

"Yes. No. . . . Sometimes." He shrugged.

She said nothing. Her silence indicated she understood.

"On a gloomy winter's day when everything is bare, I imagine I shall miss Calcutta—the humidity holding the scent of spices, monkeys chattering in the trees, the never-ending sea of green. Heat rising in an endless wave."

He paused.

"But then the British countryside bursts into bloom and lambs drop in the fields. Wisteria hangs on vines and, well, it is impossible to miss India when faced with the beauty of a full-blown English spring."

More silence, comfortable and easy.

"My father used to say there is nothing as fine as a sunny day in June," she said.

They continued to talk as they walked.

Miss Heartstone relaxed more as they went, hopefully forgetting that she had intended to send him packing. He learned that she adored Sir Walter Scott but was less partial to Mrs. Radcliffe.

"Come now. The castle scenes in *The Mysteries of Udolpho* are bone-chilling," he protested.

"I will grant you that, but I prefer my heroines with a little more pluck. Mrs. Radcliffe has them cowering in terror far too often for my liking."

Which comment devolved into them discussing the virtues of various literary characters.

With every word out of her mouth, that sense of recognition grew. Colin understood it finally for what it was: intense attraction.

Miss Heartstone was rapidly owning his heart.

No, not Miss Heartstone.

Belle. The nickname he had heard Lady Stratton call her.

Beautiful Belle.

It suited her in every way.

He admired how she didn't chatter on aimlessly. Didn't giggle. Didn't flirt or try to take advantage of the situation.

No. Miss Heartstone was just . . . herself. Open. Honest.

They had not traveled far when Miss Rutger came up the path toward them, conscientious of her charge's reputation.

Lord Odysseus was directly behind her, clearly frustrated that Colin was edging into territory that Lord Odysseus claimed for himself. The competitor in Colin welcomed the challenge. Belle was a prize worth fighting for.

It wasn't until much later—after the picnic, the oohing and ahhing over the field of bluebells, Lord Odysseus weeping over the darling lambs toddling through the grass, the long walk back—that Colin finally asked himself the question that, really, he should have asked immediately:

Why was Miss Heartstone walking the path alone in the first place?

. . . please accept my sincere apologies, my lord. I remain ill and letters have been forwarded on to you in Cornwall, but now I have heard that you are at Stratton Hall, not Cornwall, so I cannot say when my correspondence will find you. Fyfe Hall has already seen the arrival of forty children with veterans and their wives. All is said to be well with the children, but an issue has arisen with the local magistrate that I was hopeful you might address—

—letter from Mr. Sloan to Lord Blake, partially written
but not sent due to Mr. Sloan's poor health

Colin flipped through the packet of correspondence again, hoping to find another letter from LHF.

There was none. Just tardy business items trickling in to him from Cornwall.

His mind struggled to piece together the giant puzzle—LHF's

continued silence, finding his letter in Stratton's wood yesterday.

Colin felt more lost than he had in . . . years.

Part of his brain needled him, telling him that perhaps he should respect LHF's wishes and let the man retain his privacy. But the longer their dance went on, the more concerned Colin became.

Was his lengthy correspondence and business venture with LHF some elaborate hoax? To what end . . . he couldn't fathom. And why did that thought make Colin almost physically ill?

He had spent the previous evening desperate to resolve the issue, studying each of the gentlemen in attendance at Stratton Hall, looking for some small tell that would betray his hiding friend.

Not one of the guests had the initials LHF. But after the encounter with Lord Halbert, Colin had surmised the initials were most likely an alias. He had reviewed what he knew about LHF from their letters over the years. Only once had the man described himself, and that description was decidedly lacking.

Brown hair, brown eyes, average, unremarkable. At the time, the description had struck him as odd, as Lord Halbert (who he had assumed to be LHF) was headed toward gray hair. But now . . .

The description characterized at least half the population of England.

Stratton himself seemed the most likely candidate—brown hair and eyes though well above average in height. Colin could see him in the role of LHF. Though why Stratton would keep the matter secret was an utter mystery.

Frowning, Colin did the only thing he could think to do—he hunted down Stratton in his study, laying the matter before him.

"Pardon?" Stratton frowned, taking a step back. "You think I am your business partner?" His frown deepened. "How can you not know the name of your own business partner?"

Colin resisted the urge to slowly pound his head against the marble mantel. "My thoughts precisely. As I said, I thought I knew, but I was mistaken."

"And you found a letter from yourself to this LHF on *my* property?" Placing his hands on his hips, Stratton began to pace before the fireplace.

"Yes. Which is why I ask you again, are you LHF?"

Stratton paused, fixing Colin with a decidedly earnest gaze. "Unfortunately for us both, I am not." He shook his head and raised his hand, as if swearing an oath. "Upon my honor as a gentleman. I would be quite the wealthy man were I your business partner. Why is the man hiding his identity?"

"I haven't a clue," Colin replied. Frustration tasted sour on his tongue.

Stratton pursed his mouth. "It's possible that Lord Odysseus is your man."

For some reason, that thought made Colin's stomach plunge. It was hard to see the brilliant steadiness of LHF in Lord Odysseus. Besides, LHF was a man of seasoned wisdom, not a young buck. And more to the point—

"I was under the impression that Lord Odysseus is hard-pressed for funds," Colin said.

"So was I," Stratton replied. "It's one of the reasons he has been so doggedly pursuing Miss Heartstone. I thought his pockets were to let. But one never knows. The man is quite cagey when actually pressed for details about his varied past."

Colin had surmised that Lord Odysseus was courting Belle in earnest, but Stratton's assessment of the man's motives still amplified Colin's own sense of dismay.

Belle deserved more than to be feted for her father's money. How she must doubt and chafe over every man's profession of adoration.

Colin knew his admiration to be genuine. He had no need of her fortune.

"Could this LHF be a spendthrift? Could that be the reason behind his silence?" Stratton asked. "He squanders the money you make and hides behind his anonymity?"

Colin pondered the idea for a moment, thinking through all the business transactions he'd had with LHF over the years. "It seems . . . unlikely. Our dealings with each other have been lengthy. There have never been any irregularities, nor has LHF ever shown a moment's hesitation when it comes to funding new ventures. The man is a brilliant statistician and clever when it comes to predicting the ebb and flow of market goods."

Stratton resumed his pacing. "Interesting. I also wonder how your letter came to be in my woods . . . it's possible that the person here simply has a connection to LHF but isn't the man himself. It could even have been stolen from LHF and brought here because you are attending the house party."

"Yes, that thought had also occurred to me. Or perhaps the letter escaped from a mail pouch and someone intended to bring it to me? My correspondence has been somewhat straggling in nature due to all my travels."

Stratton frowned. "The Royal Mail is more reliable than that, I would think. It's most likely that the letter was dropped by someone."

For the hundredth time, Colin tried to make sense of it all and came up empty-handed. LHF had always been honest with him. He had the financial ledgers to prove it. Everything added up from the beginning. The man's brutal honesty had won him Colin's respect and affection time and again.

Why hide?

Stratton paused. The men stared at each other for a heartbeat.

A gleam lit in Stratton's eye. "Well." He rubbed his hands together. "We have quite the mystery on our hands. I have to thank you for enlivening our house party. And I had worried that this week would be dull," he laughed.

"But what is to be done?" Colin asked. "We can hardly slink about spying on your guests or riffle through their mail. That wouldn't be seemly."

Stratton winked at him. "I don't think we'll need to stoop to that. My servants are the souls of discretion. We start by asking them what they have seen."

THE FOLLOWING DAYS passed in a blur of activity.

Colin gave himself two tasks: understand how his letter had ended up in Stratton's woods and stake his claim with Belle.

The first task remained a fruitless endeavor. Despite Stratton setting his servants to snooping, they had nothing of import to report. Worse, word had reached them that the mail coach had been delayed for days due to wet weather north of London. No letters of any sort had arrived, so the temptation to spy on the post was moot.

Both Stratton and Colin were at a loss as to what to do. Short of cornering every man and questioning him point blank, there were few other honorable options available to them.

Colin was starting to doubt that the man was actually in attendance. There were just no good candidates besides Stratton himself. The Gold Miners were too young to be LHF. The few older gentlemen seemed unlikely—one hadn't been in the country long enough, having just returned from years in the West Indies; another was clearly too scatter-brained.

He refused to see LHF in Lord Odysseus' dramatic persona.

Perhaps the letter had landed in Stratton's woods through some other means. Theft or accident?

Colin had sent off several letters of his own. He had written Mr. Sloan and asked the man to pass along his wishes for a meeting to LHF. It was possible that Mr. Sloan himself was the mysterious benefactor. Why he insisted on silence, Colin couldn't fathom, but it was still a possibility.

Colin had also written several factory managers who he knew had interacted with LHF over the years. Though if the postal situation elsewhere was like that of London at present, it would be weeks before Colin received any sort of answer.

As for his second task—stake a claim to Belle Heartstone—the Desperate Debutantes and Lord Odysseus proved a determined obstacle. They interrupted Colin constantly. Anytime he found a chance to speak with Belle, one or the other abruptly appeared.

For example, one afternoon the entire party traipsed down to a large lake situated south of the house. The Desperate Debutantes had been pleading for the gentlemen to row them across to a small island in the middle for a picnic. Colin wasn't sure he wanted to attend, but Belle was going and Lord Odysseus was going, and Colin refused to cede the field to his rival.

Not until Belle had officially given him his marching papers.

So he went.

They all set out together from the front steps of Stratton Hall, Lady Stratton leading the way, laughing merrily on Stratton's arm. Belle looked particularly fetching in a sky-blue spencer and matching bonnet.

But, of course, the Desperate Debutantes intercepted him before he could make it to Belle's side. A pair of the Miss Button-Joneses chattered incessantly about India and tigers and could he describe the different types of monkeys just one more time?

By the time Colin extracted himself and turned his head around, Lord Odysseus had already been awarded Belle's hand around his elbow. Worse, the smug look Lord Odysseus shot him over Belle's stylish bonnet said it all—

He and Lord Odysseus were at war, and Lord Odysseus had triumphed in this skirmish.

Colin felt his blood rise. The competitive streak that had won him a fortune in India reared up.

Colin *would* win this battle.

Turning back around, Colin caught Stratton's eye. His friend raised an eyebrow before shooting a glance at Belle.

Colin gave a subtle nod.

Stratton smiled, slow and wicked, before raising his chin slightly.

Leave this to me, his actions said.

Colin answered with a tight grin.

As they walked down to the water, Lord Odysseus managed to pull Belle ahead, her arm still linked with his. Colin watched the swish of Belle's skirts and the bob of her bonnet as she leaned into whatever Lord Odysseus was saying to her.

He did *not* like the image of them together, cozy and nearly domestic in appearance. It caused an almost unbearable urge to put his fist through a wall. Would Stratton be able to separate the two?

Mrs. Jones-Button and her two daughters chattered by Colin's side.

"Do you return to London after the party, my lord?" one girl asked breathlessly, curls bouncing.

Yes. "Perhaps. I have not yet decided how to spend my next few weeks."

"Well, you must come for a visit, Lord Blake," Mrs. Jones-Button said.

"Oh, please!" That was the other daughter, clasping her hands in delight, skipping at his side. So young. Was she even eighteen? He hated to ask.

Colin fingered LHF's letter in his pocket, continuing to stare at Belle ahead as Mrs. Jones-Button rambled on and on about the "fine hunting" on their estate in Somerset.

He suppressed a snort. He was currently hunting a lost friend—and Belle Heartstone if she were amenable to the idea—not pheasants.

The group reached the boathouse, people bickering and laughing over who would go in which boat.

Before Colin could say a word, Stratton took charge, clapping his hands loudly.

"Allow me to make boat assignments," he boomed. "I want to ensure each boat has a strong rower in it. Lord Odysseus"—Stratton turned to the man—"you seem a strapping sort. Given all your adventures, I am confident you can take charge of the largest boat over here."

Stratton motioned to long rowboat pulled alongside the dock. In rapid-fire succession, Stratton assigned everyone else to a place.

It was a brilliantly-done, straight-forward piece of management.

Naturally, Belle and Colin were placed in the smallest skiff—one with only enough room for two people.

Hah! He owed Stratton now.

He and Belle waited patiently as the others loaded into their boats, the ladies chattering and tittering, the Gold Miners laughing loudly.

Lord Odysseus spared Colin a murderous look as he rowed out, three giggling misses and their mothers with him.

Stratton saluted him from the skiff he piloted with Lady Stratton.

Finally, Colin and Belle were alone on the dock. He was quite sure he sported a stupid, silly grin on his face.

Colin stepped into the rowboat before turning around to steady Belle as she followed him into the boat.

Her gaze flitted to his as their gloved hands met. The connection shouldn't have sent a thrumming charge up his arm, but Colin felt the jolt regardless.

And given the slight flare of Belle's eyes, she was clearly not immune. He continued to stare into her eyes as he helped her sit down on the small bench, only releasing her hand to take his own seat.

The situation with LHF might be a mess. But enjoying Belle Heartstone's company? That was utterly delightful.

She arranged her skirts around her and fluffed open a parasol to keep the sun off her head. Light tangled along the edge of her fashionable bonnet, catching the spark in her eyes as their gazes met again.

Colin's breath came in shorter bursts. Heavens but she was truly lovely.

Colin tugged off his gloves, folding them into the pocket of his coat, before shrugging out of his coat. The garment didn't allow enough movement to row a boat, which explained why all the gentlemen were currently in waistcoats and shirtsleeves.

"Allow me, my lord." Belle extended a hand, indicating she would hold his coat for him, preventing it from falling to the floor of the boat.

He willingly handed over the garment, their fingers brushing and sending another wave of awareness through him.

Steady, man.

He fit the oars into the oarlocks and pulled back, propelling the boat onto the water. Colin was in no hurry to join the others on the island, so he kept his strokes slow.

If Belle noticed, she didn't seem to care. Instead, she turned her face into the glimmering sun, sighing.

Was it a good sigh? A contented sigh?

Or was she preparing to deliver her vaunted speech, finishing what she had begun the other day?

How could he make his case?

"I trust you are well, Miss Heartstone," he began.

"Yes, thank you. Very well." A wry smile tugged at her lips. "Are we to discuss the weather next?"

Colin chuckled. "Only if you feel the topic has not utterly exhausted itself."

"My lord, you *clearly* have not spent enough time in England. The weather is wholly incapable of exhausting itself as a topic." Her laughter carried across the water.

They chatted about inanities—the Strattons, the ball on the following evening, their plans for the remainder of the London Season.

Fortunately, unlike their conversation along the forest path, Belle appeared delighted in his attention, returning it. Colin found himself hard-pressed to keep from staring at her. Her eyes sparked with life as she spoke, emotions came and went across her pretty face.

Every now and again, he caught an intensity in her look. As if he were a feast and she a starving peasant who had hungered for too long—

Colin shook his head in bemusement.

That was simply wishful thinking on his part, surely.

A lull appeared in their conversation. He stroked with the oars. Water lapped the side of the boat.

For nearly the hundredth time, Colin wondered why she hadn't chosen to marry. Clearly he wasn't the first man of consequence to court her over the years. *Was* she suddenly taken with him? Or was she always like this with men?

Which, he supposed, could explain why so many men offered for her. Colin felt somewhat burned sitting in the glow of her gaze.

Which meant that her next words caught him decidedly off-guard.

"My lord—" Belle cleared her throat. "—there is something I wish to speak with you about," she began.

What?

No! Not the speech!

Not yet!

He had just begun making progress.

Panic gripped him.

"I wonder why you are not yet married, Miss Heartstone?" He practically shouted the question, the topic dragged from immediate thoughts.

Belle's brow puckered, her shoulders stiffening.

"Pardon?"

Right. If he wished to woo her, he should probably not ask such a question. It practically invited her to continue with her practiced speech.

"Am I too impertinent?" He laughed, trying to cover his gaff. "You may tell me so. Years of living in Calcutta have rendered my manners somewhat rusty, I am afraid."

He declined to add that his upbringing had not educated him to interact with the upper echelons of the *ton*.

"Heavens, you are anything but impertinent, my lord. I was simply somewhat surprised by the question. You do not strike me as the type to care if a woman chooses to remain unmarried."

He nodded his head.

First, *hallelujah* he had distracted her again.

Second, her observation was tellingly accurate. He added *perceptive* to the list of things he admired about her.

"I did not mean to imply any criticism, madam," he hastened to clarify. "It is simply curiosity on my part. A charming woman such as yourself surely has had her pick of suitors over the years, and yet you have declined them all."

"By *charming*, I think you mean *wealthy*, my lord." Belle smiled, but it was not a delighted smile that lit her eyes. It was more of a sad, worn thing.

Something hot and searing washed through Colin, not quite anger or outrage or indignation, but some combination of all three.

How could it be? This remarkable woman *doubted* her own inherent attractions. Was that the motivation behind all her rejections? Send potential suitors packing before she had a chance to be hurt?

But, as he contemplated, he supposed he understood it.

A loud laugh had him shifting a glance toward the boat where Lord Odysseus sat, entertaining several young ladies with success, judging by the giggles that drifted across the water.

Lord Odysseus was likely the tail-end of a long line of bachelors who needed her money to bolster their coffers.

And that knowledge left Belle adrift.

"You do yourself a disservice, madam, by discounting your own personal charms," he said, turning back to her.

"You are too kind, my lord. I was not angling for a compliment." She sucked in a deep breath. "I brought up the point merely to illustrate why I have not chosen to marry as of yet. My financial reserves are not . . . insignificant and, as such, it can be difficult to trust that a gentleman's interest is for myself alone."

"So there is no tragedy in your past? No long-lost love?"

Was it his imagination, or did she wince? But as she laughed in reply to his question, he figured it must have simply been the sun on the water playing tricks with his perception.

"Well, I have considered finding a dastardly Italian count to hold me hostage in a castle tower until my true love can rescue me—"

Colin let out a bark of laughter. "Unfortunately, Italian counts are hardly as dastardly in the real world."

"'Twould appear so. Reality can be such a disappointment at times." She shot him a soft smile, subtly indicating that she excluded present company from her assessment. "And what about you, my lord. Why have you chosen not to marry? Do you have a long, lost love? Been held hostage by a wicked countess?"

Belle appeared to ask the question casually enough, but something told Colin that the question was not quite as carefree as it appeared. Though he was at a loss to explain *why* he felt that way.

Regardless, it caught him off-guard, the events of last autumn still near enough to sting—the shock of realizing how thoroughly Sarah had deceived him, how blind he had been to her true nature.

But, he reminded himself, Sarah Forrester and Belle Heartstone were worlds apart when it came to forthright, honest behavior. And as he had many times since Sarah's betrayal, he sent up silent thanks that he had learned the truth of Sarah before marrying her.

Belle Heartstone was a thousand times the woman Sarah would ever be.

Colin simply needed to convince her to not toss him aside quite yet.

17

. . . this entire situation has been utterly horrid. You have made me a laughing stock. If you had married me quickly as I had asked, we would have been safely away before all this ugliness surfaced. I cannot believe you would do this to one you professed to love . . .

—letter from Miss Sarah Forrester to Lord Blake,
on the occasion of him breaking off their betrothal

Blake froze mid-stroke, hands holding the oars parallel to the water. Belle was quite sure her question still rang between them, an awkward bell strike.

Why have you chosen not to marry? Do you have a long, lost love?

Clearly, she had struck a nerve. It was just . . . she knew *something* had happened with Sarah Forrester. What had Blake called it in his letter? A sordid tale?

She desperately wanted to hear the entire story.

Granted, she wanted to know every little thing about him. She treasured each detail she learned, putting sound and sensations to the man she knew from his letters.

She now knew that his laugh had a throaty edge. That his mouth quirked higher to one side when he smiled, giving him an endearing lopsided look. That he preferred a brisk walk to a quiet stroll.

That the warmth in his eyes when he saw her obliterated every last ounce of her self-preservation.

She was rapidly sinking into the mire of her own making. It was all she could do to keep her worshipful admiration of him off her countenance.

Belle had lost his letter. She and Anne had scoured the woods but came up empty-handed. The wind had probably carried it into Shropshire by now.

She had planned scenario after scenario to get Blake alone, allowing her to tell him the truth. The Desperate Debutantes and Gold Miners continually disturbed her plans. Of course, it didn't help that Belle's heart really wasn't in them.

And as Blake had interrupted her yet again just five minutes ago in her attempt to tell him about LHF, well . . .

Just one more day, her breathless heart whispered. *One more day to live out this fantasy.*

So even though she knew this moment on the boat was a chance to speak with him, that she should continue to press the issue despite his abrupt change of topic, she let it pass.

Belle did not offer up her biggest secret.

Instead, she said, "Forgive me, my lord. I did not mean to pry—"

"No, turnabout is fair play." Blake dipped the oars in the water again, pulling them toward the island. But, as she had noticed earlier, his strokes lacked force. Neither of them was eager to join the shrieks of laughter and loud calling that carried across the water from the rest of their party. Many of them had reached the island and were disembarking on the dock there.

"I cannot say I was held hostage in any sort of physical fashion, but a young woman did steal my affections and then used them most poorly." Fleeting sadness and pain flashed across his face.

Oh.

Belle was not given to anger, but it washed through her unbidden.

How dare Sarah Forrester have done this to him!

Of course, her conscience unhelpfully pointed out that she most certainly fit into the same category.

Shush! She pushed that nagging voice back.

"May I ask what happened?" Belle had to know.

Blake lifted a shoulder before pulling the oars out of the water again, his gaze skimming the shoreline beyond her.

"It is nothing more than a typical tale of naivety on my part and deception on hers." Blake tried to shrug away the conversation.

Belle knew she should let it go. But she just . . . couldn't.

"I would listen to the story if you wish to tell it."

Blake continued to look away. Belle waited.

She didn't want to force a confidence.

Finally, his head swung back to her.

"A young lady named Sarah Forrester arrived in Calcutta, a companion to her aunt," he began. "Her uncle had received an appointment from the Crown and was to work with the Governor. Naturally, as we moved in the same social circles, we became well-acquainted. I thought myself in love with her. She was beautiful and vivacious with a sort of disarming charm. She was also nearly ten years my junior, but as many men marry younger women, I did not let that deter me—"

Blake stopped mid-sentence as a shout of laughter reached them. He turned toward the sound, his body rotating around. Wind ruffled his brown hair.

A pair of the Gold Miners were miming boxing moves on the island boat dock, good-naturedly grappling with each other. The young ladies shrieked in delight, looking on.

Blake turned back to her with a grimace. "Not sure I want to land us in the middle of that." He nodded his head, indicating the party gathered on the dock.

Belle leaned to the side. "I believe there is a small landing area beside that weeping willow over there." She pointed to a shady area to the left of the island, well away from the rowdy group.

Blake nodded and turned the boat, aiming for the new landing place.

"You were saying, my lord." Belle prompted him. "About Miss Forrester?"

She had no intention of *not* hearing this story to completion. The trick was to hide her almost maniacal interest. In her mind's eye, she was an eager puppy, jumping up and down, begging for more, more, more.

So Belle barely managed to hold back a relieved sigh when Blake cleared his throat and continued his story.

"Yes. Miss Forrester." He pulled on the oars. "After several months of courting, I offered for her and was accepted. All was well 'til that point. News travels slowly to India, but it does reach us eventually. A casual acquaintance arrived and was astonished to find me betrothed to Miss Forrester. He had known Miss Forrester in London. She had run with a wild set and had been known for her duplicitous ways. More to the point, she had been caught in—" Blake hesitated, as if carefully choosing his words. "—a decidedly-compromising situation with an older, married man. The circumstances and witnesses involved were such that I did not doubt that the incident had occurred or the seriousness of what Miss Forrester and the gentleman had done. Needless to say, her reputation had been shattered. Her parents sent her off with her aunt and uncle in the hope that she could snare a husband before the scandal caught up with her."

"Heavens!" Belle gasped. She barely managed to avoid clasping her hands to her chest in abject horror.

"Truly." Blake shot her a knowing glance, before pulling hard on the oars. Again, thank goodness, missing the true depths of her feeling.

How unbelievably dastardly of Sarah Forrester to abuse Blake so abominably!

Though, her less-kind self pointed out, *he would not be here with you rowing in this boat had Sarah Forrester not proved a scapegrace.*

True that. She had to take her silver linings where she could find them.

Blake continued, "Ironically, it wasn't her behavior alone that caused me to break off with her. If Sarah had confessed the lot to me—if she had been honest with me—I would have moved on from the point.

People make mistakes; we learn and grow from them. I do not feel as if my wife has to impeachable. If she had been willing to acknowledge her past behavior in any way, I would have readily forgiven her.

"But, instead, Sarah lashed out at me, accusing me of meddling in her life, of not trusting her enough, of burdening her with my need for truth. In one sentence, she proclaimed her innocence, and then in the next, baldly stated that the gentleman involved had a cold-hearted wife and Sarah only wished to bring him comfort. It was . . . painful . . . to realize how thoroughly mistaken I had been in her character, how misguided in my affections."

Belle's heart sank to the bottom of the lake. How much deception could Blake's heart take?

"You broke off the engagement at that point?"

"Yes. I could not, in good conscience, continue my relationship with her. I boarded a ship back to London the following week." He grimaced and stroked hard again, the oars splashing in the water.

"You were justifiably overset."

"Yes. It was healing to spend six months at sea. It helped clear my head. After a month of anger, I realized that I had narrowly avoided a terrible mishap. It was my anger that solved the problem for me."

Belle frowned. "Your anger?"

"Yes." He let the boat coast for a few beats. "My predominant emotion over Sarah's betrayal was *anger*. Not loss or disappointment or grief—"

Ah. Belle's eyes widened, absorbing his meaning.

"If you truly loved someone, you should feel more than simple anger at their loss," she said.

"Precisely."

How was she supposed to avoid having stars in her eyes when he said such brilliant things?

They glided in silence for a moment, small ripples lapping against the side of the skiff.

Belle couldn't seem to stop herself from adding to his insights. "I've often thought that people fall into two camps: those who pass through my life and those who alter it. Some come into my life like a herd of elephants, stomping and trumpeting and thrilling to be sure, but they leave me much the same after they have passed through. Perhaps a little dusty or unsettled, but not changed. Yet on occasion, I have met a person who reshapes me, who becomes essentially woven into the fabric of my life. The loss of such a person is catastrophic, as it tears away some fundamental part of myself—"

Belle stopped abruptly, drawing in a fortifying breath, willing back the emotion that pricked at her eyes.

That list of people for her was impossibly short.

Her father.

Anne.

And . . . Blake.

For his part, he stared at her, his expression unreadable. Was he upset at her words? She most certainly couldn't ask him who was on his list. Though she had to wonder—was LHF on it?

She took in another steadying breath. "You asked why I have never married, and though trust is an issue, the greater reason is simple—no man has ever woven himself into my heart."

What a lie that was.

Ah, Blake.

A beat of silence.

"No man has ever stitched himself into your soul," Blake restated.

She managed a slight nod.

Blake pulled at the oars again. One beat. Two.

"You are a wise woman, Miss Heartstone," he finally said. "Very wise."

Belle willed herself not to blush under the weight of his praise, but it was a losing battle. Surely her cheeks were crimson.

Their boat reached the shade of the giant willow and the small boat landing at its base. The sounds of the Desperate Debutantes and Gold Miners retreated. A hush fell, as if she and Blake were the only two people on the island.

"You are right, of course, in regards to Sarah Forrester." His voice carried in the quiet. "She was a hurricane of laughter and delight, but in the end, she did nothing more than blow things around in my heart. I have come out . . . unscathed. Mostly, I am forever grateful that I did not ally myself with a dishonest woman."

Whoa.

Belle barely held back a pained gasp.

I am forever grateful that I did not ally myself with a dishonest woman.

The truthful sting of that statement cut. She had to tell him. She did. She would—

Was now the point then? Would she open her mouth and say the words at this instant?

Belle sucked in a breath. His story of Sarah Forrester was a sign. Perhaps if she were forthright, he would forgive her.

But even her most hopeful hope wasn't terribly optimistic on that score.

As Blake navigated their small boat up against the dock and tied it off, she gathered her thoughts.

You can do this. Tell him.

Blake shrugged back into his tailcoat before he stepped out of the boat and turned, extending a hand to her.

"My lord, I have something I would like to tell you," Belle began, stretching her hand to take his.

But nerves made her words tumble out in a rush. *IhavesomethingI-wouldliketotellyou* . . .

"Pardon?" He leaned toward her.

As with so many other momentous points in her life, it all happened in an instant.

Belle placed her hand into Blake's, taking a step out of the boat and onto the small wooden platform.

But she was so caught up in the burning sensation of Blake's touch and her own nervous terror that she neglected to lift her skirts high enough to clear the boat. The edge of her overskirt caught, pitching her shoulders forward while simultaneously pushing the boat away from the dock, causing both her feet to slide from underneath her.

Belle fell, her nose planting into Blake's chest. Would she never cease being clumsy in his presence?

To Blake's credit, he didn't stagger under the abrupt force of her entire weight. Instead, his arms whipped around her waist lightning fast, pulling her upright and settling her back on her feet.

It was an impressive feat of strength.

More to the point, within the space of two heartbeats, Belle found herself wrapped against the chest of the Marquess of Blake. Her arms trapped between them, pressed against his shoulders.

She gazed up into his blue eyes, expecting him to look amused or chagrined or politely . . . *something.*

Instead, his eyes burned with possessive heat and fire.

Oh!

Belle quite forgot how to breathe.

He did not release her. If anything, his arms tightened around her.

Abruptly, every sense was acutely heightened. The hard muscle of his chest underneath her hands, the scent of eastern spices that clung to him, the puff of his breathing on her cheek.

Her knees buckled. Only Blake's firm hold stopped her from melting into a puddle.

"I have you," he whispered. "You're safe with me."

A pained gasp escaped her.

I have you. You're safe with me.

Words she had wanted to hear from him for more years than she could remember.

Silence stretched between them, punctuated only by their breaths.

His eyes were everywhere. Her forehead, her eyes, her lips . . .

His head dipped slightly, as if the gravity of her mouth were too much to resist.

Belle found herself canting upward, intent on meeting him halfway—

"Lord Blake! Miss Heartstone!" A loud voice cut through the silence of the moment.

Lord Odysseus.

Of course.

Blake flinched and stepped back, releasing her abruptly. He rotated around as Lord Odysseus stepped out from the trees.

"Ahoy there!" Lord Odysseus gave a friendly wave.

The two men exchanged a glance. Dogs fighting over a bone would have been less obvious. If Belle hadn't been so shaken, she might have laughed.

But as it was, she barely stopped herself from reeling. She swayed and glanced down. She was still standing too close to Blake.

Or was that not close enough?

It was hard to say. Her mind and heart were at odds over the point.

"Lord Odysseus." Blake raised a hand, his tone anything but welcoming.

The motion allowed Belle to catch a glimpse of the edge of a letter peeking out from the pocket of his waistcoat—the initials LHF clearly inscribed.

All warmth fled from her body.

Oh no.

No. Nononononono!

It couldn't be.

The letter was lost, right?

But he *had* been walking up the path behind her that day. If anyone had been in a position to find it, it would have been him.

What if Blake had gotten to the letter first?

Blake would know. He would assume, rightly so, that LHF was attending the same house party.

He would investigate. Ask questions.

Blake turned back to her, as Lord Odysseus reached them. "I greatly enjoyed our conversation, Miss Heartstone." Blake offered her his arm.

Belle looked between Lord Odysseus and Blake, gaze surely as flustered as she felt.

This entire situation was quicksand, and she was sinking far too fast.

18

. . . I fear I have given him my whole heart and left no piece of it for myself. However shall I recover it? . . .

—excerpt of a letter from Miss Heartstone to Miss Rutger, while the latter was away visiting family, dated December 20, 1822

Colin stood at the edge of the ballroom in Stratton Hall. It was the last evening of the larger house party; the Desperate Debutantes and Gold Miners would depart in the morning. Only Colin, Lord Odysseus, Miss Heartstone, and a handful of the older guests would be staying on for an additional week.

Colin couldn't wait for a respite from the constant haranguing of the match-making set.

But for tonight, Lady Stratton had gathered all her guests and other local gentry for a grand ball. A small orchestra played diligently in one corner as couples moved through a quadrille.

The Desperate Debutantes and Gold Miners were in fine form, flirting and laughing. Belle stood at their center, clad in a gown of rich green silk with a gossamer net overlay. Matching long gloves slouched above her elbows, pearls gleamed at her throat and wrist. She looked every inch the elegant, confident lady.

Colin shook his head. She assumed all men chased her for her money, but she was so much more than her fortune. The lady herself was a brilliant prize to be won. It was no wonder men hung around her like eager pups.

Himself included.

She had reserved the first of the evening's two waltzes for him—the supper dance. A smile lit her face as she saw him approach to claim his dance. Not the fake smile she had bestowed upon the Gold Miners. But a real smile. One that said she was delighted to see him.

Surely she had no intention of sending him packing now.

Perhaps it was time to further his intentions with her. What would she do if he formally requested permission to court her?

Colin's heart expanded in his chest at the thought. How he was coming to adore this woman. Genuine. Kind. Here was someone who was as she seemed.

He bowed. She curtsied.

She kept that smile on her face as he led her onto the dance floor, wrapping her gloved hand in his, lilting into the familiar down-up-up pattern.

"You look lovely this evening, Miss Heartstone. You outshine all others. Is all well with you?" he asked.

"Yes, all is as well as it ever is. And you? Is all well with you?"

"I am dancing with you, madam. So all is quite right in my world."

She laughed, a genuine sound. "Such a pretty line, my lord."

"'Tis truth. Now if you just knew an elderly man with the initials LHF, my troubles would be at an end."

Was it his imagination, or did Miss Heartstone miss a step? No, he must be mistaken.

Though she did worry her lower lip, as if thinking. "I cannot say I know a man by that name. Has this LHF person done you harm?"

"Not precisely. More like a friend who has been avoiding me."

"I am sure this LHF values your friendship."

One could hope. "That remains to be seen."

Colin twirled her, pulling her perhaps a little closer than was strictly necessary. He adored the feel of Miss Belle Heartstone in his arms. She seemed . . . just right.

The perfect height. Not too tall, not too short. Clever without being overbearing. Forthright and honest.

Which, of course, meant that she took that precise moment to say—

"My lord, there is a matter I wish to speak with you about—"

"Do you return to London, Miss Heartstone?" he interrupted, self-preservation jumping to the forefront.

Truthfully? She was *still* intent on sending him packing? He ignored the flash of indignation that lightninged through him.

Though on second thought, perhaps it was time to address the issue straight-on? How many times had she begun this conversation?

She had stiffened in his arms at his interruption, but her face remained . . . uncertain.

Yes, you are abandoning me too soon, Miss Heartstone. I will press my case.

She opened her mouth.

He repeated his question, not giving her time to speak. "Do you return to London then?"

A pause before she replied. "Yes."

"Excellent." Definitely excellent. "I should dearly like to call upon you, if I may. Perhaps we may take a drive in Hyde Park together?"

Her eyes snapped to his, wide.

Hah! He felt like gloating.

There was a reason Colin excelled in business dealings. He knew when to show his cards. He upped the ante. "More importantly, I would like to introduce you to my family."

Belle startled, giving a small hitch in his arms.

Colin knew she was intelligent enough to understand what he was asking. He intended to court her in earnest.

Now what would she say?

"Of-of course, my lord. I would be honored, but there is a matter we should discuss—"

Truthfully?!

She accepted his offer of courtship, but she still wanted to give him her little "speech"?

No. He would have none of this.

His brow furrowed. "Perhaps you are surprised?" he offered, deliberately misunderstanding her.

Miss Heartstone floundered for a moment. Opened her mouth. Closed it. Tried again. "It is only . . . " She finally settled on a shrug. "You are too kind, my lord."

Had she admitted defeat then? Agreed to allow him to court her longer?

He smiled. "Though I am accounted quite a gracious fellow, I assure you, Miss Heartstone, I do not call upon a lady and introduce her to my family out of mere kindness. You give my altruism far too much credit, and your own personal charms too little."

That earned him a vivid blush and a duck of her chin. She shook her head, causing curls to bounce.

Raising her eyes back to his, she said, "I should be honored to accept your invitation, Lord Blake. But there *is* a matter I would discuss with you—"

"Not tonight, Miss Heartstone." Yes, he had interrupted her again. His manners were taking a beating this evening.

"But—"

"Is it a pleasant matter?"

A pause.

"Perhaps?" Why was this a question? "Maybe? . . . Possibly, no . . ."

"Will it keep? This matter?"

She blinked, eyes searching around them, finally bringing her gaze back to his.

"Yes," she swallowed. "Yes, it will keep."

"Then let it lie. If you still feel the need to discuss it with me, we can speak of it tomorrow."

Her brow dipped in a frown, but she rallied, shooting him a smile.

Had he misunderstood her wishes to speak with him after all? Was there another matter? But what could it possibly be otherwise?

He spun her around, his own head whirling, trying to see the world through her eyes.

Poor woman.

She was far too used to men only looking at her as a commodity. Something they hoped to purchase.

He almost snorted. Didn't that heiress say something similar all those years ago in Hyde Park? That her money should purchase her a husband of her choice. The idea had stuck with him.

Had that girl ever found a husband? Had she taken his advice?

What *had* been her name? Miss Lovestruck? Something about love and hard . . .

A chill chased his spine.

He glanced down at the woman in his arms.

Something very much like . . . *Heartstone.*

. . .

. . .

No.

His mind instantly rejected the idea. Belle was poised and gracious and the sole of propriety. Nothing like the brazen minx that morning.

Belle sent men packing, not the other way around.

But the more Colin pondered that morning so long ago, the more concerned he became. If Belle *had* been the woman that morning, why hadn't she said anything about it?

Was she not the person she appeared to be?

My lord, there is a matter I would discuss with you . . .

Had he misread her words all this time?

Bloody hell.

He had all but declared himself to her and then told her not to discuss her urgent matter with him.

Emotions swelled upward, racing to surface. Lingering feelings of anger and betrayal linked to Sarah Forrester.

"*How could you have lied to me about this, Sarah?*" Colin asked, *speaking past the unbearable ache in his throat.* "*Why not tell me the truth?*"

Sarah looked away, giving him her pretty profile, the window light turning her blonde hair to liquid gold.

"Why do you allow them to dishonor me so?" Her angry tone cut through him. "I am the injured party here!"

Colin shook his head, nearly baffled at her response. "There are five separate individuals newly arrived from London who all describe the same situation. I cannot accost a person for stating the truth, Sarah. Is the situation not what it appeared?"

"I am tired of this conversation." She made a dismissive motion. "It is in the past. It was nothing."

"Being caught in flagrante delicto *with Lord Hempton was nothing?"*

She flinched but brought her gaze back to meet his. Had there always been that hardness in her eyes? That coldness?

Or had he just been too blinded by her beauty and charm to see it?

"Are you at least ashamed of your behavior?" he continued.

She turned her back to him. "I'm through discussing this."

And there it was, he realized.

Sarah wasn't particularly sorry for what she had done. She was just sorry that he had found out.

The sorrow of the unrepentant soul—

Colin shook off the memory.

Having his heart and trust so thoroughly shattered had left a gaping wound in his psyche.

Sarah and Belle were worlds apart, literally and figuratively. He knew that.

But if Belle Heartstone were the woman from Hyde Park that morning—if she, too, had been less-than-truthful with him—what was he to do?

THE WALTZ CAME to an end, and Belle wrapped her gloved hand around Blake's arm. Again. Letting him lead her to a small table as he went off to collect plates for both of them.

Her emotions flitted back and forth.

How long could she keep the stars out of her eyes when looking at him? How much more could her heart take?

Guilt was a leaden weight, dragging her down.

She *had* to tell him about LHF. She did. It was just proving more and more difficult to get her mouth to form the words, and then when she finally did, Blake would inexplicably change the topic.

Every. Single. Time.

It was maddening.

And just now, he had flat-out refused to hear her speak of it.

What was she to do? Tie the man down and force him to listen to her?

Mmmmm . . .

But he had actually asked her about LHF, which was clearly a sign of his desire to uncover LHF's identity.

She would speak with him about it tomorrow. Perhaps she simply needed to approach the topic differently.

Allow me to tell you an interesting story, my lord . . .

Blake returned, setting a small plate in front of her and taking the other seat at the table, flipping the tails of his black evening coat out of the way as he sat. His eyes sparked with life above his immaculately tied cravat. Heavens, but he was a striking man.

He stared intently at her. That same fixed gaze he had adopted not long after inviting her to drive with him in Hyde Park.

As if he could see into her. Through her.

He cleared his throat.

"I would love to know more about your formative years, Miss Heartstone. Have you always lived in London?"

The question seemed innocuous, causally dropped. Hardly unusual, given the breadth of things they had discussed over the past few days.

But something inside Belle jumped to attention. Maybe it was the intensity of Blake's gaze as he asked. As if the polite question were deadly important.

"Yes, my lord." She settled a small napkin on her lap. "I have spent most of my time there. I own—or rather, my father owned—several country estates, as well."

"Ah. Do you enjoy walks in Hyde Park?"

"Yes. I do."

"Morning walks in Hyde Park?"

"From time to time."

Belle's mind churned. Had she offended him somehow? His words were polite, but a coolness had stolen over him.

They each took a couple bites of food. The silence between them stretched and strained.

What had happened? She had agreed not to speak of her pressing "matter" until tomorrow. So why was he abruptly so cool?

"You manage your own fortune, Miss Heartstone?"

She had lifted a venison puff to her lips but set it down at the question.

"Yes. I know it is unusual for a young lady to be involved in the management of her estate, but my father trusted my abilities."

Blake took a bite of raspberry tart, chewed deliberately, and dabbed his lips.

"What made you decide to undertake such a thing yourself? Certainly a husband would be better equipped to deal with the complexities of your estate?"

Again, perhaps a simply curious question, but something about his expression put her on edge.

Blake championed women who knew their own worth. Wasn't she living proof of his encouragement to that end? So why the question that implied he felt the opposite?

What to say?

"A trusted friend gave me some excellent advice once, encouraging me to look beyond a husband."

More intent staring.

Belle's throat went dry.

"Miss Heartstone, there was an incident some years ago, right before I left for India. I was approached with an unexpected offer—" Blake broke off. "—I say, are you quite all right, Miss Heartstone? You have gone white suddenly."

Belle swallowed. "The room is merely a trifle stifling. Give me a moment."

She lowered her head, somehow her face altering between a heated blush and stark-white terror.

He couldn't possibly know she was LHF, could he? He had asked about LHF earlier, but she had gathered no sense that he thought the question related to her?

But now this question about an "unexpected offer"? What offer could he mean, other than her offer to fund his venture to India?

Was this the moment then? She would tell him right now, and not wait for tomorrow?

And in front of so many witnesses? While dancing, she had tried to bring it up with the intention of moving outside to discuss it.

She wasn't sure her heart could handle an audience watching his face morph from friendly kindness to horror and loathing over her deception, no matter how altruistic her initial aims. She had let the farce go on for far too long, assuming that she was only hurting herself.

He wanted to introduce her to his family. Her. Miss Heartstone.

How could their story end like this?

What to do?

"Allow me to escort you onto the veranda. Perhaps some fresh air will clear your head." His tone lacked the warmth of their earlier conversation.

Ah.

Well then.

They *were* to discuss this right now.

You should have listened to me earlier, Blake. I do have *an important matter to discuss with you.*

Blake stood, offering her his hand, his bearing stiff and off. He was far too astute to not be putting two-and-two together at present.

Belle gently placed her gloved hand in his, allowing him to lead her toward the tall, paned doors.

Thank goodness, he had the foresight to remove them from prying eyes.

Her thoughts were a whirlwind, trying to make heads or tails of what to say once they were outside.

Of course, they were stopped every three feet by one person or another, prolonging Belle's anxiety, fine-tuning it.

Mr. Edgar, an eager MP within Stratton's district, was the first. He fawningly bowed to Blake, perspiration beading his brow, before seizing Blake's hand.

"Allow me to add my voice to those welcoming you back to England, my lord." He pumped Blake's hand enthusiastically. "We are honored to have you here."

Blake murmured something polite to the man and moved them onward.

Two elderly women Belle had met on previous visits to Stratton Hall were next.

"Lord Blake, it is an honor that you have graced us with your presence," one tittered.

"Indeed, I remarked mere moments before how blessed we are to meet such an illustrious person," the other blushed.

Belle smiled and nodded, mouth dry. These interruptions were merely drawing out her period of judgment.

They had only gone two steps further when the vicar stopped them.

"Pleasure, again, to meet you, my lord." The man's beard moved as he spoke, his gray hair somewhat askew. "Headed out to take the air?" He gestured toward the open doors.

"Miss Heartstone is feeling light-headed," Blake replied.

"'Tis a lovely night. Beautiful full moon. The air will do her good," the vicar agreed. "Though don't stay out too long. There is an impressive moon halo tonight. Did you hear about the floods that swept through Cirencester? Mark my words, there will be rain by morning."

Belle managed a wan smile. She had a feeling there was a storm coming, but of the figurative kind.

"Thank you, sir." Blake's expression was strained.

He turned, finally reaching the doors. The cool night air washed over Belle, a light breeze tugging at her curls.

Blake kept them in view of the entire ballroom, outdoors but still well within the purview of propriety.

"Do you feel better, madam?"

"Yes, my lord. Thank you."

Belle swallowed, her heart racing. What was to be done? Would he allow her to plead her case before passing judgment?

And how large would the scene be, given that every third head in the crowded ballroom kept swinging their way, observing their conversation. No one could hear, but the tenor would not be missed.

"So back to my question, Miss Heartstone." He studied her for a moment, eyes narrowed. "As I said, before I left for India, there was an incident in Hyde Park involving a young lady and the Long Water—"

The comment dowsed Belle as quickly as a bucket of cold water. Her head snapped back, eyes flying to his.

"Par-pardon, my lord?"

She had been wandering off in her concerns over LHF, and here he was asking about . . .

What *was* he asking precisely?

He turned to overlook the garden, gesturing for her to do the same. Placing their backs to the open door, hiding their conversation from those inside. Belle looked up to the sky, stars bleached into mere pinpricks beside the bright full moon.

There was indeed a moonbow. Softly colored bands surrounding the moon.

Would that it were an omen of good luck . . .

"I see guilt on your face, Miss Heartstone. It *was* you," he whispered. "That morning. In Hyde Park."

Belle's breath hitched.

He had seen guilt on her face but from another, arguably more serious, transgression.

What was that line from Sir Walter Scott?

Oh, what a tangled web we weave . . .

She bit her bottom lip. And then nodded.

"You proposed marriage to me." He said the words without looking at her. His face turned to the garden beyond. Tone dead and flat.

She choked. A sound somewhere between a laugh and despair.

Oh, Colin!

"Yes, I did," she managed to whisper. "I was the young woman that morning."

Silence.

The sound of murmured voices and crystal clinking drifted out from the room behind them.

"I am at a loss as to what to say, Miss Heartstone. What has been your aim over this past week? To attempt again to purchase my affections, perhaps through entrapment this time?"

Belle flinched. "That was beneath you, my lord."

"What would you have me believe, given your past behavior?"

"I was young and foolish—"

"An understatement."

"—and I felt desperate. My mother pushed me into the arms of this lord and that. I wanted to have a measure of control over my life."

"How could you say nothing about this? You had only to open your mouth and indicate that we had a prior acquaintance. There was no need for a lengthy introduction to the topic—"

A bolt of righteous indignation jolted through Belle. "Had you shown a flicker of recognition, I would have said something immediately."

"So you claim."

"Heavens! What would you have *had* me say?"

"Anything other than this condemning silence—"

Belle let out an embarrassing cross between a snort and a huff. "So when I stumbled into you that morning in Hyde Park some weeks past, I should have said, 'Pardon, my lord, but this reminds me of the time I proposed marriage to you in nearly this precise spot seven years ago—'"

"I do not appreciate your sarcasm, madam."

"'—you know, the woman you do not remember and were quick to dismiss?'"

"How long were you going to withhold the information from me?"

Belle *blink, blink, blink*ed. "I have been *trying* to speak to you! Besides for all I knew, you did not remember the incident at all."

"For future reference, Miss Heartstone, a man *never* forgets that a woman proposed to him."

"Duly noted."

"So all the other men you proposed to were sensible enough to refuse as well?"

Belle turned her head, finally fixing him with such a *look*—

"Do not glare daggers at me." Blake kept his gaze sternly on the garden before them, bathed in bright moonlight. "Might I remind you, *I* am the injured party here."

Belle turned back, mimicking his pose, willing the people in the ballroom behind them to miss the abrupt tension between them. "There have been *no* others, as I am sure you can see."

"Why give up so easily? Surely, you could have purchased at least the title of viscountess—"

"Enough, my lord. There is no need to be vulgar." Belle managed to keep her voice low. "You have made your point. I know I acted brazenly seven years ago. You offered me excellent advice at the time, which I took. You were not outraged then. Why are you so upset now?"

Blake didn't look at her. He kept his head firmly directed forward. Belle pressed her lips together.

How ironic that *this* should be their conversation . . .

In the grand list of *The Ways Belle Heartstone Has Wronged the Marquess of Blake*, the time she had proposed marriage to him barely merited a mention.

How terrible would his anger be when he knew the whole truth? Though at this point, what did it matter?

"As I have been trying to tell you, my lord, there is a matter I would discuss with you—"

"So your proposal of marriage to me is *not* this mysterious matter?"

Belle bit her lip. "No, my lord, it is not. There is another item, that might be tangentially related—"

"Enough," Blake laughed, bitter and angry. "Save your rehearsed lines, madam. I do not care to hear them."

"But, my lord—"

"What more can you have to say to me? I will not allow you the last word in this. I will not be sent packing with one of your practiced speeches."

She took a step back, trying to gather her words. She noted more than one curious head turned their way.

Oh, dear.

Their conversation was clearly gathering attention.

Belle leaned forward, voice low. "My lord, perhaps we could still speak tomorrow as you mentioned earlier—"

Blake shot a glance at their onlookers. "There is nothing more to say at present, madam. I bid you good evening, Miss Heartstone."

With a curt nod, Blake turned on his heel and strode down the stairs and into the dark garden beyond.

Never once looking back.

BELLE EXCUSED HERSELF early from the ball, claiming a head-ache. But even by that point, rumor was running rife that she had some-how displeased the Marquess of Blake. His curt leave-taking had been well-observed. Some even asserted that he had given her the cut-direct. Whispered conversations followed Belle out of the ballroom.

Belle shut herself in her room. Clouds now raced across the night sky, blocking the moon. The winds had picked up, the vicar's promise of rain rapidly materializing.

After pacing her bedroom for nearly an hour lost in sluggish thoughts, Anne knocked on her door. Her expression was sympathetic as she slid into the room and latched the door.

Without saying a word, Anne personally helped Belle undress and slip into a cotton night rail. Wind gusted, rattling the window. A spatter-ing of rain quickly followed.

"Would you like to talk about it?" Anne looked at Belle in the vanity mirror, running a brush through Belle's hair.

Belle pondered her own reflection for a moment. Lightning flashed, followed quickly by rumbling thunder. "I feel like a fox with the hounds closing in."

Anne paused and then resumed her brushing. "Your discussion appeared quite heated."

"That is an understatement. Blake finally remembered the incident from Hyde Park seven years ago."

"He realized you proposed marriage to him?"

"Yes."

"That cannot have gone over well."

"No." A hiccuppy sigh. "It did not."

A harsh gust of wind hammered the window; rain pummeling the glass. Lightning flashed.

"This is a fine fettle you have landed yourself in."

"H-he has asked to sever our acquaintance."

"Given that you still have business interests tied up with his, that might be easier said than done."

Thunder crashed, vibrating the room.

It seemed fitting somehow. That the very heavens should unleash such anger and frustration, as if Nature herself was feeling Belle's anguish.

Anne brushed in silence.

Who knew that heartbreak literally felt like one's heart was being torn asunder. She had never realized that the figure of speech was actually excessively accurate.

Anne set down the brush and braided Belle's hair into a long rope, tying it off with a bit of ribbon. She placed her hands on Belle's shoulders before meeting her gaze in the reflection.

"I will tell him tomorrow. I have tried to be circumspect and polite about it, but I cannot wait any longer. I will be bold." Belle's shoulders slumped. "And then take my punishment."

"Perhaps if he knows the entire truth, it will soften his heart."

Belle brushed a tear away. "No. He already felt so betrayed by Miss Forrester. I am sure I will only make him angrier."

"That is also a definite possibility."

"I was so foolish to think that he might forgive me. That we might—" Her voice cracked.

Anne sighed. "Sometimes you cannot have your cake and eat it too."

"But I so enjoy cake."

A weak smile. "Don't we all, my dear."

Belle sniffled, lifting a handkerchief off the vanity. Silence hung in the room, broken only by the popping of the fire.

"Oh, Anne." Belle's chest heaved. She dabbed her wet cheeks. "Until tonight, I had thought that I was s-simply avoiding the messiness of c-confronting him, that I f-feared having his anger and scorn heaped on my head. I feared losing his friendship. But now . . ."

Silence.

"But now?" Anne prompted.

"B-but now I realize that it's more than fear of losing him." Another gasping breath. "Somewhere along the way, I gave Blake so many p-pieces of my soul, I feel as if I am l-losing m-myself."

"My dear friend." Anne pulled her into a tight hug.

"H-how shall this ever be put to r-rights?"

Belle sobbed her grief.

After shattering into a thousand jagged shards, how was she ever going to piece herself back together again?

And at the end of it all, would she be like a broken mirror? Hundreds of fractured versions of herself with no way to see the whole?

Long after Anne left and Belle cried herself to exhaustion, she stared at the ceiling, listening as rain pummeled the house and lighting crashed and wind howled.

All of it echoing the despairing ache of her own soul.

. . . I have reached an impasse with the magistrate near Fyfe Hall. It appears that several of the local gentry have raised objections to having an orphanage in their jurisdiction, citing the children as being an unsavory influence in the area. They wish to evict the children and veterans. My illness has exacerbated the situation, as I was unable to reply in a timely fashion. I have sent an inquiry to Lord Blake, as well, but I am unsure how to proceed. I await your reply . . .

—letter from Mr. Sloan to Miss Heartstone, sent but languishing
in the mail coach due to poor weather

Colin strode down the main staircase the next morning, tapping a ledger against his thigh. He skirted two footmen hauling a trunk out the front doors to a waiting carriage.

Rain continued to fall, having morphed from the drenching

downpour of the night before into a steady drumming. The footmen ducked their heads as they strapped the large trunk onto the back of the carriage.

The chattering sound of the Desperate Debutantes floated down the central staircase. Theirs were the carriages currently being prepared, though it seemed they were in disarray over a lame horse and sick footman. Colin knew it was uncharitable of him, but he hoped and prayed they would not be delayed on their journey.

The Gold Miners had already departed earlier in the morning, Lord Odysseus accompanying them as far as Warwick. He would attend to some business in Warwick and return that evening.

"I do hope the roads aren't too horrid." The voice of one of the girls floated down to Colin.

"The rain was so terrible last night, I could hardly sleep," another said.

"Indeed. And my maid mentioned that the river through town can become nearly impassable after a good rain," a third joined in.

"Just think," the first said, "we might have to return and spend another few days with Lord Blake."

Laughter greeted that statement.

Heaven help him.

Colin stepped into the music room adjacent to the entry hall, not wishing to engage in small talk with the gaggle of debutantes.

Would Miss Heartstone stay on now? After the events of the night before, he had to wonder.

He had no intention of quitting the field. He would remain with the Strattons through the end of the week, shoring up his friendship with Stratton himself and catching up on some business, hence the ledger he currently carried. Besides, there was still the matter of LHF to suss out.

Even without the raging weather, he would have found sleep elusive, staring at the ceiling for hours.

Miss Heartstone . . .

Aptly named, that one—

No. That was being unkind.

His thinking brain clearly understood the facts. Belle had been so young seven years ago and, obviously, had taken his words to heart. She should be *commended* not excoriated, assuming her motives—then and now—were as innocuous as she claimed.

It was just . . . he had truly begun to care for her. The slap of realizing she was the girl from Hyde Park so many years ago—

It had definitely caught him off guard.

Worse, that haunting sense of rightness would not leave him. The feeling that she was somehow already a part of him. What had she called such connection? Woven into the fabric of one's heart—

Enough.

He steadfastly refused to examine the turmoil of emotions she caused.

Yes. He had reacted badly last night. This whole business with LHF left him on edge, betrayal scraping him raw and making every other prick hurt so much worse. He was a wounded tiger lashing out at those around him.

Colin would speak with Miss Heartstone later today and see if there was anything to salvage from the situation.

He was in the process of crossing through the music room when a hand touched his elbow. He turned to find a footman at his side.

"I was asked to give you this, my lord."

Colin took the neatly folded missive with a nod, glancing at his name on the front.

Lord Blake stared back at him in a bold, loopy script he knew as well as his own.

Gooseflesh instantly pebbled his arms.

He unfolded the note.

Forgive me, my friend. I know the puzzle of my anonymous identity has weighed on you. The reason for my silence on this matter is breathtakingly simple. The time for a full disclosure has long passed. I await your pleasure in the library, should you care to join me.

Your true friend,
LHF

Colin froze. Eyes wide.

And then the words sank in.

Hallelujah! At last.

The man had come to his senses.

Colin walked through the music room and subsequent drawing room, intent on the library door at the opposite end.

Finally, his friend had seen reason. His heart sped up as the door drew near.

Who would he find?

Had LHF truly been here all week?

Blood thundered in his ears, his throat abruptly scratchy and dry.

Taking in a deep, fortifying breath, Colin pushed the door open and stepped into the shadowed interior.

Dark skies and rain made the room dimmer than normal. Books lined the walls from floor to ceiling on three sides, broken only by a marble fireplace and mantel. A cheery fire popped in the hearth. Two tall paned windows made up the fourth wall, bleary and rain-streaked. A large map table stood in the middle of the room.

At first he did not see the slim figure staring out of the farthest window. But then Miss Heartstone turned to face him, drawing his attention.

Colin froze, brows drawing down. He was intent on meeting his business partner, not resolving past romantic entanglements. Though he was resolved to discuss the matter with her, he was not in the proper frame of mind to do so at present.

"Pardon me, Miss Heartstone." He gave a short bow. "I was to meet someone here."

"Lord Blake." Her voice soft and low.

He shook his head, glancing down at the note in his hand. What game was LHF playing now? Colin needed to find the man. "I am afraid I do not have time for a conversation at present. May I ask, was there another individual here before you?"

A brief hesitation and then, "No, my lord."

Ah. Colin backed toward the closed door. "If you will excuse me then—"

She stopped him with an outstretched hand. "My lord, as I said last night, there is another matter to discuss between us. Forgive me for calling you here, but I need you to hear me out—"

"Calling me here?" Colin frowned. "I did not receive a summons from you."

Her shoulders sagged. Weariness flashing across her face.

She waved a hand toward the paper in his hand.

Colin glanced at LHF's note.

And then back up at Miss Heartstone.

She did not appear confused or bewildered.

Was it possible—

"You admit to having a hand in this?" He brandished the letter at her.

"Yes. If you will please listen—"

Colin held up his hand, palm out.

Stop.

Miss Heartstone instantly silenced.

He looked down at the missive. It *was* LHF's handwriting. His mind reeling, punch-drunk, trying to fathom how there could possibly be a connection between his business partner and this . . . woman.

He felt the entire situation spooling out of his control.

He forced himself not to notice the white knuckles gripping the edge of her morning dress. The strain of her mouth. Her red-rimmed eyes.

Marveling that, even now, he found her attractive.

She took his prolonged silence as permission to continue speaking.

"You want answers. I wish to provide them." She clutched her dress tighter.

"What answers could you provide, Miss Heartstone?"

She motioned toward the letter again.

He sighed. "I asked you point-blank last night if knew anyone named LHF. You said no. Did you lie to me?"

"Not precisely, my lord. You asked me if I knew a *man* by that name. I merely answered truthfully." A deep breath. "I do not."

"Semantics, Miss Heartstone?"

"If I must."

A strained silence. Rain pattered against the window panes. Colin snapped the letter against his thigh with one hand, the ledger still in his other.

"Yet you claim to have something with the sending of this letter?" He held it aloft.

"Yes."

Grimacing, he stuffed the letter into his coat pocket.

"Miss Heartstone." He sagged, pinching the bridge of his nose with his free hand. "Will you please just get to the point? I am a busy man and do not enjoy being led a merry dance."

She sucked in another deep breath, as if readying herself for battle.

"I hoped this moment would never come. Please understand, I was in the middle before realizing it had begun—"

"What in heaven's name are you referring to?"

"—I only wished to help. If you hear nothing else from me today, please remember that much. My heart and motives were always pure."

He gestured toward her with his ledger.

"You are still not making sense, Miss Heartstone. I fail to see what any of this has to do with my business partner, LHF."

Silence hung heavy.

She opened her mouth, as if to speak.

Shut it.

Opened it again.

"Really, my lord," she finally said, spreading her hands wide. "You are being somewhat obtuse. Allow me to repeat. Last evening, I said I did not know a *man* with the initials LHF."

She rolled a hand. *Ergo* . . .

Colin frowned, sifting through the information.

LHF was not a man.

Which meant . . . what?

"Do you mean to tell me LHF is not a gentleman? He is a commoner?"

Belle threw her arms up in the air and shook her head.

Looking at him like he was twenty-times a fool.

Oh.

Oh!

His entire body went numb. Surely this wasn't what he was thinking—

She continued, her voice hushed. "As I said, I did not want you to know the truth of me. Because I feared you would look at me as you are right now—eyes wide with horror."

"Miss Heartstone, I—"

She stretched her hand to him. "Please, my lord, hear me out. I stayed up most of the night composing an excellent speech. I have been trying to tell you this all week, but I have allowed you to change the topic each time. Let me give my apologies first, and then you may have at me."

Colin froze.

This was what she had been trying to tell all week? She hadn't been attempting to refuse his courtship?

His mind was literally too stunned to comprehend the magnitude of this conversation. Colin could scarcely string two thoughts together.

She shot him a beseeching look. "I realize that mere fear or discomfort on my part is hardly a valid reason for not divulging all to your purview. I should have told you my name years ago. I have begun countless letters laying the entirety of my situation before you without finishing them. It has been selfish cowardice in me to keep this information from you."

"Pardon a moment." Colin held out a staying hand, his languishing thoughts struggling to catch up. "You . . . you admit to being the illusive LHF?"

"Yes." She nodded.

"And you have *always* been LHF? From the beginning?"

Once more, "Yes."

Colin pulled the note from his pocket. Yes. It was LHF's handwriting. Plain and clear. Proof. Evidence. He tucked it back away.

So . . .

Belle Heartstone was LHF.

He blinked. Shook his head.

No, the sentence still struggled to settle into his thoughts.

He began pacing, setting down his ledger, picking it up again. Back and forth.

Miss Heartstone! Belle! LHF?!

She was far too young. Far too female. Far too . . . beautiful.

Why beauty would be a barrier, his scrambled wits could not say. But . . .

She could be brazen, forthright. If any woman could pull off such a thing, it *would* be her.

How was this possible?

He paused and stared at her, trying to see his elderly, trusted friend in her pretty face, desperately trying to reframe the past *seven* years of his life.

With little success.

"A woman. LHF. You!" he spluttered.

Colin was starting to worry that the shock had dislodged something vital in his brain. Would he become like the vagrants in Kings Cross, shouting random words at passersby? *Turnips! Upholstery! Repent ye!*

"B-but why? And . . . how?" He began pacing again, a thousand thoughts chasing each other through his brain. "I have been writing an unmarried, young *gentlewoman* all this time?"

She nodded, catching her bottom lip with her teeth. "Therefore, you will hopefully understand why I have been reluctant to reveal myself to you—"

"Reluctant? That seems a monumental understatement!"

He had to give her credit, she squared her shoulders and faced him, even as he continued to walk back and forth.

"You must know I have only ever wanted your success and happiness," she said. "I originally intended to just provide you with your needed capital and send you on your way—"

Colin stopped and lifted his hand, palm out, averting his head. *Give me a moment.*

In all his mental attempts to sort the puzzle of LHF, he had never once considered that his good friend might be a woman.

Was Belle toying with him? Had she *ever* been true?

He mentally skimmed back through their letters over the years. How had she described herself?

I am neither tall, nor short in stature. Neither thin nor stout. My hair and eyes are a simple brown. In summation, I am utterly unremarkable.

Which, though on the surface might be true, he would give serious argument against her *unremarkable-ness*.

"We have been corresponding for . . . for . . . for *years*." He said the word as if it were particularly repugnant.

"Yes."

"You are still so . . . so *young*." He gestured toward her. "When we began writing, you were practically in the schoolroom."

"I am perhaps not as young as you may think me."

"You could *not* have been a day over nineteen when this began."

A beat.

"That is true."

More pacing. Colin threaded a hand through his hair.

So young. How was all of LHF's wisdom possibly contained within her slight frame and pretty face?

He felt like a lake trout, gaping and gasping on dry land, trying to make head or tails of this strange world. "You have given me sound business advice, provided breathtaking mathematical calculations, guided our investments."

"Yes."

"By yourself?"

"Mostly. Mr. Sloan has provided some help from time to time."

"But . . . you are a—"

"A woman? Yes. But . . . my father was a veritable financial wizard. He never saw my sex as a barrier to my abilities." Was there accusation in her tone? "I learned everything I know at his knee."

He turned away and returned to his pacing.

It was too much to absorb.

Pacing.

Back and forth, shifting the ledger from hand to hand.

A solid, *manly* activity.

The perfect thing to do when one was desperate to reorient the last seven years of one's life.

His very sense of reality had shifted around him. He ran a trembling hand over his chin.

"We have exchanged drawings." He plucked the words out of the air, as if scribbled pictures of cheeky monkeys were the issue here.

"Uhmm. Yes."

"W-we founded charities together."

"Indeed. They have helped a great many people. It's been a source of tremendous satisfaction for us both."

More pacing. His hands still shaking.

"You have sent me books, discussed philosophy, laughed over dreadful gothic novels." His voice rose with each syllable.

"Yes."

"You came up with devilishly clever riddles." He flung the words at her.

"Thank you. Yours were quite clever, too."

He stopped and pinned her with his gaze.

She squirmed. "Uhmm . . . to be completely honest, Miss Rutger may have helped somewhat with the riddles." She bit her lip again. "She has a knack for them."

"You cheated?" He could hear the outrage in his tone.

"Uhmm, I would not use the word *cheated*, my lord. I'm not quite sure one can cheat at riddles. Shall we say I *sought professional advice?*"

And there it was.

That dry humor he had experienced in letter after letter. The same gentle wit he had been enjoying all week.

How could it be?

How could this woman be LHF? How could Fate have dealt with him like this?

His chest heaved. Something that tasted strongly of panic choked him.

"Why?" he finally gasped.

Why me? Why you?

How did this happen in the first place?

She walked forward a few steps, placing a tense hand on the map table between them. "You were kind to me that morning in Hyde Park—"

"I was?" Colin stopped, trying to recall exactly what they had said.

"You were. You needed funds. I wanted to help. Truthfully, I simply wished to pass along my father's excellent advice. I honestly never intended to write you again. But then you wrote me, and I wrote back, and we were in the middle of it all before . . ."

"But you did not know me."

"Well, that is not precisely true. I did have a Runner research you."

"Right." Sarcasm edged in. "To decide if I was husband material."

She squirmed again, obviously not appreciating the reference to her behavior that day.

"But we had never met before that morning in the park." He angled his head. "Had we?"

"We were introduced at a musicale in London right after you rose to the marquisate."

A beat.

"I have no memory of that."

"Yes. I gathered as much." Again with the dry humor.

It was an unwelcome reminder. He cared deeply about LHF. Colin had considered the man to be his Mentor, his guru . . . practically a second father.

An older, wiser, patriarchal figure.

Miss Heartstone was . . . not that. She was youth and feminine and beauty. A love interest. He had been intent on courting her.

He simply could not reconcile the two people into the same body.

His life currently sprawled before him, a shattered mass of expectations and reality.

Some dry part of his brain unhelpfully noted that his thinking was perhaps a smidge melodramatic.

No more gothic novels then.

That same dry voice also pointed out that he usually championed women who seized the reins of their own destiny. So why was he now upset that someone he had looked up to and admired proved to be female?

Colin blew out a frustrated breath.

That was true.

But . . . but . . . *her* reins were connected to *his* team of horses. He was fine with women in general being liberal and free. But when one controlled his journey like this . . .

And . . .

And . . .

And . . . pondering this personal hypocrisy was consuming too much brain power.

He shook all thoughts loose.

"Again, why?" he asked "You didn't need to help me. I refused you, after all."

She looked down at her hands on the table, studying her fingers.

"As I said, you were kind to me that morning."—She gestured toward him.—"I know my behavior was rash and unseemly. But instead of castigation or mockery, you gave me gentleness and encouragement. You changed me. I merely wished to return your behavior in kind."

Her fingers curled in agitation, gripping the edge of the table. She still did not raise her head.

A wet splash dashed her hand. Followed by another.

Blast. He had made her cry.

Well, given her deception, she probably deserved to cry. The sorrow of the guilty.

She was a quiet crier, he would give her that. Loud hysterics would not be her style.

Emotions thrummed through him. Memories of Sarah's betrayal surged forward, his emotions then and now converging into a hardened mass of . . . of . . . of—

Colin let out a harsh breath. "Though I understand that our initial friendship might have begun in an unanticipated way, there surely was a point in the past *seven* years when you might have told me that You. Were. A. Woman!"

She flinched, chest hiccupping.

Clearing his throat, he shifted his ledger, slapping it against his thigh.

His heart pounded in his chest. His hands shook.

How could this be the answer to LHF?!

Why was his throat so tight? Why was he so blindingly overset?

How could Belle be LHF? How could his two separate worlds have collided so thoroughly? After Sarah, he had thought to avoid such women in the future.

He ignored the unhelpful prick of his conscience that pointed out the differences between the women.

Sarah's bold refusal to accept the consequences of her behavior.

Belle's quiet owning of her actions—

She dabbed at her eyes. "P-please know that I am genuinely sorry we have come to this—"

Pain whipped him, lashing deep. "I do not wish for your apologies, madam. You have used my affections and friendship most abominably."

Quiet.

"Understood." Her voice was barely above a whisper. "What shall we do about our business?"

"Our business?!" Colin barely avoided flinching. "You throw this . . . this . . . information at my feet and then ask me to think about such things?"

"Of course not. Of course—"

"I trust you will, at least, do the right thing and retreat back to London immediately. You will not suffer us to remain in close proximity to each other for the next week. And as the wronged party here, I should not be forced out."

"Naturally." Another whisper.

"As for our business, I cannot say at present. When I am ready to speak on it, I will contact Mr. Sloan, and we will proceed from there."

He shot her one last glance. One last look at her pretty face and soulful eyes. How could this be his answer?

Too many emotions clogged his throat. Too much to sort through—

"Goodbye, Miss Heartstone."

Colin turned on his heel, practically stomping from the room, gritting his teeth at the sounds of soft sobs behind him.

PART III

CONSEQUENCES

20

. . . The magistrate grows bolder. I fear the orphaned children will be cast into the street and set adrift before we can intervene—

—letter from Mr. Sloan to Lord Blake,
sent but not yet delivered due to rain

The door slammed behind Blake, the noise reverberating through Belle's chest, shattering what remained of her heart.

Blake was gone. Their friendship in tattered ruins. He had said nothing more. Merely bowed and stomped out.

She had never considered how much *hope* she had secretly harbored. That somehow, against all odds, Blake would *see* her. That he would discover the truth about LHF and not run off in horror. But, instead, look at her with admiration.

What had she thought would happen? That he would fall down on one knee, profess his undying devotion, and sweep her off on his noble steed to a castle in the sky?

Oh!

Yes, please.

That would be so lovely.

Ugh.

She really needed to reassess how much bad literature she consumed.

She was fifty—no, a thousand—ways a fool.

Somehow, Belle managed to wipe her eyes and save the ugliest of her crying until she had retreated to her bedroom.

Once there, she didn't collapse onto the bed as much as it came upwards to meet her. She sprawled across it, just as she had as a child. Resting her arms on her pillows, she let it all out.

The guilt of keeping her secret for so long.

The relief of finally having told him.

The pain of knowing she had lost him forever.

A barren emptiness stretched before her.

Belle knew, in the way of knowing things, that she would forever consider this moment to be both a death and a birth.

A pivot point.

One's existence could alter so quickly. A breath. A word. A mistake. A boon.

She knew the rest of her days would flow from the actions of the past hour. Just as the events of the past seven years had been sparked by another morning in Hyde Park.

Nothing would be as it had been.

Every person was forever only one day away from an absolutely different life.

Hers had now arrived; this had shattered her in truth.

Blake was lost to her. Worse, he had taken more than just her heart with him. His loss had fractured something deep within her. She was at sixes and sevens, not knowing how to glue herself back together. And even if she did, she would forever bear the scars of where she had broken.

Anne found her a while later.

Belle's sobs had moved into hiccupping breaths by that point. Her handkerchief had devolved into a dripping rag, her face surely red and splotchy. She had never been an elegant crier. When she was little, her nurse had said she looked like she had run through a patch of stinging nettle after a good weep.

"Well, that's done then, isn't it?" Anne murmured, running a soothing hand down Belle's spine.

Belle could only nod, chest still heaving in ragged gasps.

"It appears to not have gone well."

Belle nodded again, hiccupping. "It went q-quite poorly."

"I see."

"H-h-he asked me to l-leave." Belle managed to raise her head.

"Yes, that is not unexpected. As the wronged party, he should be allowed to continue the week with the Strattons and not be forced to leave on such short notice."

"I-I know."

"We should leave him in peace. 'Tis the honorable thing for us to do."

Belle hiccupped again. "I-I shall h-have to g-give my apologies to G-Georgiana."

"Yes." Anne nodded. "Simply tell her that an urgent matter has arisen. Your face will speak for itself."

Belle set a hand to her forehead.

"You speak with Lady Stratton." Anne rubbed a comforting hand along Belle's shoulder. "I'll start packing our bags and have the carriage readied. I think we should be able to leave within the hour."

Belle nodded again.

Anne looked at the rain setting a steady rhythm against the window glass.

"Let's just hope the weather holds enough to keep the roads passable," Anne sighed. "At least Mother Nature has the good sense to be dreary."

COLIN TOOK A leisurely sip of cognac, savoring the slow burn down his throat. Stratton's library hung with hushed silence, the only sound being the continual pitter-patter of the rain. Bluish, gloomy light shrouded the room.

Setting down his drink, Colin angled the book in his lap toward the dim window light, turning the page. His mind had been too chaotic to focus on his ledger in the end. So he had turned to reading. But he had ignored Stratton's well-worn copy of *Ivanhoe* and had chosen a sensible treatise on modern farming techniques instead.

Reading overly-wrought novels was a little painful at present.

Though, for the record, modern farming techniques were appallingly dull. He steadfastly held on, refusing to even glance toward the novels dotting the room.

Belle and Miss Rutger had left nearly two hours previously, returning to London, giving him some much-needed time and space to sort through his mental state.

Caustic anger, betrayal, grief, disappointment, disbelief . . . the toxic combination of emotions rode him hard.

Worse, little bursts of Belle Heartstone wiggled past his mental defenses.

The divots that bracketed her lips when she smiled.

The lingering smell of lemon and lavender that eddied in her wake.

The porcelain beauty of her face.

The soft shine of kindness in her gaze—

Stop, he commanded himself. *You must cease this. She lied and deceived you.*

Though once the initial shock had faded slightly, Colin struggled to wrap his brain around the truth—

LHF was Miss Belle Heartstone.

The same Miss Heartstone who had proposed to him in Hyde Park all those years ago.

The same Miss Heartstone who had rejected every able-bodied member of the *ton* for the past seven years.

The very Miss Heartstone of the lovely eyes and pretty face who had been slowly burrowing her way into his heart all week—

Bah! His budding affection for her had been a weak puppy love at best. A passing fancy.

True love took years. Lasting love grew through shared experiences, through trust built on a thousand joint decisions and discussions. Through trials surmounted and one's deepest ideals exchanged.

Much like he had done with—

Damn and blast!

That tight achy feeling in his chest threatened to choke him.

Enough.

How was he to reframe his relationship with LHF?

How was he to now imagine a *young (!), beautiful (!!) woman (!!!)* in the role of his elderly mentor and confidant?

It boggled the mind.

He turned another page in his book, eyes seeing words but not comprehending them.

All he saw were Belle's eyes, anguished and desperate, owning her mistakes and pleading for his forgiveness—

Stop!

Were all women intent on deceiving him? First Sarah and now Belle? How was he ever to trust a member of the opposite sex again?

He brutally repressed the dry voice that whispered Belle's explanation made sense, that she had tried to tell him—too late, but still— that, he too, might have acted the same way, if presented with a similar situation—

No!

But the voice would not be silenced. It continued on, pointing out her brilliance as a business advisor. Women were so capable. It was an eternal shame that they were forced to remain closeted in such a narrow sphere of life. To see one woman break free in such a spectacular fashion—

Enough! Stop!

He didn't want to think on his hypocrisy or the peal his mother— God rest her soul—would ring over his head if she could see him at present.

No. He would wait out the rain and then he would go for a bruising ride. A satisfying gallop cross-country would do wonders for his mood.

And if he found the thought of another week of contemplative silence somewhat daunting, well . . . he would overcome it.

There were many other women in the world. No need to hang on to a woman who masqueraded as a mentor and best friend that he could open his heart and soul to—

Colin slammed the book shut and tossed it aside. He drained the rest of his cognac in a quick gulp.

Enough of Belle Heartstone.

He would soon be rid of her, once they managed to disentangle themselves financially. He would never have to see her again, to think about artifice and subterfuge that had shrouded every letter she wrote to him as LHF.

Part of him hated that it was all tainted now. The stain of her deception spread through everything they had created together.

Somehow he had to move past it—

The rattle of loud voices drifted in from the large entrance hall.

Women's voices, agitated and excited.

Far too many women to be the housemaids or Lady Stratton.

He thought he heard Stratton in the midst, calling for his horse.

Frowning, Colin stepped out of the library, moving through the music room.

The voices became more distinct.

His stomach plummeted as he recognized them.

"—bridge was swept clear away." Mrs. Jones-Button was saying. "The carriage became mired another two times before we managed to arrive back here."

"I was so frightened." That was a younger Miss Jones-Button. "The water was rushing so quickly."

"Aye," her mother agreed. "The coachman declared that the old stone bridge was simply no match for the current. The gentlemen crossed earlier before the water rose so dramatically, or at least that was the report of the tollman."

"Heavens!" Lady Stratton exclaimed.

Given the clamor in the hallway, it would seem that all of the Desperate Debutantes had returned.

His mind instantly careened to Belle Heartstone. She had left before the younger women in the end, as the Desperate Debutants had spent hours sorting their problems with the horses. What had happened to Belle? Had she crossed the bridge in time?

He ignored the flare of worry. He reminded himself that he did not have charitable feelings toward Miss Belle Heartstone at present.

Colin walked into the entryway. The chaos was just as it sounded. Fluttering ladies and their mothers. Stratton and two footmen shrugging into greatcoats.

"Blake!" Stratton exclaimed as he caught sight of Colin. "There you are, thank goodness. Miss Heartstone's carriage was caught in the current and swept downstream."

Terror flooded Colin's body. Which surely was the wrong feeling for the moment. Concern, certainly. But terror?

Every head turned his way.

"Oh, Lord Blake! It was horrifying!" Mrs. Button-Jones pressed a shaking hand to her bosom. "I don't know that I shall ever forget the sight. Miss Heartstone's carriage crossed the bridge, just as an enormous tree came sailing downstream—"

"It took the bridge right out," her daughter continued. "The noise was astounding."

"Yes," said a third. "Miss Heartstone's horses had just reached the opposite side and the force of the impact snapped the hitch right in two, setting the horses free."

"The postillion managed to keep the horses in check."

"True, but her coachman and two footmen were sent tumbling into the water. One managed to cling to the side of the carriage as it bobbed downstream."

"Like a cork in a torrent! The whole carriage could be in the ocean by now!"

"We're off," Stratton met his stunned gaze. "You're coming, right?"

Colin didn't trust himself to respond beyond a curt nod.

Belle.

He had to reach Belle.

There was too much unsettled business between them.

As he raced for his coat and horse, Colin refused to examine the strongest emotion pummeling his chest—

Breathtaking, mind-numbing panic.

21

. . . How could you have deceived me so? How could you not have told me the truth? I trusted you with everything that I am, every hope and wish, every profound thought. I loved you as a child loves a parent. Your betrayal has been a death. You killed LHF and the person he was to me. I feel like I have lost my father all over again . . .

—*letter from Lord Blake to Miss Heartstone,
written, brooded over, and then tossed into the fire*

They should never have attempted to cross the bridge.

Belle realized this too late.

It was just . . . she had been so desperate to reach London and home. So when the driver was hesitant to cross the bridge, Belle had urged him forward. She couldn't imagine having to return to Stratton Hall and endure Blake's stony gaze and censorious looks. Anything seemed preferable.

Careful what you wish for.

Belle clung to the inside of the carriage, clenching her chattering teeth, sternly telling herself not to panic over the rising water.

After being swept off the bridge, the carriage had floated downstream, being tossed and turned in the current. Her carriage was well-made and strong, and so it took to the water, bobbing up and down, instead of shattering. Anne and Belle had clung to the leather straps hanging from the ceiling, desperately keeping their heads above the swamping water.

Fortunately after only a few minutes, the carriage had whirled to a stop. A large island divided the river and the carriage had snagged on a tangle of logs and other debris at the island's edge, pushing the vehicle into a slow, circular eddy nearer the bank.

The good news? They were no longer careening down the raging river, and Belle was quite sure neither she nor Anne had any broken bones. Just some scrapes and bruises.

The bad news? They were still too far from shore to attempt to reach it alone, not to mention the freezing cold water swirling around them.

"H-hold on, Anne," Belle ordered from her side of the carriage. "We c-can both hold on 'til help arrives."

Anne nodded her head, clutching her leather strap tightly. But Belle could see that the cold water was getting to her friend.

They had been in the water for what felt like hours.

"You st-still th-there, Henry?" Belle called to the young footman clinging to the outside of the carriage.

"Yes, madam," he replied, his voice muffled.

Henry had managed to crawl onto the carriage roof and shout for help. He said some passing farmers had noticed him and then disappeared, hopefully running for reinforcements. The current was too strong for him to attempt to get across alone and the debris surrounding the island made it impossible to land there.

Belle and Anne remained trapped in the carriage. Their waterlogged skirts would make clinging to the outside of the carriage fraught at best, not to mention the difficulty of having to crawl through the carriage window and scale the carriage without upsetting it. Their position on the snag of debris was tentative at best.

No, better to remain inside.

Belle wasn't sure how long they clutched to the inside of the carriage. Her wool pelisse thankfully provided some protection from the frigid water, but her chattering grew so bad, she struggled to keep her hold.

Anne, however, was in worse shape. Her pelisse wasn't as thick as Belle's and more of her body was submerged. Belle became truly alarmed as Anne's shivering subsided and a sort of strange lethargy took her over.

"Th-think warm thoughts, Anne," she encouraged. "India in the h-hot sun. A r-roaring f-fire—"

"Don't know how much longer I can manage," Anne whispered. "So tired. Must . . . let go."

"D-don't you d-dare!" Belle chattered. "You m-must remain strong."

"So tired." Anne's eyes drifted closed, her grip slipping.

"No! Anne!" Belle tried to shift, needing to move to support her friend, but even the slightest movement jostled the carriage, threatening to dislodge it.

"No!" Belle cried. "Anne! Do not fall asleep!"

Anne struggled to open her eyes, hands slipping further. She would sink into the water and drown if Belle didn't do something.

"Anne! L-look at m-me—"

A whoop rose from Henry above her. "Here! Over here!"

Then . . . Belle heard it.

The shouts of men and horses.

The noise roused Anne, who lifted her head in a groggy circle of motion.

"Anne, p-please!" Belle begged. "H-help is here. J-just a little longer."

Anne barely nodded, but she did use her remaining strength to clutch her leather strap tighter.

After an infinity of heartbeats, Belle heard voices outside the carriage.

"Tie off the carriage, man." Lord Stratton said. "It could break loose at any second. And if it does, I want to ensure it won't go downstream."

"Aye, my lord," an unknown man replied.

The carriage jostled as men moved around it, shouting orders.

"Can we get the carriage door open?" a painfully familiar voice asked.

Oh! Belle closed her eyes.

Lord Blake.

Blake was here.

He had come.

She didn't know whether to be thrilled or mortified.

Honestly, at the moment, Belle was too relieved to care. Later, she would allow herself to feel the full weight of embarrassed horror over this situation.

"No, the pressure from the water is too great. We'll have to go through the window," Stratton replied. "Fortunately, most of glass is already broken."

"Miss Rutger? Miss Heartstone?" Blake called.

"We're h-here," Belle said. "Anne is in d-dire need of help."

An eternity of minutes passed. Hearing the gentlemen talking outside, Belle surmised that they must be roped together and were being held up by a string of men stretching from the riverbank.

Finally, a gloved hand reached in and carefully removed the last of the glass from the window nearest Belle, pushing past the sodden window curtains.

Blake's face appeared, hair plastered to his head, rain streaming down his face, blue eyes hard, jaw clenched.

Their gazes locked. A muscle twitched in his cheek, but he gave nothing else away.

Belle swallowed.

No need to ask if he was still furious with her. If she had even an ounce of energy left, she would have blushed from the intense embarrassment of it all.

This poor man. All he wanted was to be rid of her.

"Do you think you can crawl through the window, Miss Heartstone?" he asked.

"Yes, b-but Anne is in worse shape." Belle half-turned, looking back at her companion who held on, but just barely. "I'll need to assist her through from this side."

Blake's jaw hardened further. "I didn't ask that, Miss Heartstone—"

"Anne needs help—"

"You are nearest to the door—"

"I won't leave her."

"I didn't ask for your opinion."

Oh!

"My lord, I manage thousands of people and make decisions that affect whole counties." Belle hissed. "It doesn't take a genius of probabilities to understand that I am more physically able to hang on here. I *will* survive. Anne, however, may not!"

Without waiting to hear his reply, Belle turned to Anne who was in danger of falling asleep again. Whatever the men had done, the carriage felt more stable. Belle moved across the carriage, her limbs shaking and numb in the cold water. Wrapping an arm around her friend's waist, Belle used the last of her energy to move her the few feet to the window. Stratton and another man appeared behind Blake. With Belle's help from inside, the men managed to pull Anne out.

Belle expected Blake to move off with Anne, but instead, Stratton and the footman supported her friend into the water.

"Miss Heartstone." Blake extended his hands.

Too tired to fight any longer, Belle took his hand. Despite the barely leashed tension of his face, his hands were infinitely careful with her. He reached through the window and wrapped an arm around her torso, easily lifting her out, sodden skirts and all.

For her part, Belle clutched to his neck, assisting with what strength she had left.

Once free of the carriage, Belle expected him to pass her off to one of the waiting men, but again, Blake surprised her. He kept her cradled in his arms. His expression may have been grim, but his arms told a different story. He clutched her to him with astonishing gentleness, as if she were treasured. As if she were something precious.

"Hold on tight," his voice rumbled in her ear, his tone clipped.

Belle nodded, not trusting her voice to speak.

Ah, Blake.

Even disliking her as he did, he couldn't allow her to suffer. He still had come to her rescue.

A line of men stretched from the riverbank, all tied to a rope and holding on to each other for support in the current.

She clung to Blake as they inched their way through the churning water back to shore, the men keeping them upright as they passed.

Dimly, Belle noted the strength in Blake's upper body, the hard muscles flexing underneath her hands, adjusting constantly to keep her protected and safe.

Finally they reached solid ground, sending a shout of relieved joy from the gathered crowd. Instead of setting her on her feet, Blake clutched her more tightly. He climbed the riverbank and carried her to a waiting carriage.

Stratton himself opened the carriage door. "Let us get you home and warm, Miss Heartstone."

"I d-don't want to be a bother, Lord Stratton," Belle protested as Blake set her carefully down in the waiting carriage. A hot brick was instantly placed at her feet, a wool blanket wrapped around her shoulders. "I'm h-happy to go to a l-local inn. I simply need to w-warm m-myself."

Belle held Blake's blue eyes as she said this, trying to communicate through her gaze that she had not intended this outcome, that she respected his right to privacy and a Belle-free existence.

Blake's eyes gave away little, their blue depths stormy and turbulent.

"Nonsense!" Lord Stratton shook his head. "I'm appalled you would even suggest such a thing. You are welcome at our home for as long as you wish to stay, Miss Heartstone. I will not hear another word on this matter."

"Yes, Miss Heartstone." Blake remained stony faced, but his tone was gentle. "You need rest. Let us care for you."

The door closed and Stratton rapped on the carriage, signaling the driver to move on.

Belle met Blake's gaze one last time as they pulled away, the intensity of his blue gaze scouring her soul.

Had he meant to include himself in his final statement, she wondered? Let *us* care for you?

It was a testament to her shattered state that she only fretted and analyzed his words for the ten minutes it took for the rocking motion of the carriage to lull her to sleep.

22

. . . You have been angry with me for days, and I find myself crying incessantly. When will you forgive me? Mamma says you are like a tea kettle when overset, prone to outbursts of words until you have let off your steam. Then common sense reigns again. So I ask you, brother mine, how steamy are you feeling today?

—*letter from Cecily to her brother, Colin,*
on the occasion of having ruined his favorite coat

Colin sat at dinner the following evening, contemplating the nearly comical turn of events of his week.

No, the past month, really.

He took a sip of wine. A burst of giggling laughter carried down the table. He set down his wine glass, forcibly not turning his head toward the sound.

The Desperate Debutantes were still *in situ* at Stratton Hall.

The Gold Miners and Lord Odysseus—who was unable to return due to the washed-out bridge—were not.

Colin met the gaze of Miss Rutger across the table, sitting beside the vicar, sternly telling himself to ignore the presence of Miss Heartstone seated at his right elbow.

The women were well, he was relieved to say.

However, the road to London was impassable, the bridge washed out and the rest a flooded bog.

Which left Colin stranded at Stratton Hall with five increasingly desperate debutantes, one woman's companion, and one duplicitous lady who had been, at times, an unsuccessful suitor, a business partner, his best friend and confidant, a damsel in distress, and a potential love interest . . .

. . . but was now no one to him.

His life had become a runaway carriage, and he worried he was now in a wild vehicle headed straight for disaster—

He winced at the metaphor. It was too soon to be casually thinking of runaway carriages.

Colin knew from past experience that it only took a little rain to turn a docile stream into a raging torrent. Though England was well used to rain, it usually came and went as gentle pattering, giving the ground and surrounding landscape ample time to lap it up. Violent cloudbursts where water poured from the heavens were a rarity, ironically.

The past storm, however, had swelled the river that ran through the town to monster proportions in a matter of hours, culminating in the moment when Miss Heartstone's carriage had attempted to cross the bridge, causing the entire structure to collapse. The swift current had quickly overflowed its banks, drowning the village green in three feet of water.

That first look at Belle Heartstone's face, ashen and desolate, peeking out from the interior of the sunken carriage, eyes desperate but hands still holding on to the leather strap, refusing to give in . . .

Her defiant insistence on helping Miss Rutger first, heedless of herself . . .

Then, the feel of her in his arms . . .

He ignored the involuntary vise that grasped his lungs at the thought. It was just—

Her body had been so slight. How had he not realized that her personality loomed larger than her actual person? But holding her against his chest, he had understood, first hand, how fragile she truly was. Her trembling arms clinging to his neck, her wet hair pressed against his cheek . . .

He swallowed back the surge of . . . feeling that wanted to swamp him.

Enough.

Yes, he was still attracted to Belle Heartstone. Despite her perfidy, she remained a beautiful woman. That's all this emotion communicated.

He would be damned if he allowed animal instinct to rule him in this.

Belle and Miss Rutger had stayed in their rooms the previous day. The doctor had visited and proclaimed that both women were in decent shape. They both simply needed warmth and rest.

He and Stratton managed to keep to the billiards room for most of the afternoon, but one could only play so many games of billiards in a day. The rain at least had let up, but the saturated ground was a boggy mess, making riding or walking a muddy chore.

However once he and Stratton left the protection of the billiards room to join the ladies for tea, the Desperate Debutantes had showed their true skill.

"Lord Blake, I have dropped my thimble. Could you help me find it?"

"Do you prefer the waltz or country dances, my lord? Perhaps, we should practice a bit."

"Lord Blake, I do believe I have an eyelash in my eye. No one appears to have keen enough eyesight to see it. Perhaps you could look as well?"

That inspired a whole host of similar problems.

"My wrist seems to be twinging. Can you feel it?"

"I fear I have twisted my ankle. Could you possibly carry me, Lord Blake?"

That last request had sent Colin scurrying for a footman and pleading a headache.

Damn and blast.

He was well familiar with the concept of *karma* from his time in India. A part of Hindu thought, *karma* referred to sowing the rewards of one's past deeds. Usually good deeds led to good rewards and vice versa. But given his current situation—stranded with a woman who had betrayed him and a bevy of misses who would delight in trapping him into marriage—he had to wonder what heinous thing he had done in the past to merit such a present.

Belle and Miss Rutger had both emerged this evening for dinner. Colin told himself that it was irrelevant, but his thundering heart seemed to disagree. He told himself she wasn't *that* beautiful. That her actions made him immune to her physical charms.

He was a terrible liar.

'Tis attraction, nothing more, he sternly reminded himself.

"Belle dear," Lady Stratton was saying, "have you told Lord Blake about your orphanage near Swindon? I must say, your stories about the plight of the children there have touched me to no end."

Lady Stratton obviously wished to act as matchmaker.

Hah!

If she only knew—

"Yes, Miss Heartstone," Colin said turning to her, "pray tell me about the orphanage."

His tone might have had a slightly mocking edge to it.

Belle raised her head. That first glance of her eyes gutted him, a quick blow to his mid-section. So many emotions swam in her gaze, it was hard to isolate just one.

Hurt, sorrow, remorse, resignation.

And why was *he* the one suddenly feeling like a cad?

No. He was the wronged party here. He refused to feel guilt for his actions.

"What do you wish to know, my lord?" Belle's voice remained steady, her smile brittle.

"Tell me how the orphanage came about," he managed to say.

He knew *exactly* how the orphanage had come to be. He had approved the plans himself.

Colin knew he was behaving poorly. Perhaps this *was* his karma.

To her credit, Belle merely straightened her spine and stared him down, that same brittle smile remaining firmly in place. Only the tightness around her eyes and the slight shake of her hand betrayed her unease.

Her clear distress did something odd to his breathing, like a vise wrapping around his heart and squeezing.

Colin gritted his teeth.

He disliked the sensation.

How could her pretty face also be that of LHF? How could his friend's voice be hers?

No matter how much he contemplated it, he struggled to put her into the role of LHF.

"It was inspired by a—" She broke off, clearly trying to reframe her thoughts. "—a friend." She swallowed and turned her head toward Lady Stratton. "A good friend, someone who I greatly admire and respect. Together we formulated the structure of the orphanage . . ."

Belle continued talking for several minutes, describing how the children were placed in family groups with 'parents' to watch over them. She praised his clever ideas and wisdom several times.

Not that anyone else in the room knew she was speaking of him.

Even more, her description reminded him of all the thought and effort they had both put into Hopewell Manor and Fyfe Hall. All of LHF's clever suggestions and ideas wrapped into a project with such noble heart—

Stop! He didn't want her words to soften his heart. To see the goodness and care showing through with every turn of phrase.

He didn't *want* to be charmed.

No, this little charade was theirs alone.

But as she spoke, Colin found himself disquieted.

It was just . . .

... he could *hear* LHF's ideas and turns of phrase in her speech. How had he missed it before? It seemed obvious now.

And what, if anything, was he to do about it?

THE NEXT DAY dawned bright and sunny, the air heavy with humidity from the evaporating damp.

Colin took advantage of the change in weather and spent several hours touring the estate with Stratton on horseback. They rode out to assess the damage from the storm, but aside from several water-logged fields, Stratton's lands had fared well.

The village, with its missing bridge and flooded streets, had not survived as neatly.

Also, as was typical, the waters were slow to subside. A gentleman had tried to ford the river on his horse earlier in the day and had nearly been swept to his death. Until further notice, the magistrate had banned all attempts to cross the river as, "We haven't the manpower to rescue every bloody fool who thinks he must return to London immediately."

Colin clearly wasn't going anywhere anytime soon.

After returning to the hall, Stratton retreated to his study, meeting with his steward, the magistrate, and the local mayor. The men wished to formulate a plan to repair the damaged bridge, at least temporarily. Until then, the town was effectively cut-off from London.

Colin had offered his help, but Stratton had waved him away with a not-so-subtle wink and a comment to, "Please spend some time with the ladies."

Which meant Colin was left to his own devices, ensconced at the dining table, eating lunch.

Belle and Miss Rutger were seated opposite him, murmuring things to each other. Colin pondered how the sunlight tangled in Belle's hair, catching highlights of gold and copper—

Damn and blast!

Enough!

No poetic thoughts about *hair*, of all things.

Belle Heartstone was a lying little minx who had abused his good nature with her clever wit and self-sacrificing ways and . . . ehr . . . generous charity work—

Gah!

Colin turned his head away from the pair.

Unfortunately, the Desperate Debutantes occupied the rest of the room. They were in fine form, chattering loudly, every third comment referring to the warm weather of the day and how they should best enjoy it.

Seeing his gaze turned their way, they pounced.

"My lord, we were so hoping you would join us for a game of boules on the back lawn after lunch," one of the Miss Jones-Buttons said, leaning forward. "I have heard it said that you are a prime bowler, and I am in desperate need of help."

The *desperate* part . . . he did not doubt.

As for the rest . . .

"What a brilliant idea! I shall speak with the footmen after lunch," another girl said, all but bouncing in her chair.

"Here, here," a third girl chimed.

Heaven preserve him. Visions of a decidedly uncomfortable afternoon swam before his vision.

Belle lifted her gaze to his, clearly not missing the alarm there.

Later, Colin would wonder why he said it. Surely, he hadn't simply panicked.

Or perhaps it was another rogue impression of Belle's charming beauty.

Or just his wayward heart catching his mouth at the wrong moment.

Regardless, he had to admit the idea had been his.

"I am terribly sorry to disappoint you, ladies." He smiled at the debutantes, before shifting his gaze back to Belle. "But Miss Heartstone has already agreed to a long stroll this afternoon." He gave Belle a look that hopefully said, *You owe me this much.* "But please enjoy your game of boules, ladies. It is a lovely day for it."

To her credit, beyond a small flaring of her eyes in surprise, Belle nodded.

She was intelligent; *that* he had never doubted.

"A walk! We would enjoy a walk, as well—" Miss Jones-Button began, voice eager and rushing.

"No, I won't hear of you cutting your enjoyment short on my account. You have spoken of nothing else but boules these past ten minutes. 'Tis clearly close to your hearts. Miss Heartstone and I will enjoy a more sedate afternoon, won't we, madam?"

A small, wistful smile tugged at Belle's lips. "Quite right, my lord." She turned to the ladies. "I wouldn't dream of interrupting the activities you already have planned."

Relief flooded Colin.

Why *relief* . . . he couldn't say.

Shouldn't he *dread* spending an afternoon with Belle? Why hadn't he made up some nonsense about Stratton needing his help after all?

Mmmmm.

Yes . . . why *hadn't* he said that? That would have been the better choice.

He could send Belle a note, begging off.

Or . . . he would tell her he had decided to walk alone.

But he knew those were all lies.

When faced with the choice, it appeared he would choose Belle every time.

And what was he to make of that?

23

. . . I cannot say the exact hour or moment when I realized I loved you in truth. All I know is that you are utterly threaded through my soul. My heart will always be tethered to yours . . .

—*note from Miss Heartstone to Lord Blake,*
written and sealed with a kiss, then tossed on the fire.

*I*t is simply a walk. Nothing more.

Belle sternly talked to herself, ordering her heart to, *Stop thundering this instant!* as she finished tying her sensible walking boots and tightened her bonnet on her head.

She knew Blake well enough to understand that he saw her as the lesser of two evils. That when faced with a choice between herself and a pack of title-hungry misses, he would choose her.

It wasn't a particularly flattering point.

Unfortunately, her miserable heart didn't care about the logic involved. It sang and skipped and raced with glee over the prospect of spending time with him—

Ugh.

It had been a most trying couple of days.

First, having to watch her friendship with Blake crumble.

Then, the carriage accident and becoming stranded here.

Moving on to watching Blake with the other women.

The worst part was seeing the distaste and anger in Blake's eyes every time he looked at her. She had looked upon spiders with less disgust.

For the record, Belle truly disliked spiders.

But . . . this was her penance. A vile physic that she needed to take and allow to run its course.

Blake's anger was well-justified.

She did not expect forgiveness.

She simply hoped that at some point she would be able to think about this entire interlude without devolving into noisy tears.

Anne bustled into the room.

"I intend to walk with you as a chaperone," she said, "but I will hold back."

"Are you quite up for it?" Anne had been slower to recover than Belle.

"Yes, I feel nearly back to normal today."

"I'm not sure I even need a chaperone at this point." Belle turned to her friend. "There is no need for such discretion, Anne. Lord Blake is not interested in spending time with *me*, per se—"

"I think you sell your own charms short, my dear."

"Anne, I grievously abused the poor man's trust—"

"Perhaps he wishes to mend fences?"

Belle gave a decidedly un-ladylike snort. "No. He wishes to avoid the Desperate Debutantes."

"I am not entirely convinced." Anne had on her skeptical eyebrows. "He could have avoided asking you on a stroll today."

"Perhaps, but—"

"I believe some discourse between you would be beneficial. You two need to clear the air."

"Anne—"

"Trust me."

Belle pursed her lips and snatched her gloves off the bed. She was quite certain Blake had no desire to 'mend fences' or 'clear the air.'

She half-expected him to cry off at the last moment.

But no. Lord Blake was waiting for her at the bottom of the grand staircase, top hat in hand, tapping his walking stick on the marble flooring. He looked painfully dashing in his fitted blue-green coat, Hessian boots gleaming.

He looked up as she approached, his expression . . . guarded? Beleaguered? Displeased?

How odd it was, Belle thought for not the first time, to know someone so well and yet know them so little at the same time.

"Shall we?" Blake swept a hand forward, toward the front door.

He did not, however, offer Belle his arm, as he had in times past.

Ah.

She bit her lip, sternly telling the sting in her eyes to *go away.*

His social chilliness was to be expected, intent on putting her in her place.

Again, not undeserved.

Belle swallowed and nodded.

They strode out the door and progressed along the gravel drive leading to the wood and lake beyond, the silence heavy between them. Anne walked behind, keeping a discreet distance.

Belle pinched her lips shut, angling her head to block the bright sun with the brim of her bonnet. If Blake didn't want to speak, she would not force him to do so.

They moved off the gravel drive and onto a smaller path that cut through the trees.

After few more minutes, Blake sighed.

"Thank you for accompanying me, Miss Heartstone. I appreciate you quickly going along with my scheme." His tone was stiff.

Belle's heart thundered.

His honest sensibilities wouldn't allow him to withhold praise where it was due. If anything, her heart broke a little more.

He came to her rescue at great personal risk, even though she had abused his trust. He thanked her for her small kindnesses.

Oh, Blake.

"'Tis the least I can do, my lord," she murmured. "I have always been sincere in my professions of friendship between us. I still consider you one of my best friends."

Belle bit her lip, instantly regretting her words.

"True friends don't keep enormous secrets—like, for example, their very *gender*—from each other," Blake snorted.

His words cut, lashing deeply.

Belle blink-blinked, willing the sting in her eyes away.

"Perhaps not, my lord," she agreed, swallowing back the justifications that crowded her throat. "I can only apologize for my behavior yet again."

Blake swung his walking stick, lopping the top off several dandelions. He seemed to find the exercise satisfying, as he instantly repeated the motion, attacking a clump of spent poppies.

Finally he stopped, whirling to face her.

"Why did you do it?" he hissed. "Why lie to me for so many years? You *knew* I assumed you to be a man. You *knew* that my assumptions about your identity were wrong. And You. Said. Nothing!"

Belle swallowed.

Mmmm.

So kindness aside, he was clearly still a little angry.

Scratch that.

A lot angry.

How could she defend her decisions? He was justified. She deserved his scolding.

"You are right," she said. "I should have, at the very least, indicated that you were mistaken in your assumptions—"

"Yes, you should have!" He thwacked another dandelion before abruptly turning on his heel and continuing onward.

Belle followed behind. They moved into the deep shade of the woods. A quick glance behind showed Anne strolling far off, barely close enough to chaperone. Sunlight glinted off the lake, sending shards of light through the trees.

Blake went only a short way before he stopped and stomped back to her.

"I trusted you!" His face was mere inches from hers, eyes wide and shooting sparks.

"I know," Belle nodded.

"I told you things I have never told another soul!"

"I know. I did the same."

"How could you act so brazenly?!"

Unbidden, Belle felt her own temperature rise.

Enough was enough.

Yes, she had lied to him.

Yes, she had betrayed their friendship.

How many different ways could he call her out on these points?

He didn't need to devolve into a complete arse over it.

"As I said, the entire situation got away from me!" Belle threw an arm upward. "You weren't supposed to write me so prolifically. You weren't supposed to befriend me!"

"You cannot seriously be accusing *me* of this deception!"

"No, of course not. My actions are my own. But I had not anticipated you wishing to further our acquaintance. And by the time I realized that we were going to be friends in earnest, the point for mentioning my age and gender had long passed."

"Usually one *leads* with age and gender, not the other way around."

"When would you have had me tell you, my lord? After you accepted my bank draft and had set off for India? Would you have thrown my money back in my face at that point? Of course not! That would have left you stranded in Ceylon."

Blake pinched his lips together, a stern slash in his face.

But he had lit a fire underneath her, and Belle refused to be snuffed out.

"Should I have told you after that first shipment of spices came in? No? Perhaps, I should have derailed your talks with the tribesmen and endangered your life?" Belle snapped her fingers. "No, wait! Maybe I should have told you right before we opened Hopewell Manor. I could have turned scores of veterans and their families out into the street—"

"Enough!" Blake barked.

"I valued what we were doing. I valued our friendship. I didn't want you to abandon your dreams and goals because of *my* unfortunate gender."

Blake scoffed. "That's a convenient excuse you tell yourself. Your gender wouldn't have stopped me—"

"Perhaps, but you would have felt honor-bound to refuse my financial capital once you knew. I didn't want your sensibilities as a gentleman to stop you from succeeding. It's what a good friend does!"

He reared back, brows drawing down into a solid line, expression flinching as if her words had struck a sensitive spot.

They regarded each other for a tense moment, their breathing loud in the forest hush.

"A true lady would never stoop to such behavior," he finally spat out. Blake turned on his heel and stomped onward.

Oh!

Belle barely resisted a hiss of outrage.

His words were a glove-slap to the face.

Arse-headed, imbecilic, stubborn . . . Argh!

The green of the forest rushed by as Belle hurried after him. His long strides and her cumbersome skirts—hems dipping into the damp and mud of the path—made it nearly impossible to catch up to him.

Grrrr. Yet another disadvantage that women faced!

Finally, she stopped and hurled her words at his retreating back, chest heaving, hands fisted. "Over and over, I tried to tell you this past week! You silenced me every time. I would never dream of impugning your honor, my lord. How dare you insult *mine!*"

That got his attention.

He whirled back to her, stomping closer until she could see the whites of his eyes, the flare of his nostrils.

Belle folded her arms and stood her ground, craning her neck up to meet his gaze.

"You are a woman! You have no honor!" he said.

OH!

"How dare you! I am a person, too! And, more to the point, I have *always* dealt with you most honorably!"

Blake at least had the decency to slightly flinch at her words. "Miss Heart—"

"Your mother, God rest her soul, would turn over in her grave to hear you say such a thing! She raised you better than this—"

"How dare you bring my mother into this argument!"

"You do not deny my sentiment!"

"My mother did not tell falsehoods."

"Perhaps." Belle took a steadying breath. "But from all you have told me, she was a remarkable woman who didn't stand by tradition. She saw women as people of valuable worth. I do not doubt that she considered my sex to have honor. I thought she taught you to do the same—"

"Don't you dare twist my mother's teachings to justify your poor behavior!"

"You yourself all but *ordered* me to abandon societies niceties that morning in Hyde Park! Now you cry foul when I have done so!"

"That is not the point of my anger, madam. You choosing to manage your *own* business affairs is admirable. You inserting yourself into *mine*"—his voice rose again—"and then neglecting to inform me of your youth, gender, and . . . and *beauty* is not!"

He turned away from her, stomping onward, slashing his walking stick at the brush as he went.

Belle stood, frozen in place, lungs heaving, heart racing, hand pressed to her mouth.

Her poor brain sputtered and spun, trying desperately to understand what Blake had just said.

You neglecting to inform of your beauty . . .

Surely she had simply misheard? Surely he didn't find her . . . beautiful? Did he?

Did he?!

A glance behind her showed that Anne had stopped, pretending to examine a patch of wild roses nestled in the trees. When their eyes connected, Anne flapped her hand at Belle. *Go on. Follow him.*

Dazed, Belle nodded and started up the path after Blake.

COLIN SLASHED ANOTHER dandelion with his walking stick, throat thick, tongue tangled.

Why was he so furious over Belle's betrayal? Why did the mere sight of her wide brown eyes and lush mouth set him to raging?

She had no right to be so beautiful.

She had no right to own so many pieces of his soul.

He sliced again with his stick.

That *some* of her points were true grated even more.

That dry part of his brain pointed out that she was right. If she had told him about her gender early on, he would have pulled out from their joint venture, feeling honor-bound as a gentleman to do so. All their future success would have been snuffed before it ever began.

But . . .

But—

Dammit!

He hated the morass of confused *feeling* that tumbled through his chest.

All too soon he heard her footsteps closing in on him.

He ignored her as she drew abreast of him again. Not that he could see more than the tip of her nose and the curve of her lips extending past the edge of her poke bonnet.

The fact that it was a darling pert nose and soft-looking lips only stoked his anger.

They strolled in silence, emerging from the trees and beginning to walk around the lake. The rain had swollen the water, causing it to overflow in places. Ahead, the dock where they had launched their boats the week previous was partially underwater now. Fortunately, the path was more or less intact.

"Is it possible to call a truce for a minute?" Belle asked, voice taut and restrained.

"A truce?"

"Yes. There are many items to discuss. Regardless of the problems between us personally, we do hold the lives of thousands of people in our collective hands. It would behoove us to move beyond ourselves for a moment or two."

Colin grunted.

He didn't wish to be polite and accommodating. He wanted to fume and slash a few hundred more dandelions.

But . . . as he was an adult, no matter how childish the current situation made him feel or how petulant Belle rendered him . . .

He nodded.

"Let me start with the worst," Belle grimaced. "I have reports of some improprieties involving the manager of the factory outside Bristol—"

"Who? Michael Brown?"

"Yes. I received a letter last month from the village midwife, and she recounted some disturbing reports regarding Mr. Brown and several of the village girls."

"Brown has been a most conscientious manager. His reports are detailed and thorough—"

"I do not disagree, but a talent for management does not preclude the man from also being a lech and using his position of authority to demand *other* services from his laborers."

Colin frowned. "Why are we to assume the worst of Mr. Brown based on a midwife's letter?"

"Of course, I agree. I hired a Runner to look into it—"

"You seem quite fond of using them." Bitterness laced his tone.

If she noticed it, she did not respond.

"I received the report from the Runner last week, and he confirmed the midwife's words," she said.

A sick feeling settled in Colin's stomach. "Mr. Brown preyed on the women under his employ?"

"Yes. Many were not willing participants, but Mr. Brown tied their continued employment to his demands, so most felt they had no other choice."

Colin closed his eyes. "How despicable. All of our other managers have been men of honor. How did we get it wrong with Mr. Brown?"

A long silence greeted his statement. Long enough that Colin stopped, turning to Belle.

She paused with him, raising her eyes to meet his. She licked her lips.

Briefly, Colin remembered letters in the past, small asides that LHF would mention.

I have found it necessary to change managers for our York investments . . .

The captain of the merchant ship Marigold *has decided to seek employment elsewhere . . .*

"Mr. Brown is not the first, is he?" Colin asked.

Belle shook her head. "Not even remotely. We actually employ a midwife at each factory who looks for this very thing. I am decidedly determined to keep the women in my employ safe from such harassing behavior. Their lives are hard enough, as is."

Colin bit back the curse that threatened to escape. His blood roared.

He knew that some men behaved like this. He had heard enough from his mother and sisters, not to mention the atrocities he had witnessed as a soldier. But he vehemently recoiled from knowing that his own agents had been participating in such things.

Worse, Miss Heartstone was a gently-bred *lady*. That she had to so actively work to protect other women—

He whirled around, not trusting himself to speak for a moment or two. He switched his walking stick once, twice. Belle instantly fell back into step with him. They circled around a flooded portion of the path, hopping from rock to rock in an effort to keep their shoes dry. Colin leaped to drier ground and then turned back intent on helping Belle, but she had already nimbly jumped crossed.

"You shouldn't even know of such things," he bit out, "much less discuss them with *men*—"

"*I* am the problem in this situation? *My* reaction, not Mr. Brown's behavior?"

Yes, why *was* he fixated on that point? He stopped again, placing his hands on his hips.

"Why was none of this brought to my attention?" he countered, waving a hand. "You never once mentioned these sorts of issues in your letters?"

"It would have taken a *year* to ask your advice and receive an answer. For items that needed more immediate action, I simply made the decisions myself. That is part of being a business partner."

Colin ground his teeth. He knew LHF was doing that. Colin had done the same thing himself in India.

But now he knew that it had been a *young woman* all along dealing with such grim decisions. And somehow that changed everything. He glared down at her.

"I should have known. I should have been the one to write those letters of dismissal, not you."

Belle gasped, head recoiling. "Why? Because I'm a *woman*? Because you consider me incapable of dealing with difficult situations?"

"Yes!" Colin practically shouted and then realized what he had said. "I mean, no—"

"You *cannot* be sincere in your protestations. Are we right back where we started?" She gazed up at him, eyes flaring wide. "You are supposedly a champion of the rights of women, remember?"

"I am!"

He was. It was just . . . somehow he wasn't quite as progressive when it came to *his* woman.

Wait—

No.

No, Belle was *not* his woman.

Damn but she had him so confused!

She continued on. "I must be honest, my lord, your words over the last hour have sounded anything but encouraging of my capabilities—"

"I do not doubt your abilities, madam," he managed to say through clenched teeth.

He simply needed to find some clarity with regards to her.

Belle was not done. "Do you? Sincerely? I stand by what I said earlier. Remember all those lessons at your mother's feet?"

He paused, clenching his jaw, nostrils flaring. Belle had struck true.

She read as much in his expression. "Do you still believe the words you parroted back to me that morning so long ago in Hyde Park?" She was ticking points off on her gloved fingers now. "Women are not even *persons* under the law once we're married. We are not educated, as a rule. Horses have more legal rights than a married woman."

"Belle . . . pardon, I mean, Miss Heartstone—"

But she was still talking, arms gesturing wildly. "Women go through horrific pain and uncertainty at every point in their lives, Blake. They give birth to children. They raise the next generation and worry and fret. The vast majority of us influence events through the meager indirect means we have, which takes strategy and verve. Women, as a whole, deal with more ugliness than men on a regular basis, but we are not allowed to even *own* that much because men deem such capabilities 'unladylike.'"

Belle pulled ahead of him, feet eating up the ground, shoulders heaving.

Colin said nothing, mind a jumbled mess. Part of him knew he deserved her blistering set-down. But another part fumed that she had put herself into situations like this one with Mr. Brown.

But . . . she had called him Blake. He had called her Belle. It seemed this argument was blasting through all the barriers between them.

He started after her, his walking stick swinging.

She reached the partially flooded dock and the large puddle surrounding it. Gathering her skirts, she prepared to leap onto the dry portion of the dock to circumvent the standing water. But the distance was far greater than the one she jumped earlier.

Grimacing, Colin held out a hand to her, offering to help steady her balance.

Belle paused, glaring at his hand before huffing. "I am a woman. I can solve this problem without a man's help."

"I'm not offering my help because you are a woman. I offer it because your legs are too short to bridge the gap."

She sniffed.

"Take my hand, madam. You don't want to tumble into the lake."

She ignored his hand and took a hopping jump up onto the dock. Of course, her heavy skirts hampered her movements, causing her to pitch precariously to the side.

Tossing aside his walking stick, Colin instantly leapt into action. He sprang onto the dock, wrapping an arm around Belle's waist, heaving her backwards just as she stumbled toward the water.

"You stubborn fool." He pulled her upright and, in the process, ended up with her in his arms, her chest flush against his, her hands resting on his shoulders.

Heat flared between them.

"Of course, I'm stubborn," she snapped. "It's what makes me an excellent business woman."

"I know that! But take my help when it is offered!"

"You are not my master to decree when I should do something. You are not my father or my brother or my husband, so you have *no* say—"

Colin only barely resisted the urge to shake her.

And then her words truly sank in.

You are not my father or my brother or my husband . . .

That lack of any real claim over her bothered him.

Belle Heartstone was *his*. A strange sense of possessiveness filled him. Not in a covetous, bilious way, but more of that sense of rightness.

Of course, she chose that moment to finally lift her head. She fixed him with her watery gaze. Pools of rich chocolate. Her palms seared him where they touched his shoulders, scorching brands.

Abruptly, all his anger morphed and changed, metamorphosing into something infinitely more warm-blooded.

Damn but she was beautiful. Color flooding her cheekbones, her eyes sparking with fire—

No!

No more poetry.

She bit her lip, defiantly meeting his gaze, her voice quiet. "You don't get to tell me what to do."

"I know." Was that deep husky tone his own?

"I do not belong to you. I belong to no one."

"I know." His voice fell to a whisper.

But . . . what if she did belong to him? Not an ownership sort of thing, but what if he continued to pursue her?

The thought filtered through the addled mush of his brain.

No! He instantly rejected the thought. *She lied to me. She deceived me.*

But the idea remained, persistently stuck in the forefront of his mind.

LHF was his *best* friend.

Belle was LHF.

Ergo . . .

It didn't escape his notice that Belle wasn't precisely eager to escape his embrace either. She stood still in the circle of his arms, gaze guarded.

How could this woman be LHF in the end?

The elderly business partner who had led him to success with keen insights. The gentle humor and kind intelligence and heart of a lion—all in the form of a young slip of a woman.

Who said women couldn't do anything they put their minds to? Here was the ultimate proof. Somewhere in his anger and betrayal, profound admiration lurked.

"You are better than this anger over my actions with Mr. Brown and all the rest," she said, tone tight. "You should be cheering me on, not castigating me. You have not been like this in your interactions with other women. Why are you singing a different tune now?"

Colin clenched his teeth. The truth of her words grated.

Why did he care now? Was it because she had betrayed him?

Or was it more that he had begun to think of her as *his* lady that changed the dynamic?

Belle wasn't done. She stepped out of his arms, putting space between them, hugging her waist. "That morning in Hyde Park . . . you altered the course of my life for the better in a matter of minutes. You opened my eyes to what my life *could* be. Given the situation, you did not need to be so kind. I was grateful. Investing in your trip to India was simply the only way I could think of to adequately thank you. I only ever wanted your happiness." She sniffed, voice barely a whisper. "I truthfully didn't mean for the entire situation to be carried so far."

Silence hung between them.

"Why LHF?" he asked.

She smiled. Not a true smile. More like a distant cousin of one.

"It was you who named me. That morning."

He angled his head. *Go on.*

"I will forever remember your words: 'God has granted you wings. 'Twould be a shame if you never learned how to fly.' And so that has been my aim all these years. I have been learning how to fly."

"LHF."

The simplicity of her statement moved him, deeply.

"Precisely. I chose to heed your advice." Belle brushed past him on the dock, intent on the path opposite, lifting her skirts as she went. "You don't get to decide *now* that you don't like how I have chosen to go about fly—AHH!"

Belle's muddy, slippery boots slid out from underneath her, sending her pitching sideways, tumbling into the lake.

Desperately, Colin lunged for her, reaching for her arm.

Her eyes met his, wide and startled.

Their hands connected, but his strength was no match for her weight and momentum.

He followed her head-first into the water.

24

. . . My lord, I humbly implore you to reply. I do not know if you are receiving my letters. The magistrate is now threatening transportation for the orphans, which is absurd, but I do not have the authority to do anything about it . . .

> *—letter from Mr. Sloan to Lord Blake,*
> *languishing with all the others, undelivered*

The cold water shocked the air out of Belle's lungs. She floundered, stroking her arms, trying to right herself. She broke the surface, gasping.

A strong hand wrapped around her elbow, pulling her upright, water pouring off her pelisse. Coughing, she floundered and then got her feet underneath herself.

The water was actually only waist deep.

Still coughing, Belle staggered sideways and would have fallen over again had Blake not had a firm grip on her. His fine coat and boots were drenched, his hat bobbing away on the surface of the lake.

"Are you quite all right?" Blake asked, his blue eyes wide with concern, hair plastered to his head, water streaming off his body.

Belle brought her gaze back to his, nodding her head as she continued to violently cough.

"Are you sure?" he asked.

She nodded again.

Frowning, he carefully helped her step through the muddy lake bottom and stagger ashore.

Wheezing, Belle glanced down the path to see Anne. Her friend was doubled over with laughter, sitting on a bench. The wretch.

Belle collapsed onto a sunlit spot of grass along the shoreline. Pulling her bonnet off her head, she began to wring the water out of her sodden skirts.

For his part, Blake waded back out into the lake to retrieve his hat. After a few minutes slog, he rejoined Belle on the bank, water sluicing off him as he walked out of the water. He hung his hat on an obliging tree branch.

He struggled out of his drenched coat, peeling it down his arms, leaving him in waistcoat and shirtsleeves. His fine linen shirt had plastered to his chest, rendering the garment utterly transparent. He turned away from Belle and twisted the water out of his coat.

Belle sternly ordered her eyes to look away from the clearly defined muscles she could see working in his shoulders.

But as it was a fairly glorious sight, her eyes stubbornly refused to obey her.

So Belle stared, transfixed, as she removed the pins from her hair and began to wring the water out of it.

Blake finished getting as much water as possible out of his jacket and turned back to her. His gaze racked her up and down, eyes searching.

Was it her imagination or did his eyes linger on her hair and the dripping skirts clinging to her legs?

Belle's teeth began to clatter. Even with the warm sun, being dripping wet was cold business.

"Here." Blake sat down beside her, wrapping his coat over her shoulders. "It's wet but it will provide some warmth."

"T-thank you," she chattered, pulling through her hair with trembling fingers, meeting his gaze.

He sat close to her. So close she could see herself reflected in his pupils and feel the heat of his body. All of her longed to cuddle closer to him.

She wisely stayed put.

The poor man was simply struggling to accept her actions as a human being. He most certainly was not interested in anything *more* from her.

"You have some, uhm . . ." He made a wiping motion down the side of his face.

"Pardon?" Belle asked.

"You have mud on your cheek," he said more clearly.

Oh!

On a positive note, the scalding blush currently scouring every inch of her body was effectively warming her up.

Belle used the dripping hem of her pelisse to wipe her cheek.

Blake surveyed her. "You missed a spot."

Without asking permission, Blake took her pelisse from her hands and, very gently, wiped a section of her face near her ear. His fingers brushed her skin in the process, leaving a burning brand in its wake. He tucked a wayward curl around her ear before handing the pelisse edge back to her.

Belle swallowed.

His eyes dipped to her mouth.

Later, she would wonder if she had imagined Blake canting toward her. The tilt in his head, the dilation of his pupils—

Was he truly leaning in for a kiss?

But he pulled back abruptly and relaxed back onto his hands, shaking his head.

The moment lost.

"We make a fine pair, you and I?" He motioned down his legs, indicating their sodden state.

"I'm so sorry I dragged you in with me."

He shrugged. "I have always tended to be the one following you into schemes, not the other way around."

A beat.

"That is true," she said. "I was the one who suggested we invest in Kashmir goats."

"Even though they smelled horrid and the price was exorbitant."

"Yes, but it paid off. Our cashmere shawls have been the Season's must-have for years now."

"You were the one who always went on and on about bonnet ribbons."

"They *are* monumentally important."

Colin groaned. "In hindsight, I was an idiot not to realize you were a woman."

Silence hung between them.

Abruptly, Blake chuckled. "The look on your face as you fell into the water—"

Belle smiled, a giggle escaping. "You mean this?"

She flared her eyes wide and pulled her mouth into a round 'O' while windmilling her arms.

Blake laughed harder. "Exactly! You screeched like a banshee."

"Your expression was so startled." Belle mimicked his stunned surprise. "Like you could scarcely believe that the Marquess of Blake should have to suffer such an indignity!" She laughed with him.

Blake mimed his flailing, panicked look. "I suppose I didn't expect you to take my admonition to fly quite so literally."

Belle laughed harder, stuffing a hand over her mouth, trying to keep it in. But the harder she fought, the more vigorous her laughter, until both she and Blake were guffawing in great huffs, tears rolling down their cheeks. The laughter was quick-silver in her veins, lightening the grim desperation that had sat there for weeks.

Eventually, Blake wiped his tears away, still chuckling. "Blast it all, Belle, I'm still furious with you for not telling me you were LHF. How can I be laughing with you, too?"

Belle sighed, swiping at her own cheeks. She studiously ignored the thrill she felt at his use of her given name. "If it makes you feel better, I seem to inspire such feelings in others, as well."

He shook his head, resting his forearms on his knees. "What am I to do about this?" He motioned at the space between them.

"I don't know, my lord. Must something be done?"

"I don't know," he parroted her words. "I honestly don't know."

COLIN WAS STILL pondering the conundrum of Belle Heartstone the following afternoon.

The post had finally been able to reach Stratton Hall via Bristol, saddle bags, and a pair of stubborn donkeys. An avalanche of delayed correspondence followed. Stratton's butler had resorted to bringing it to him in a punch bowl instead of the more customary silver tray.

Colin ensconced himself in the library, reading letter after letter from Mr. Sloan and his own man of affairs, dismay growing. Phrases leapt out at him:

Fyfe Hall has already seen the arrival of forty children . . .

I have reached an impasse with the magistrate . . .

I fear the orphaned children will be cast into the street and set adrift . . .

He had scarcely finished the final one when the door snicked open.

Belle hastily entered and cautiously pushed the door nearly closed.

"I assume you've received the same news." She waved a sheaf of papers at him.

"Fyfe Hall and the magistrate?"

"Oh! Well, yes. That, too, I suppose." She bustled over to him, motioning for him to sit back down. "I was referring to the problem of transport out of Lisbon. As it's a logistics issue, I wished to confer with you about it."

Belle shuffled through the papers, rereading bits here and there. Unwittingly, Colin acknowledged that she was quite adorable when she read correspondence. A dent appeared between her eyebrows and her lips moved, silently repeating the occasional word.

Colin was puzzled, however.

"I would have thought you would be more concerned about Fyfe Hall," he said.

She raised her gaze to his, brow drawn down. "I am most concerned about Fyfe Hall. I leave within the hour to address the issue; I simply wished to discuss the Lisbon matter with you before I departed."

It was Colin's turn to frown. "You will journey to Fyfe Hall yourself?"

She nodded, most matter-of-factly.

Colin nearly sat back in . . . what? Dismay? Apprehension? Surprise? "How will you address the issue with the magistrate? Surely you don't deal with such things yourself? It's unlikely the magistrate will listen to an unmarried woman."

Though if the man *would* listen to a woman, Colin would put his money on Belle.

Belle tipped her head. "Of course the magistrate will not listen to me. I will send word ahead to have my man of affairs in Bristol meet me at Fyfe Hall with several assistants. It may take a day longer, but—"

"The matter has already been left too long."

She rolled her eyes in clear exasperation. "I understand that, Blake, but this is the only way I can accomplish the task. It's what I always do—"

"I had already determined to leave for Swindon immediately."

Belle paused, staring at him. She blinked, two slow sweeps of her eyelashes fluttering up and down.

Silence.

"Oh," the breath escaped her.

"You appear surprised." Colin couldn't keep the amusement from his tone. "Why should my journeying to Fyfe Hall surprise you?"

More silence.

Belle swallowed, expression still dazed. "To be honest, my lord, the thought hadn't even occurred to me."

"You hadn't thought to ask your business partner to help deal with this problem? Fyfe Hall is just as dear to me as it is to you. We created these charitable organizations together—"

"Yes . . . but . . . I never think to have help. I always do these things—" Belle broke off, blinking more rapidly now, looking quickly away.

Alone. Colin finished her sentence in his head.

I always do these things alone.

What was it Belle had said yesterday?

I belong to no one.

Oh!

He had been so blind to the obvious.

In his head, LHF was a man. Colin had simply assumed that his business partner had a life that he never mentioned: a wife, children, parents, friends, etc.

Belle had precisely . . . who? Miss Rutger, surely.

But who else? Hadn't LHF mentioned a mother once or twice? Something about helping his—no, *her*—mother build a large house, mostly to keep her mother occupied.

Oh, Belle.

A painful rawness settled into the back of his throat.

"Who—" Colin began. "Who cares for you, Belle?"

Belle shook her head.

"Your greatest fear is being left alone," he whispered.

A tear tumbled onto her clenched hands. She did not wipe it away.

"But you already are alone," he continued.

Understanding scoured through him, leaving a fragile sort of tenderness in its wake.

Belle Heartstone was accustomed to having the enormous weight of their joint affairs entirely on her slim shoulders. She was used to confiding in no one.

Except, perhaps, her business partner and proclaimed close friend.

And even that had been taken from her, in his anger and betrayal.

"How long have you been alone, Belle?"

She sniffed before letting out a long, slow breath. "A very long time." She lifted her eyes to his, pools of damp earth. "Since my father's death."

"Ah."

A pause.

Belle notched her chin higher. "I do not need your pity, sirrah. My life is full of friends."

A beat.

"Truly bosom friends?" He had to ask it. "Friends who know the extent of the business you run with me?"

A pause. "No," she whispered. "Besides yourself, only two others meet that criteria."

Anne and Mr. Sloan, he supposed.

He was starting to see why she had clung to his friendship long past the point of propriety. And why did that thought cause the pang in his heart to fluff itself out and grow several sizes?

She shook her head, as if banishing her tears. "Friends aside, I do much good. I find our charity work enormously satisfying."

"But not as satisfying as possibly having a family of your own?"

She bit her lip, not denying his words.

"Lord Odysseus?" He had to ask it.

She did not misunderstand his question. "Among others," she shrugged. "If I wish to have a family of my own, I must marry."

Colin nodded. The betting books at White's had it right.

She would marry this year. Some other man would have her at his side, would know her thoughts, would hear her laughter.

The thought made him want to pummel something.

"Why have you not married until now?" he asked. "You are somewhat notorious for refusing an entire army of men."

She laughed, a sad, breathy sound. "I suppose I have just been waiting for the right person."

As far as answers went, that one was lackluster. She looked back at the letters in her lap. "You will truly go to Swindon and help our poor orphaned children?"

Colin knew that she had said the words without conscious thought, but her phrasing stuck with him.

Our poor orphaned children. As if he and she were parents of a large brood. Which, he supposed, they were in a way.

"Yes, Belle. Count on me. We'll sort this together," he replied.

"Thank you."

"No, thank you. I shall write when I have word."

25

To LHF
Swindon, England
June 26, 1823

Dear Friend,

Silence your fears. All is set to rights with Fyfe Hall. I called upon the magistrate and was able to allay his concerns. As things turned out, I had served with his son in the Belgium action, so we had much to discuss. His son perished at Waterloo, so once I explained the full extent of our aims with Hopewell Manor and Fyfe Hall—how we help veterans, as well as children—he was more amenable to our schemes.

As for the matter of Mr. Brown and our factory, I have set out from Swindon to resolve the matter, as Bristol is close at hand here. I shall report when I have news.

I have attached several sheets of notes about the transport problem in Lisbon. Please let me know if you approve of my plans. I value your input.

Still yours in friendship,
Blake

P.S. *Least you heap recriminations upon my head, I did think of you as I completed these tasks and the effort you must have gone through to address these problems over the past seven years. I would be ungrateful to not say thank you. So . . . thank you.*

P.S.S. *I miss our riddles.* There is a word and six letters it contains. Take one away and twelve is what remains. What word is it?

P.S.S.S. *No cheating with Miss Rutger this time.*

To Lord Blake
London, England
June 29, 1823

Dear sir,

Thank you for your letter. I sincerely appreciate you addressing the issue with Mr. Brown. It has weighed heavily upon my mind.

As you can see, I am returned to London. Repairs were made to the bridge, and Anne and I were able to leave the Desperate Debutantes behind. I have enclosed some correspondence from Mr. Sloan regarding an opportunity outside Manchester. There is talk of building a steam railway. I would like to invest in this new technology, but I understand if you still wish to separate our business interests. Perhaps we can meet to discuss particulars when you return to Town.

I also must admit to some confusion. I had thought you would feel honor-bound to cease all correspondence with me. I enjoy our letters enormously, but do not wish to encroach on your sensibilities.

Your true friend,
LHF

P.S. I must admit that I have missed our riddles, as well. I shall place my fingers in my ears and sing, 'la, la, la' if Anne tries to intervene. (Secretly, I think she enjoys the riddles more than both of us).

To answer yours: Dozens

Mine: What has a face and hands but not a nose or arms?

P.S.S. Thank you for your kind words. Though it has taken some creativity over the years, I have tried my best to resolve all problems, no matter how thorny. Thank you for your trust in me.

To LHF
Bristol, England
July 3, 1823

Dear Friend,

The sun shines hot here. I hope your day in London is bright and sun-filled. I have enclosed documents regarding our latest shipment from Calcutta.

As for why I continue to write you, I have moved past my initial shock over your identity and have realized that true friendship should not simply be tossed aside when I discovered that my supposed elderly friend was in fact a pretty, young woman. I am still struggling to re-align the past seven years of my life, but for some reason, when I am writing you, it feels all set to rights again.

For now, I am content to continue as partners in our various business interests.

Take that statement as you will.

Sincerely,
Blake

P.S. A clock! Hah! You nearly stumped me with that one. Are you sure Miss Rutger isn't helping you?

26

. . . It was an unexpected pleasure to see you in Hyde Park this afternoon. Lord Odysseus looked well. Though were those swans he was weeping over? Do you go out driving with him often? And does he always cry over poultry?

—letter sent from Lord Blake to Miss Heartstone,
dated July 12, 1823

C olin stood aside, allowing the noise of the ballroom to wash over him. Lady Atterson's annual ball was well underway. Couples moved through a stately minuet on the dance floor. Women gathered around the edges, whispering behind fans. A loud series of whoops and groans drifted out from the card room.

Colin wasn't entirely sure why he had come. He was behind in tending to his business affairs. He had a mid-morning meeting with his solicitor the next day, and a late-night ball would not afford him much sleep.

But . . . Cecily had insisted he accompany her and George and—here he was even more honest with himself—he hoped Belle might be in attendance. He knew he simply needed to call upon her.

But calling upon her would be a marked attention. And did he want to be numbered among her swains now?

He had seen his odds listed in the betting book at White's.

Apparently, the bloods of the *ton* did not hold him in high favor.

A burst of laughter drew his eye sideways. A group of men, each more dashingly dressed than the next, stood around a figure. The Gold Miners in their element.

No, wait. There she was in the middle of them.

Belle Heartstone.

She looked impossibly lovely this evening in soft rose satin, long evening gloves extending up her arm. Her hair piled high and studded with her usual pearls, another strand of pearls around her slender neck.

She smiled and nodded at something one of the men had said. Was her smile forced? Why was she allowing the Gold Miners to pay such attention to her—

And that's when Colin realized. The men around her were not the Gold Miners, per se. *That* group of men were young fortune hunters.

No, the men around Belle tonight were slightly older—the more mature gentlemen that a man would prefer to see his daughter marry.

Lord Odysseus, of course, was closest to her, leaning in and whispering in her ear. She laughed.

Something lodged in the back of Colin's throat. It tasted like panic, but surely that was the wrong emotion here.

Yes, she was his friend, but that didn't mean he was interested in her as anything more than a friend.

A business partner was all well and good. Belle had always been an excellent business partner. A wife was something else entirely. He was not interested in Belle Heartstone as a wife. Not anymore, at least—

"If you watch her any more intently, my friend, you are liable to set tongues wagging."

Colin startled at the wry voice at his elbow. Turning his head, he met the gaze of Lord Stratton, grinning impudently and holding a tumbler full of a mahogany-colored liquid.

"Stratton. You are returned to town, it appears."

"Of course. Lady Stratton insisted on seeing how your little drama plays out."

"My drama?"

Stratton lifted his glass in Belle's direction, waggled his eyebrows, and then took a sip of his drink which looked suspiciously like Scotch.

Damn. Colin was quite sure he would give away an entire shipload of tea for a solid three fingers of Scotch right now.

"How did you come by that at a ball?" Colin's eyes narrowed, pointing at the drink. "I thought there was only watered-down ratafia on hand."

"I am accounted a close friend of Lord Atterson. It comes with certain . . . privileges." Stratton took a deliberately loud sip. "He has a well-stocked liquor cabinet."

Colin shook his head.

Stratton sipped again.

"You are a cruel, cruel man," Colin said.

Stratton shrugged. "Perhaps, but I am hardly heartless."

With a flourish, Stratton produced another tumbler from behind his back.

Colin was quite sure he heard angel song and hosannas.

"You looked like you needed it," was all his friend said.

Colin nodded in glum agreement.

Both men turned to study the gathered crowd, slowly sipping their Scotch whiskey.

Of course, Colin's eyes went right back to studying Belle.

Did she *have* to lean toward Lord Odysseus as he spoke? And had she put gold dust in her hair? What else would cause her curls to sparkle so in the candle light?

And had he actually just compared her hair to gold dust?

Stratton chuckled.

"Pardon?" Colin turned toward him.

"Nothing." Stratton sipped his Scotch, but a smile tugged at his lips.

Colin glowered at him.

"You really should just put everyone out of their collective misery and announce your intentions toward the lady," Stratton continued. "Or should I say, *your* lady?"

"She is not my lady." Colin said the words reflexively, but an ache in his heart belied them.

He told himself that for the next solid hour as he watched Belle flirt and laugh and make merry with what seemed to him like half of the male population of London.

Did no one else see what a spectacle she was making of herself?

BELLE SLIPPED OUT of the over-heated ballroom, intent on the lady's withdrawing room.

The evening had been exhausting, and Lady Atterson's ball was far from over. Lord Odysseus and the other gentlemen were tireless in their pursuit of her. Lord Odysseus, in particular, clearly already considered her to be his. He remained firmly attached to her side.

She wanted to escape from it all.

Or, at the very least, retire to the soothing quiet of her own townhouse.

For now, however, the withdrawing room would have to suit.

Belle thought she would be ecstatic to be so close to finally choosing a husband. Instead, the thought made her throat tight and her eyes sting and her limbs so very heavy.

She had a difficult time envisioning Lord Odysseus in that role. Whenever she thought of married life, all she could see was a cozy fire, a pot of tea, and Blake in the chair opposite her.

Blake had stalked the ballroom all evening, darting glances her way on occasion, but not braving the gauntlet of suitors to speak with her. She had allowed her stupid heart to hope, that perhaps his letters to her were a sign of him moving toward forgiving her.

That perhaps he might care for her as more than simply a friend.

Hah! How wrong she had been.

She passed through the large entrance hall and along a side corridor.

A rustling noise caused her to turn her head. She let out a barely repressed yelp as a hand wrapped around her elbow, pulling her through an open doorway.

Everything came at Belle's senses in a rush. The dark room lined with books. The snick of the door behind her. The fire flickering in the hearth. Blake's finger pressed to her lips, urging her to be quiet.

She blinked.

Blake's *finger* on her *lips* . . .

"Hush," he whispered before removing said finger. But the burning brand of his touch remained, leaving her mouth bee-stung.

The room cast him into shadowy shapes, his white waistcoat and cravat, his dark tailcoat, the intent glare in his eye.

Belle knew she should be giddy to see him. She should feel grateful that Blake was tossing her what scraps of friendship he felt he could.

And a part of her hummed in joy to be so close to him.

But a larger part of her was . . . angry.

Yes, that was the precise emotion.

She was angry. Furious even.

He could have called on her at *any time* if he wished to speak with her. Why was he doing so now? And in such a clandestine fashion?

Had the man no respect?

"Why have you dragged me in here?" she all but hissed at him. "Have you no thought for our reputations?"

"I needed to speak with you."

"And it couldn't wait until tomorrow?"

"No!"

Alarm bells sounded in Belle's mind. "What happened? Was there some tragedy?"

"Pardon?" Now it was Blake's turn to look confused. "No, nothing like that."

Silence.

"So . . . what then?" she asked.

He folded his arms across his chest. "You cannot be serious about Lord Odysseus?"

"Pardon me?"

"First driving with him in Hyde Park and now allowing him to squire you to a ball—"

"You dragged me in here to speak about Lord Odysseus?" Belle barely kept her voice low.

"Yes, and as I was saying—"

"You risk my reputation and standing in the *ton* to speak to me about Lord Odysseus?"

"Yes—"

"And this conversation had to happen right this instant?"

"Yes! I am concerned you haven't thought through the consequences of your actions with him—"

"*I* haven't thought through the consequences of *my* actions? Do you even hear yourself speaking?"

"There's no need to be snippy. It's a valid concern."

"He's courting me," Belle whispered, hand waving. "That's what men do when they're courting. We've already had this conversation, remember—"

"Of course, I remember." Blake took a step forward. "When are you going to give him your little speech?"

"My speech?"

"Yes," he came another step closer. "The one where you tilt your head and say, 'I have something I wish to speak with you about,' and then give the man in question his *congé?*"

"I do *not* do that."

"The bloods at White's say otherwise."

"Truly?"

"Well, are you? Going to send Lord Odysseus packing?" Another step closer.

"Not at present, no."

Belle refused to budge. Instead, she folded her arms, mimicking his stance. She tilted her head upwards to meet his gaze.

"What will become of *our* business once you marry?" he asked.

"Hah!" Belle huffed. "That's your concern here? That I will somehow sabotage our business through this?"

"Will you? Do you have a plan?"

"I-I will when I need to!" she spluttered. Truth be told, she didn't have much of a plan. "I assume my new husband will be well-aware of the extent of my business dealings before our wedding day. We will simply have to sort through it all and ensure that the marriage contracts take everything into account—"

"And what about me?" He took another step toward her. Belle notched her chin higher.

"What about you?"

Another step. "I cannot imagine that your new husband will allow you to continue your association with me."

A beat.

"That is likely true," Belle whispered.

Mere inches separated them now. Belle could feel the heat of his chest, the scent of pine and woodsmoke eddying around her.

"I don't like the thought of losing you as a partner."

"You cannot keep changing your mind like this, Blake," her voice breathless. "Such vacillation is unlike you."

"It is." His eyes darkened, face a morass of flickering shapes. "You seem to scatter my good sense."

"Oh."

The air between them sparked. Belle was unsure whether he reached for her first or if she leaned into him.

But his hands were suddenly on her waist, and Belle found herself pressed against him, her hands reaching for his shoulders. The one place she had dreamed of being more often than any other.

His head descended and she rose upward.

Their lips met in the middle.

She wasn't sure what she had expected kissing Lord Blake would be like, if and when she allowed herself to even consider it.

Tentative? Tender? Reserved?

His devouring hunger was unexpected.

He kissed her like she was his lifeline. His sanity.

His very breath.

It only took the barest fraction of a second for Belle to eagerly return in kind.

Part of her brain shrieked in amazement.

Blake.

She was *finally* kissing Blake.

The sheer relief of it was staggering.

But her second thought blew away the first:

How was she ever to recover her heart after this?

COLIN HADN'T INTENDED to kiss Belle.

Perhaps Stratton's Scotch had been stronger than he thought.

Or perhaps his brain was simply addled.

It was just . . . watching Belle flounce around Lady Atterson's ballroom, dancing away the night with one eligible bachelor after another . . . it had all been a form of acute torture.

Kissing her seemed the only logical place for this *feeling* to go.

But now that he had her in his arms, Colin had to wonder why he hadn't been kissing her all along.

She returned his kiss enthusiastically, hands wrapping around his neck, lips pliantly soft.

Heaven help him.

He pulled her even closer, losing himself in the plush softness of her mouth. She felt vital to him, as necessary to life as breathing.

How could this be? How could he be *kissing* her?

The same sense of reason seemed to blow through Belle, too.

She stiffened and pulled away from him, staggering a step backward.

They stared at each other, his lungs a bellows.

Her own breathing was no less steady.

The sounds of women chattering drifted down the corridor outside.

"Why did you kiss me?" Belle pressed trembling fingers to her lips.

A pause.

"I don't know." He blew out a long breath, lifting his hands to his hips again.

That was his truth.

She shook her head. "You can't kiss me because you dislike my decisions."

"I know."

"You don't get to decide who I am with. I am not your possession."

"I know. You belong to yourself."

"Exactly. You don't have the right to march in and out of my life at your will. I understand that I wronged you, but I have at least been consistent in my actions. I dislike this tug-o'-war that you seem to be playing with me."

"Belle—"

"No! I have not remained unmarried this long because my emotions are an easy target." Her eyes shone in the dark. She swiped a shaking hand across her cheekbone. "When I care for someone, I do not do it lightly."

Silence.

The fire popped. Somewhere in the house, a lady screeched with laughter.

Colin held very still. "Do you care about me then?"

He *had* to ask it.

Belle stiffened. "Of course, I care about you. You're my business partner—"

"No, Belle. You know what I meant by that question. Do you care for me as *more* than a business partner?"

More silence.

"You have been my close friend for seven years. I have remained unmarried for seven years. You are an intelligent man. Put the puzzle together," her voice low.

Colin froze. Her reply was mind-numbing.

"But I refuse to be your plaything, Blake," she continued. "True friends do not behave like this. You cannot run hot and cold." She turned and listened at the door, ensuring the coast was clear.

She turned her head back to him. "Figure yourself out, my lord."

And then she was gone.

27

. . . I must sincerely apologize for my behavior last night. I find myself ~~helpless to resist you~~ at sixes and sevens with regards to my ~~deep-felt~~ emotions for you . . .

—letter from Lord Blake to Miss Heartstone, written but unsent

Colin passed the next few days in a haze of his own making. First . . . that kiss.

Had any other kiss ever rattled his composure to such a degree? He could feel her yet in his arms, her body rising to meet his, the lush softness of her pressed against him—

Over and over, he shook the memory from his mind. But Belle's words after the kiss were just as tenacious.

I have been your close friend for seven years. I have remained unmarried for seven years. You are an intelligent man. Put the puzzle together.

Did she really mean what he thought she did? That she had loved him for so long? She had waited for him?

And why did the thought swell inside him?

The smallest thing reminded him of Belle, from the ragged orphans begging in the streets to the swishing laughter of debutantes at an evening soiree.

It was unbearable.

He knew that she wasn't lost to him, per se. He had yet to hear of her betrothal to Lord Odysseus.

He was an eligible bachelor. He could woo her.

But Sarah Forrester and her betrayal still loomed large in his mind's eye. How could he trust Belle? It seemed the height of foolishness to cast off Sarah because of her lies, but then forgive Belle her trespasses.

He found himself retreating more and more from society, preferring to spend his time at White's, enjoying long evenings chatting with elderly members of parliament and drinking far too much brandy.

Three days after seeing Belle at the ball, Colin sat at White's staring into the fading fire when a voice stopped him.

"Pleasure to see you here, Blake."

Colin turned, surprised to find Lord Halbert at his elbow. Aside from a heartfelt note of thanks, Colin hadn't heard from the man since their meeting in Bath.

"May I?" The older man gestured toward the empty chair beside Colin.

"Please."

Lord Halbert settled himself down. "I really must thank you again for your assistance, my lord. You have set my mind to rest."

"I am happy to have been of help."

They spoke of other matters for several moments: Lord Halbert's sudden trip to London, an outrageous bet in the betting book, the outlook of the corn trade.

Colin thought he was answering adequately until Lord Halbert stopped and fixed him with a puzzled look.

"If I may be so bold, Blake, you appear to be somewhat depressed of spirit."

Colin narrowly avoided a grimace.

"I am as well as could be expected," he replied, downing a large gulp of brandy.

"Did you ever resolve the problem with that LHF?"

"Yes, I solved it." Colin nodded.

"But it is not the cause of your current melancholy, I think." Lord Halbert smiled knowingly. "In my experience, usually only a woman can cause such gloom."

"You are a man of wisdom." Colin gave a mirthless chuckle.

"No. A man of experience." Lord Halbert sighed. "There is a difference, unfortunately."

They sat in silence for a moment. Colin had thought of this man as LHF for so long, it was difficult in the moment to remember that he *wasn't* LHF.

So it felt only too natural to ask: "What should I do?"

"Aside from apologize? Usually that is all a man needs do."

Colin snorted. "I am the wronged party."

"Are you sure of that?"

Colin opened his mouth to reply and then frowned. A vision of Belle's face right after their kiss. Her stricken gaze. *I refuse to be your plaything. True friends do not behave like this.*

Seeing Colin's hesitation, Lord Halbert nodded. "Regardless of fault, my lord, there are only two questions to answer. Do you love her? And is the pain of losing her greater than the humility required to forgive her?"

Colin blinked, the air rushing out of his sails.

Do you love her?

Is the pain of losing her greater than the humility required to forgive her?

The questions pummeled him.

"I don't know," Colin replied. "It's more than humility, I think. I fear to trust her again. I have been wronged and deceived in the past. It is . . . difficult . . . to move past those feelings of betrayal."

Lord Halbert tapped his hand on the arm of his chair, eyes too knowing. "That's the rub, isn't it? If you trust her, you leave yourself open to this lady hurting you again. But if you don't trust her, you may lose her forever."

Colin nearly flinched over the bald statement. It was a serrated truth.

"I find that dishonesty takes two forms," Lord Halbert continued. "There are those who live and breathe dishonesty through to their inner core. And those who make a genuine mistake, apologize, and grow from their experiences. The first type you should root out of your life. But the second . . ."

Lord Halbert waited until Colin met his gaze fully.

"The second," Lord Halbert repeated, "well . . . we're all the second type from time to time. We all make mistakes. We all need forgiveness. We all deserve a chance to be trusted again. If you were ever to heed advice from an old man, take it now. Holding on to wounded pride is a cold comfort . . ." Lord Halbert drifted off with a shrug. "I wish you luck, my lord."

LORD HALBERT'S WORDS stuck with Colin for days afterward, refusing to be silenced.

He found himself reading Belle's letters to him over the years. Every missive from LHF, written in her distinctive, loopy script. Her words leapt off the page to snare him.

I deeply appreciate your kindness in sharing your experiences with me through your words and drawings . . .

I cannot express my abiding sympathy at the passing of your dear mother . . .

I fear being left alone in the world, of losing the trust and friendship of those I hold most dear . . .

How had he ever considered her handwriting to be that of a man? It appeared so clearly feminine to him now.

We all make mistakes. We all need forgiveness. We all deserve a chance to be trusted again.

Holding on to wounded pride is a cold comfort.

Was his pride the thing holding him back, in the end?

And why had he not felt this conflicted over Sarah's behavior? Once he learned of her deception, he couldn't put distance between them fast enough.

He had been angry and hurt, but never once had he regretted his decision. In fact, the more his pain and anger receded, the more grateful he was that he had *not* married Sarah.

But with Belle . . .

Is the pain of losing her greater than the humility required to forgive her?

Her words came back to him, ones spoken as he rowed her across Stratton's small lake.

Some people pass through my life like a herd of elephants, stomping and trumpeting and thrilling to be sure, but they leave me much the same after they have passed through. Yet on occasion, I have met a person who reshapes me, who becomes essentially woven into the fabric of my life. The loss of such a person is catastrophic, as it tears away some fundamental part of yourself.

In a moment of painful insight, he finally understood.

Sarah had been an elephant, noisy but easily forgotten.

Belle . . . Belle was nearly the air he breathed. She was the very fabric of his soul.

The only answer left him was to decide how to act.

28

. . . It is three a.m. and I cannot sleep for thoughts of you. What am I ever to do, Blake? You have utterly ruined me for anyone else other than yourself . . .

—*letter from Miss Heartstone to Lord Blake,*
written, wept over, and then torn into tiny pieces

After the incident at Lady Atterson's ball, Belle had briefly considered retreating for the rest of the London Season. She could hide away in one of her country houses, maybe rent a hunting lodge deep in the Scottish Highlands.

But running from this problem would not solve it. She needed to face her decisions rather than run from them.

And so she soldiered on. She cried into her pillow at night and breakfasted with a heavy heart. She accepted callers each afternoon, greeting the pack of Gold Miners still hanging on as a form of penance before whittling away each evening at some *ton* entertainment or another.

Everything bled together into a mass of gray nothingness.

Flashes of sharp awareness occurred when someone mentioned Blake's name. Or when she caught a reference to the charming Lord B— in the scandal sheets. He had been seen driving in Hyde Park. Attending the opera. Belle had even seen him once at a distance, standing next to Cecily's carriage, enjoying flavored ice outside Gunther's.

She hated how her heart leaped every time his name escaped someone's lips. Hated how she lived for even the smallest glimpse of him.

The memory of his kiss seared her.

Which is how she found herself poking at her eggs over breakfast one morning a week later, wondering how long hearts took to heal. Hers felt just as jagged and raw as it had after confronting him at Stratton Hall.

At this rate, she would begin to feel better in perhaps a year's time.

"You need to eat more," Anne murmured from behind her teacup.

Belle suppressed a sigh. "We should both be grateful that I lose my appetite when I am upset, not the opposite. This year's fashions will continue to fit me."

"Perhaps. But I think you will want a more solid breakfast in your stomach this morning."

"Anne, this morning will end like every other morning this week. I do not see—"

A loud knock interrupted whatever scolding Anne was to have received. A moment later, the butler shuffled into the breakfast room. He presented her with a letter on a silver tray.

Belle politely took the proffered letter and nodded in thanks. And then properly looked at the folded paper.

Every thought scattered from her brain.

There, in that bold, beloved handwriting she knew so well:

To LHF

The trembling started with her fingers, but quickly traveled up her arm and settled firmly within her thumping heart. She opened the note.

My dear friend,

Answer this riddle: When I blow up, I become more whole. What am I?

Please meet me in one hour in Hyde Park in the open meadow just north of the Queen's Temple.

I await your answer there.

Still your friend,
Blake

Belle stared at the letter for a solid two minutes, words jumping out at her.

. . . my dear friend . . .

. . . become more whole . . .

. . . await your answer . . .

Was this it then? Would Blake finally break with her entirely?

But . . . he had included a riddle. The entire tone of the missive was playful. What did he mean by the riddle?

Her mind might have urged caution, but her rapid pulse said otherwise.

Belle finally shifted her gaze to Anne. "It appears I shall be going for a walk this morning."

Belle donned a pelisse, bonnet, and walking boots in record time. She did not wait for the coachman to hitch horses to her barouche or for a groom to saddle her mare. She barely waited for Anne to strap a bonnet on her own head.

As they hurried down Upper Grosvenor Street, Belle mentally sorted through Blake's motivations. Why reach out to her now? He wouldn't request her company merely to publicly humiliate her.

. . . still your friend . . .

And what was the answer to the riddle? What was blown up yet became more whole?

Once she and Anne reached the park gates and walked into the trees,

Belle still hadn't arrived at any conclusions. Surely if Blake intended to simply inform her of their business split, he could have asked her to meet at Mr. Sloan's offices.

By the time they reached the Serpentine, Belle was regretting not eating breakfast as Anne had urged. Her stomach twisted and churned. What did he want with her?

Curse his riddle, too.

She couldn't think clearly enough to come up with the answer.

Once they reached the Long Water and crossed over to the path leading to the Queen's Temple, Belle had decided she was grateful for her missing breakfast after all. She surely would cast up her accounts from nerves alone.

Morning dew clung to the grass, dampening her boots and the bottom six inches of her pelisse. The park was sparsely populated. Thank goodness. No witnesses to her hurried, nearly panicked, walk.

She and Anne topped the final rise, an expansive meadow before them.

Belle stopped, eyes flaring wide.

She wasn't sure what she had expected. But *this* . . .

This was not it.

"Good heavens!" Anne exclaimed at her elbow. "What a sight!"

A flurry of activity hummed through the meadow. Men holding ropes, others calling instructions. Spectators gathering.

Belle clapped a hand over her mouth, blinking through her tears.

In the middle of it all, a giant balloon rose. Blue silk edged with gilt designs. A small basket sat underneath.

Surely he hadn't . . .

Of all the extravagant gestures . . .

But it appeared he had.

When I blow up, I become more whole. What am I?

Hah! A balloon.

It didn't necessarily mean anything, she firmly told her pounding, silly, *hopeful* heart. He probably merely remembered how much she had enjoyed the balloon exhibition all those weeks before. That was all.

Or he thought himself clever with his riddle—very well, it *was* quite clever, she owned—and had to have a balloon to match it.

Swallowing, Belle crossed the last few yards. Down the hill, into the meadow, weaving her way through the men tying off thick cords of rope.

Until everyone parted and she saw *him*. Hatless and coatless, talking earnestly with another man. Dark green waistcoat pulled smartly down, chestnut hair catching glints of the morning sun. Shoulders broad and inviting.

Oh my.

And then he turned around.

That first moment when their gazes tangled. How his eyes lit from within. His warm, welcoming gaze.

He instantly strode toward her, everything and everyone fading away to just him and her and *this* and *now*.

Her stupid, optimistic heart gave another painful lurch. Surely this could only mean good things.

More than just "good friend" things.

"You came," was all he said, stopping in front of her, grasping both her hands in his.

"Of course. How could I not? I had to make sure that your balloon was blown up properly."

He smiled then. A slow grin that gradually expanded to overtake his face. Joy in his eyes.

Belle was sure her own echoed his.

And she knew.

She *knew* . . .

Something had changed within him.

"Come." He offered her his arm. "As you can see, I have a task for you."

With a smile far too large, Belle nestled her gloved hand in the crook of his elbow, allowing him to lead her under the large balloon. It was a wonder to view it close up.

Belle peered into the wicker basket and then looked around at the gathered men.

"Who will be ascending this morning?" she asked.

Blake returned a slow spreading smile.

"No!" Belle's eyes flared wide. "Heavens, how shall we ever return to earth?" She remembered the balloon from April, how it had sailed away until it was nothing more than a speck on the horizon.

"Not to worry." Blake leaned closer to her. "See the gentlemen there and there. They will tie off the ropes once we climb over the rooftops. At my signal, they will pull us back down. So it is all quite safe."

"We won't drift away?"

He paused, staring down at her, eyes so very soft. "No, my dearest friend, we won't drift off. Not now. Not ever."

Only his firm grip prevented Belle from melting on the spot.

FIFTEEN MINUTES LATER, Belle found herself standing in a wicker basket, an enormous balloon over her head pulling them into the sky.

Just her and Blake. Alone. Drifting toward the clouds.

As soon as the basket left the ground, Blake claimed her hand, holding it low where no one else could see. Belle clung to him. The ground was receding at an alarming rate. Now was not the time to realize she suffered from a fear of heights.

He had donned his coat, but he remained hatless. With his free hand, he clutched one of the ropes securing the basket to the balloon, a crazy grin on his face.

Belle was torn between enjoying the wonder of flight or merely staring at his beloved face.

She had always thought Blake had set her free to float into the sky, himself remaining the perceptive voice, grounding her. But was that to change, too? Her soul ached to be tethered to him permanently. To soar to great heights together.

Belle squeezed his hand. He gave a reassuring smile in return.

She reminded herself to breathe. This dramatic gesture did not express *more* than mere friendship—though he *was* still holding her hand.

And he had kissed her under a week ago.

And she suspected she was seeing something more than just friend-ship in his eyes when he looked at her.

The world appeared so different from above. People crawled across the ground. Enormous ox carts shrank to the size of children's toys. As they cleared the London roof line, a sea of chimneys extended before them, broken only by the rising bell towers of various churches. Looking back across Hyde Park, the enormous dome of St. Paul's cathedral rose to her left. The high steeple of Westminster Abbey to her right.

Even more miraculously, the sounds of the city retreated to a soft hum, leaving them to float in an ocean of hushed quiet.

"Thank you," she whispered, leaning closer to him. "This . . . this is as marvelous an experience as I will ever have."

It was true. She was quite sure as she lay on her deathbed, she would remember flying through the sky, holding hands with her dear friend, the Marquess of Blake.

"You are most welcome. As you have been flying quite competently in a figurative sense all these years, I figured it would only be fair to add *actual* flying to your repertoire."

Belle shook her head. Wonder spilled through her veins, bubbling like champagne.

"Why have you done this?" she asked.

"Well, after my words and behavior at Lady Atterson's ball, I figured I needed to beg for your forgiveness."

"No, 'tis I who should ask for forgiveness. I was unnecessarily harsh—"

"No. I needed to hear what you said." He smiled down at her. Eyes kind and gentle. "I have thought of you and the past seven years almost constantly. I sat down and re-read every letter you have written me."

"You kept them?"

"Of course. They came from the hand of a dear friend, you see."

"Oh!"

"While reading the letters, I finally understood. Yes, you were perhaps wrong to not correct my erroneous assumptions early in our correspondence. But without that small omission, I would never have come to know you as I have. Sometimes a mistake *can* transform into something beautiful. And I would be a great fool to let my pride stand between me and the company of my best friend."

Belle gave him a wobbly, watery smile. "I do not deserve such grace, Blake."

"I fear I would strongly disagree. Though you should probably call me Colin. I came to my title later in life, so I never lost my preference for my given Christian name. I know I intend to only call you Belle from this point on."

Her voice caught on a gasp.

Oh! Did he mean what she thought he did?

"I have quite thoroughly compromised you. Look at us." He spread his free arm wide. "Here we are, sailing above London, entirely unchaperoned."

"Perhaps it is I who have compromised you, Colin." The last came out on a whisper. Saying his given name felt almost like a benediction. A holy hallelujah. "I lured you into the sky—"

"No, I did the luring in this case."

"True. Though I did come quite willingly."

"Shall I consider it a summons then, Belle?"

"Please. But given that nearly all of London can see us, how have you compromised me? Aren't we now being chaperoned by thousands?"

He made a grand show of looking over the edge of the basket, scanning the ground below, smiling rather wickedly as the basket rocked, causing Belle to cling to his arm in terror.

"I suppose you are correct, my love."

Love?! Had he truly just said that?

He stood upright, that wicked grin still in place. "Well, I shall just have to ensure I do the deed properly."

Hope burned ragged and bright.

Before Belle could blink, he raised their joined, gloved hands. "But this will not do at all." Staring at her, he slowly pulled off his own gloves. First one. Then the other, stuffing them into his pocket.

Then he moved on to her gloves. Gently unbuttoning the single button at her wrist. Tugging on each finger. Sliding the soft leather off her palm. Planting a scalding kiss on the back of her hand before moving on.

He repeated the actions with her second hand.

Belle's mouth had gone quite dry by the time he finished. The balloon, the city before them, everything faded.

It was only Colin's eyes that held her. The sound of his breathing. The feel of his warm hands against hers.

"Much better," he whispered as her second glove disappeared into his coat pocket. He threaded the fingers of his right hand through hers. His thumb moving in lazy circles across her palm.

His other hand moved to cup her cheek, lifting her gaze to his. She had heard the cliché of a lover gazing with his heart in his eyes . . .

She could quite literally see her whole world in his.

"Belle . . . my dearest, most beloved friend." He stroked her cheek. "I should have realized sooner that I wanted LHF in my life permanently. I am determined to be quite persistent, if I must."

"Colin . . ."

His thumb brushed across her lips. "You darling, beautiful woman. Everything good in my life began the day you entered it."

He bent down. Or she raised up.

Belle could not recall afterward.

But, somehow, they met in the middle.

His lips : . . warm and soft and giving. Yielding under her own.

It only took a second for his hands to move around her waist, pulling her closer to him. For her part, Belle wrapped her arms around his neck, threading her fingers into his hair.

Finally! How could this *finally* be happening?

"Oh, Colin . . ." She pulled back with a hiccuping gasp. "I have loved you for so very, very long."

He cupped her cheek again.

"Belle, my darling, beautiful Belle."

They kissed and kissed and kissed. Until Belle's knees had quite melted. And surely the entire city of London had spied them.

Colin held her tight to him. Forehead to forehead. "One last riddle, my love. What short word is the longest promise of happiness?"

Belle shook her head, licking a tear off her lip.

Colin kissed her forehead. "You asked me first. But, Belle, I intend to ask you last." He kissed the tip of her nose. "Marry me, my love. Say you will be mine?"

Later, Belle had no memory of actually saying, *Yes!*

All she remembered was kissing him over and over, tasting tears of happiness as they flew through the sky.

EPILOGUE

. . . I already miss you, my dearest wife. Shall I tell you precisely what I miss? In no particular order: your laugh, the skipping bounce in your step when you are excited about something, your soft hand in mine, your frigid nose pressed against my cheek when you are cold, the way you sigh when I embrace you after a long day. Please hurry home after finishing your business at Hopewell Manor. I ache to see you . . .

—excerpt of a note from Lord Blake, tucked into Lady Blake's reticule,
which she finally noticed when twenty miles outside London

. . . I cannot wait to hear how your speech went today in Lords. I am utterly positive it was a rousing success and will set the bar for Parliamentary speeches for years to come. I believe in you, my love, and the good that we are trying to do in the world.

—a note from Lady Blake, hidden in Lord Blake's waistcoat pocket,
which his lordship found just before delivering a speech in the
House of Lords on the necessity of child labor reform

You look exhausted." Colin tucked his wife closer to his side in the rocking carriage. "Come, Lady Blake. I won't have anyone saying that I am neglecting you. Imagine the horror."

Belle laughed softly, burrowing her nose into his shoulder, wrapping her hands around his elbow.

He wasn't wrong about her feeling exhausted, however. Everything had required so much more effort as of late.

The past eight months of her marriage to Colin Radcliffe, Lord Blake, had been idyllic. Their joint business and charitable endeavors had grown by leaps and bounds. Their presence in London was sought out and curried; Belle quickly found herself as one of the premier hostesses in Town.

But the external success paled when compared to the soul-deep adoration she had for Colin and their life together. Marriage to her best friend had shown her true joy.

She and Colin weren't just tethered together now. They had created their own air-ship and were able to control it, sending them soaring into unknown countries. Together.

Just the thought had her wiping away tears.

Granted, nearly everything brought her to tears recently. Hadn't she cried over a glowing report from Fyfe Hall just two days previous? And then there had been that pair of darling puppies in Regent's Park. And the wisteria in such beautiful bloom—

She was officially an emotional mess.

"Did you enjoy yourself this evening?" Colin asked. "I know Cecily delights in having you as a sister-in-law."

Belle smiled and snuggled closer. "I adore how much your sister adores you. I know that you have at times assumed she cares more for your title than yourself, but that is not true. She loves you as you are."

He snorted. "Though the title doesn't hurt."

"No," she giggled, "it does not."

"Lord Halbert was charming, as usual."

"I cannot believe you thought him LHF all those years."

"Neither can I."

"Though I do admit he makes an excellent alter ego."

"I thoroughly enjoy his company." Colin pulled her tighter against him as the carriage rocked back and forth. "All those years in India, I would imagine Lord Halbert at dinner with Cecily and George, laughing and making merry at Christmastide. It made me dreadfully homesick."

"You longed for that yourself," she murmured, blinking back the emotion in her throat. Was everything determined to render her a weeping pot?

"Yes."

"And now?"

"Now?" She heard the smile in his voice. "Now I am the happiest of men. Though I'm afraid I will insist on you retiring instantly when we arrive home," Colin continued. "I would see you well rested, my love."

Belle sighed and cuddled closer. He brushed a loose curl off her forehead, placing a tender kiss there.

"It will be of no use, Colin," she replied. "I fear exhaustion will play a large part in my life for the foreseeable future."

She felt more than saw Colin's alarm. He pulled back, looking down at her in the dim carriage light.

"Are you unwell?"

Belle shrugged. "No more than is to be expected."

"Belle love, you're frightening me. What is wrong?"

She placed a gloved hand against his cheek. "There is nothing to be frightened over. It is a simple riddle."

"A riddle?"

"Yes. When does one plus one equal three?"

Belle emphasized the question by placing a hand over her stomach.

Colin's astonished expression sent her straight into tears.

Of course.

"Truly? You're with child?" he whispered.

Belle could only nod, her eyesight blurry.

"Ah, my love." He tenderly kissed her. "*Now* I am the happiest of men. Of all our adventures together, this one will be the most precious."

Naturally, Colin's words took Belle's weeping from gentle to torrential. But she didn't care. She smiled through her tears.

Because he was right.

AUTHOR'S NOTE

This story has always been one of my favorites. I knew when I wrote it initially that Belle and Blake had a much more involved tale to tell. It's been so fun to deep dive into the Regency era again.

If you struggled with the riddles where no answer was given, I've listed them here for you:

At night, they come without being fetched. By day, they are lost but never stolen. What are they?

    Stars

Four days start with the letter 'T.' One is Tuesday. The other, Thursday. Can you name the other two?

    Today and tomorrow

What is so delicate that even saying its name will break it?

    Silence

What occurs once in every minute, twice in every moment, but never in a thousand years?

The letter "M"

A couple more fun facts:

Despite what many suppose, there were wealthy businesswomen during the Regency era. In fact, two of the largest banks of the time— Coutts Bank and Child's Bank, now the Royal Bank of Scotland—had women as their largest shareholders and active managers. Though much rarer than today, of course, women were not quite as invisible as we might assume today.

The history of ballooning is fascinating. It began in France in the late 1700s and was all the rage in Regency London. That said, balloon rides were notoriously unsafe for the first hundred years or so of their existence. Many of the first balloon enthusiasts died in crash landings or other related catastrophes. Charles Green, who is mentioned in passing here, was not one of them, fortunately. But he was the first to pioneer using coal gas (a fuel produced through the gasification of coal) to fill balloons. Though I didn't bring this into the story, one of the most famous balloonists of the era was a French woman—Sophie Blanchard.

Streams and rivers do vary tremendously in size depending on rainfall. It seems weird, but most rain in the U.K. falls gently and slowly. So a heavy, torrential downpour can quickly cause a small stream to turn into a raging torrent.

I have created an extensive pinboard on Pinterest with images of things I talk about in the book. So if you want a visual of anything, pop over there and explore. Just search for NicholeVan.

As with all books, this one couldn't have been written without the help and support from those around me. I know I am going to leave someone out with all these thanks. So to that person, know that I totally love you and am so deeply grateful for your help!

To my beta readers—you know who you are—thank you for your editing suggestions, helpful ideas, and support. And, again, an extra-large thank you to Annette Evans and Norma Melzer for their fantastic editing skills.

Again, I cannot thank Rebecca Spencer and Erin Rodabough enough for their insights. And a shout-out to Julie Frederick for her keen observations.

And, finally, thank you to Andrew, Austenne, Kian, and Dave for your endless patience. I love you.

READING GROUP QUESTIONS

Yes, there are reading group questions. I suggest discussing them over lots of excellent chocolate (solid, liquid, frozen, cake . . . I'm not picky about the precise state of matter of said chocolate. Chocolate in any form is good chocolate.)

1. This book has a clear, three-act partitioning. Why do you think the author did this? Do you like the division? Why or why not?

2. What do the titles of each of the subsections refer to? What proposals do you see in the first section? How many betrayals in the second? What are the resolutions in the third?

3. What does the title—*Seeing Miss Heartstone*—refer to throughout the book? How many different types of "seeing" can you infer?

4. As a character, in what ways does Belle Heartstone change throughout the novel? In what ways does Blake change?

5. Did you figure out what the initials LHF stood for? If not, what did you think they referred to? Did you find the mystery initials to be an interesting addition to the story? Why or why not?

6. The metaphor of flying is also strung throughout the book. Did you like how the metaphor played out? How do you think the concept of flying could be connected to the title, *Seeing Miss Heartstone*?

7. How did you feel about Belle's reluctance to tell Blake about LHF? Did she procrastinate too long? Was Blake too quick or too slow to forgive her? Has there been a situation in your life like this—where you knew you needed to tell someone something hard, but you procrastinated doing it?

OTHER BOOKS BY NICHOLE VAN

THE BROTHERS *MALEDETTI*

Lovers and Madmen (Cesare and Judith)
Gladly Beyond (Dante and Claire)
Love's Shadow (Branwell and Lucy)
Lightning Struck (Chiara and Jack)
A Madness Most Discreet (Tennyson and Olivia)

THE HOUSE OF OAK SERIES

Intertwine
Divine
Clandestine
Refine
Outshine
An Invisible Heiress (a novella included in *Spring in Hyde Park*.)

OTHER WORKS

Vingt-et-Un | Twenty-one (a novella included in *Falling for a Duke*.)

If you haven't yet read *Intertwine*, book one in the House of Oak series, turn the page for a preview.

Intertwine

HOUSE OF OAK, BOOK 1

PROLOGUE

The obsession began on June 12, 2008 around 11:23 a.m.

Though secretly Emme Wilde considered it more of a 'spiritual connection' than an actual full-blown neurosis.

Of course, her brother, Marc, her mother and a series of therapists all begged to disagree.

Thankfully her best friend, Jasmine, regularly validated the connection and considered herself to be Emme's guide through this divinely mystical union of predestined souls (her words, not Emme's). Marc asserted that Jasmine was not so much a guide as an incense-addled enabler (again, his words, not Emme's). Emme was just grateful that anyone considered the whole affair normal—even if it was only Jasmine's loose sense of 'normal.'

Jasmine always insisted Emme come with her to estate sales, and this one outside Portland, Oregon proved no exception. Though Jasmine contended *this* particular estate sale would be significant for Emme, rambling on about circles colliding in the vast cosmic ocean creating necessary links between lives—blah, blah. All typical Jasmine-speak.

Emme brushed it off, assuming that Jasmine really just wanted someone to organize the trip: plan the best route to avoid traffic, find a quirky restaurant for lunch, entertain her on the long drive from Seattle.

At the estate sale, Emme roamed through the stifling tents, touching the cool wood of old furniture, the air heavy with that mix of dust, moth balls and disuse that marks aged things. Jasmine predictably disappeared into a corner piled with antique quilts, hunting yet again for that elusive log cabin design with black centers instead of the traditional red.

But Emme drifted deeper, something pulling her farther and farther into the debris of lives past and spent. To the trace of human passing, like fingerprints left in the paint of a pioneer cupboard door. Stark and clear.

Usually Emme would have stopped to listen to the stories around her, the history grad student in her analyzing each detail. Yet that day she didn't. She just wandered, looking for something. Something specific.

If only she could remember what.

Skirting around a low settee in a back corner, Emme first saw the antique trunk. A typical mid-nineteenth century traveling chest, solid with mellow aged wood. It did not call attention to itself. But it stood apart somehow, almost as if the air were a little lighter around it.

She first opened the lid out of curiosity, expecting the trunk to be empty. Instead, she found it full. Carefully shifting old books and papers, Emme found nothing of real interest.

Until she reached the bottom right corner.

There she found a small object tucked inside a brittle cotton handkerchief. Gently unwrapping the aged fabric, she pulled out an oval locket. Untouched and expectant.

Filigree covered the front, its gilt frame still bright and untarnished, as if nearly new.

Emme turned the locket over, feeling its heft in her hand, the metal cool against her palm. It hummed with an almost electric pulse. How long had the locket lain wrapped in the trunk?

Transparent crystal partially covered the back. Under the crystal, two locks of hair were woven into an intricate pattern—one bright and fair, the other a dark chocolate brown. Gilded on top of the crystal, two initials nestled together into a stylized gold symbol.

She touched the initials, trying to make them out. One was clearly an F. But she puzzled over the other for a moment, tracing the design with her eyes. And then she saw it. Emme sucked in a sharp breath. An E. The other initial was an E.

She opened the locket, hearing the small pop of the catch.

A gasp.

Her hands tingled.

A sizzling shock started at the back of her neck and then spread. *Him.*

There are moments in life that sear into the soul. Brief glimpses of some larger force. When so many threads collapse into one. Coalesce into a single truth.

Seeing *him* for the first time was one of those moments.

He gazed intently out from within the right side of the locket: blond, blue-eyed, chiseled with a mouth hinting at shared laughter. Emme's historian mind quickly dated his blue-green, high collared jacket and crisp, white shirt and neckcloth to the mid-Regency era, probably around 1812, give or take a year.

Emme continued to look at the man—well, stare actually. His golden hair finger-combed and deliciously disheveled. Broad shoulders angled slightly toward the viewer. Perhaps his face a shade too long and his nose a little too sharp for true beauty. But striking. Handsome even.

Looking expectant, as if he had been waiting for her.

Emme would forever remember the jolt of it.

Surprise and recognition.

She knew him. Had known him.

Somehow, somewhere, in some place.

He felt agonizingly familiar. That phantom part of her she had never realized was lost.

The sensation wasn't quite deja vu.

More like memory.

Like suddenly finding that vital thing you didn't realize had been misplaced. Like coming up, gasping for air, after nearly drowning and seeing the world bright and sparkling and new.

She stood mesmerized by *him* until Jasmine joined her.

"Oooh, you found him." The hushed respect in her voice was remarkable. This was Jasmine after all.

Emme nodded mutely.

"Your circles are so closely intertwined. Amazing."

Jasmine turned the locket in Emme's hand.

"What does this inscription say?" she asked.

Emme hadn't noticed the engraved words on the inside left of the locket case. But now she read them. Her sudden sharp inhalation seared, painfully clenching.

Oh. *Oh!*

The words reverberated through her soul, shattering and profound.

Emme didn't recall much more of that day—Jasmine purchasing the locket or even the little restaurant where they ate lunch. Instead, she only remembered the endless blur of passing trees on the drive home, the inscription echoing over and over:

To E
throughout all time
heart of my soul
your F

Visit www.NicholeVan.com to buy your copy of
Intertwine today and continue the story.

ABOUT THE AUTHOR

THE SHORT VERSION

NICHOLE VAN IS a writer, photographer, designer and generally disorganized crazy person. Though originally from Utah, she currently lives on the coast of Scotland with three similarly crazy children and one sane, very patient husband who puts up with all of them. In her free time, she enjoys long walks along the Scottish lochs and braes. She does not, however, enjoy haggis.

THE LONG OVERACHIEVER VERSION

AN INTERNATIONAL BESTSELLING author, Nichole Van is an artist who feels life is too short to only have one obsession. In former lives, she has been a contemporary dancer, pianist, art historian, chore-ographer, culinary artist and English professor.

Most notably, however, Nichole is an acclaimed photographer, winning over thirty international accolades for her work, including Portrait of the Year from WPPI in 2007. (Think Oscars for wedding and portrait photographers.) Her unique photography style has been featured in many magazines, including Rangefinder and Professional Photographer. She is also the creative mind behind the popular website Flourish Emporium which provides resources for photographers.

All that said, Nichole has always been a writer at heart. With an MA in English, she taught technical writing at Brigham Young University for ten years and has written more technical manuals than she can quickly count. She decided in late 2013 to start writing fiction and has since become an Amazon #1 bestselling author. Additionally, she has won a RONE award, as well as been a Whitney Award Finalist several years running.

In February 2017, Nichole, her husband and three crazy children moved from the Rocky Mountains in the USA to Scotland. They currently live near the coast of eastern Scotland in a medieval barn conversion. Nichole loves her sea views while writing and long walks through fields and beaches. She does not, however, have a fondness for haggis.

She is known as NicholeVan all over the web: Facebook, Instagram, Pinterest, etc. Visit http://www.NicholeVan.com to sign up for her author newsletter and be notified of new book releases. Additionally, you can see her photographic work at http://photography.nicholeV.com and http://www.nicholeV.com

If you enjoyed this book, please leave a short review on Amazon.com. Wonderful reviews are the elixir of life for authors. Even better than dark chocolate.